J.E. BIRK, RACHEL EMBER &

USA TODAY BESTSELLING AUTHOR

LESLIE McADAM

ISBN (paperback): 979-8-9884871-5-9

Cover Design by Cate Ashwood Designs
Edited by Kari Shafenberg

A NOTE FROM THE AUTHORS

Hello, Dear Readers!

Thanks for joining us for Doug, Max, and Zeke's journey! This story is fun, sweet, sexy, and low-angst: think queer holiday rom-com. With that said, this tale does include references to past bullying, fistfight-level violence (there's a quasi-evil twin involved), and a role-play scene depicting CNC, power exchanges, and feminization that may not be every reader's cup of tea—or eggnog. As always, please take care of yourself when determining if this read is right for you.

We're fully aware that we pushed the boundaries of reality in this story. Jury is still out, for example, on whether any cow could *actually* be born with that many thematic markings at once. We suggest suspending disbelief before beginning with chapter one. That's what the holidays are for, right?

On another note, deep, deep thanks for all the love so many folx have sent to *ILYBSM*, the first holiday title the three of us wrote together. It means a great deal to us that Jeb, Adam, and Embry have reached so many readers. We hope you all enjoy Doug, Max, and Zeke just as much.

Finally: while we loathe typos as much as all writers, they do happen. Should you find an error somewhere in this book (we're clutching our imaginary pearls just thinking about it), rather than report it to Amazon, please email info@lesliemcadamauthor.com so we can fix it!

All our love,

J.E., Rachel, and Leslie

PART ONE
FML

AIRBNB HOST

Hi, I wanted to confirm your reservation for seven
nights in La Fierte, Vermont. There was a note
that said to contact you about length of stay.
How can I help?

MAX

Girl, my balls hurt. It's been so long since I got
laid. Holy fuck.

AIRBNB HOST

Oh, I don't think I can help you with that.

MAX

OH MY GOD.

I am so sorry. I meant to send that to my best
friend. I replied to the wrong thread.

AIRBNB HOST

I figured it was something like that. It happens.
No worries!

MAX

I'm so embarrassed. I sincerely apologize.

Now I'm low-key considering canceling my
booking so I don't have to look you in the eye.

AIRBNB HOST

Oh, please don't! We have our most comfortable
room ready for you.

MAX

Thank you. I promise I'll be a drama-free tenant.
I've been told I'm incredibly easy

As a guest, I mean

Okay, can we forget this text thread ever existed,
and I'll see you when I check in?

AIRBNB HOST

Absolutely!

CHAPTER 1

MAX

"So, what brings you to the area?"

Dante, the rideshare driver, turns to me and smiles. He looks vaguely familiar, which is a strike against him. He's probably around my age, and anyone in range of my hometown who I might have encountered in high school gets my guard up. Another strike: he keeps grabbing his phone from its dashboard holder and looking back and forth between it and the windshield while he steers us through the winding Vermont roads. I wish he'd put the phone down, because I'd like to make it to my destination safely.

But beggars can't be choosers, and people who land at airports need to get to their Airbnb somehow.

I think about how to respond to his question. *What brings me here?* There are a number of answers, all of which are true. "I'm from here, for starters," I finally say, pushing up my glasses and looking out the window. The Green Mountain State at this time of year is winter bare and gray-brown—decidedly *not* green.

"Yeah? Which part?"

"Atherton, actually. My mom still lives there."

"Um. Cool." He trails off.

I chuckle. "It's not cool, it's okay. I was happy to get away from there. High school sucked." I study him. "Where did you go to school?"

"I went to Atherton High," he says, as he glances back down at his phone.

Shit. I'd already suspected as much, but the confirmation makes my heart sink. I knew coming back here meant taking the risk that the old, bad things would catch up to me, but I hadn't expected to come across someone from high school so quickly. Although if I'm being objective, Dante doesn't seem like much of a threat. He seems more likely to join a drum circle than a gang of bullies.

Still, my guard goes up around anyone bigger than me, or with anyone who I associate with my past. I have the approximate muscle tone of a toothpick, and no matter what I eat, my body stays small. While my slim stature is good for, say, running from mall cops and slipping through slats in a fence—not that I've done those things more than twice, each—it's no good for self-defense. So, I spend a lot of time anxiously avoiding confrontation.

The problem is that, for me, Vermont equals confrontation. My years at Atherton High School were the worst, thanks to Jonah James, who bullied me daily.

So aside from a few trips to see my mom, I've avoided Vermont almost entirely since I escaped to college and then settled in DC. My high school's a place I'd like to burn down to the ground. Not that I'm an arsonist or anything. I just have some bad memories there.

A memory bonfire. That's what I want.

"When did you graduate?" I ask, trying to keep a wary note out of my voice.

When we establish that he graduated four years after me, I breathe a sigh of relief. He's probably never heard of me. But he's a local, so maybe he can help me out with my project. The thought flips a switch in my head, and I feel like a talented journalist again, not a scared kid.

"Do you know Mayor McEmbirk?" I ask.

"Doug? Yeah! He's the best!"

"Oh, excellent. I'm a journalist, and part of the reason I'm here is to interview him. Did you see that article? The viral one?"

"Pfft," Dante says, waving his hand. "Who didn't? So weird to see something from La Fierte *everywhere*, man."

I'm referring to an article in the local newspaper called "Child Mayor to Bankrupt Town for Holiday-Off?" It portrayed a not-so-flattering picture of Doug McEmbirk, the twenty-eight-year-old mayor of La Fierte, Vermont, which is one town over from Atherton. Doug won a special mayoral election, and apparently he has pissed off at least one local. One who happens to be the editor of *The Pigeon*. Yes, that's the name of La Fierte's local paper.

That article probably wouldn't have been read by anyone outside the county, but one of my favorite online influencers, Adam O'Connor, posted a rant on his socials denouncing the *Pigeon* article and supporting Mayor McEmbirk. Now, people all over the planet are reading about the political machinations of my hometown and its tiny neighbor. As a freelancer, I couldn't resist the opportunity for a story of my own. Hence, my trip here. Old memories be damned.

"Do you have an opinion about the Holiday-Off?" I ask. I'm not sure a quotation from a random rideshare driver is going to make its way into my article, but maybe if he's occupied by talking to me he'll keep his eyes on the road and off his phone.

"Not really," Dante says, shrugging. "And I'm probably the only person in the county without one. I'm sure you know how competitive La Fierte and Atherton can be."

I nod, because I'm familiar with the old Atherton-La Fierte rivalry. Although when I lived here, that rivalry mainly funneled its way through sports, and I've never cared much about bats and balls—well, I definitely care about balls, but *not* in the traditional athletic sense.

"So, you aren't bothered one way or the other about the expenditures? According to the article, the budget for the annual

Christmas Eve celebration in the town square has tripled thanks to the contest."

"No. Atherton and La Fierte have always held big town parties on Christmas Eve. If they want to hold a competition this year and really go all out to see whose party is better, I say let the people celebrate."

"Do you know why the editor of *The Pigeon* wrote such a scathing article about Mayor McEmbirk supporting the increases to the event budget? Did the mayor tick him off?"

Dante shakes his head. "No way. I mean, Doug is Doug. How could anyone get mad at him? Everyone likes him, but he's not a mental heavyweight, if you know what I'm saying. You should talk with him. He's nice."

I write down in my notes app, "Not an intellectual heavy-weight." And my source, Dante the texting rideshare driver.

"I'll be talking with him," I say. "I'm staying at his Airbnb."

And I *really* hope he's not the one monitoring the messages for that Airbnb, seeing as how I accidentally texted my blue balls status to that number. But blurting embarrassing things is a way of life for me, so I'll deal, I guess.

"Oh, cool! I thought I recognized the address," Dante says. "I'll get you there soon."

I know the way to La Fierte by heart. We take the slightly longer route to avoid construction, which means we drive right down the main street of Devon Falls, the other closest major town to Atherton. It's not a bustling metropolis by any means, but another small Vermont town. There's the coffee shop I used to bum rides to when I was in high school. There's the doctor's office I had to go to when I broke my big toe in that graduation incident with Jonah. I shudder. Time to think of better thoughts.

Like this one: Doug McEmbirk is a firefighter, and I have a *thing* for firefighters. He also looked especially gorgeous online. So, I can interview him *and* drool over him. Sounds like fun to me.

La Fierte is such a minuscule town, I almost miss it. There's a bend in the tree-lined road, a sign signaling an abrupt drop in the speed limit, and then a short row of well-tended but worn one-story buildings that are all at least a hundred years old, most of which are still in business. After that block of what passes for downtown, Dante turns onto a sloping street uphill, where a grand old house with white clapboard siding and green trim overlooks the town. I recognize the house from my own memories of La Fierte way back when, and from the Airbnb listing.

Up close, the place gives me a good feeling. There are lace curtains up in the windows, a wide, friendly porch, and a hand-painted sign by the door that reads "Home is where the heart is."

Grabbing my bags, I say goodbye to Dante and head up the steep porch steps. This house feels old in the best way—comforting, established. Safe.

I raise my arm to knock on the door when it swings open, and the most handsome guy I've ever seen stands in the doorway.

No joke. The pictures I looked at online didn't do him justice. Doug McEmbirk is ridiculously beautiful.

He's very tall, with medium brown hair that's cut short. His muscles strain against his shirt sleeves, and his legs are like tree trunks. I notice all of this because I'm helplessly checking him out. Hey. I have a license to twink, okay?

My walking daydream gives me a broad smile, his light brown eyes friendly.

"Hi! Are you Max Rivers?" Mayor Doug's eyes are intent on me, and energy radiates from him. Being the center of his attention makes me briefly forget my name.

Max? Max who? Max me?

After a moment, I manage a stunned nod.

"I'm Doug! Come on in! I have your room ready for you. And I can't wait to tell you all about La Fierte!"

I follow him inside, recognizing the decor from the photos on the Airbnb website. There are quilts draped over the shabby furniture, pastoral needlepoint is displayed on the walls, and doilies clutter every surface. This place is grandma chic.

"Um," I start, collecting myself. *You're a journalist, Max.* "Is this your house?"

Doug grins at me. "No, it's my grandma's. I just live here." He opens a door to a spacious but old-fashioned bedroom. "She moved to Florida a couple of years ago. I'm renting out the spare bedrooms to help her make some extra cash."

"Interesting." I make a note of that for my article as I set my bag down on the floor and look around. There's a large, four-poster bed with a blue and white quilt. A braided rug lies on the hardwood floor. A wooden rocking chair sits near the bed, and under the window there's an old-fashioned sewing machine. A plethora of cross-stitched pigs hang on the wall, and I notice three crochet pigs lined across the side of the bed. I have no idea what decade it is, and I don't care. This is perfect.

I hear someone clearing their throat and I turn around, ready to tell Doug how much I like the room. But Doug isn't the only one standing in the hall.

My stomach sinks to the floor and my pulse starts racing as I blink my eyes, hoping I'm hallucinating and not seeing my worst nightmare come true.

But it's real.

Jonah James, my high school bully, stands in the doorway. And he's glaring at me.

DOUG

Hi, I just wanted to confirm you're on your way.

ZEKE

WTF are you talking about? I'm in the sheep room.

DOUG

Shoot, I meant to text our Airbnb guest. His plane should have just landed. Sorry, Zekers.

ZEKE

You know I hate it when you call me that

DOUG

Awww, we both know that's not true! You love it! Just like how you secretly love Meg Ryan rom-coms.

ZEKE

I hate those movies.

DOUG

Sure you do, buddy.

UNKNOWN NUMBER

Um, hi. Sorry, but I think you accidentally added me to this chat? I'm your Airbnb guest. I'm on my way.

DOUG

Whoopsie! See you soon! And now you know not to ask my roommate to watch Sleepless in Seattle with you.

UNKNOWN NUMBER

No problem. When Harry Met Sally is better anyway.

ZEKE

You're categorically wrong, but that's okay.

DOUG

I knew you loved Meg, Zekers!

CHAPTER 2
ZEKE

I never should have agreed to this stupid fucking Airbnb idea. Now, instead of spending the evening pretending I don't want to watch *You've Got Mail* with Doug, I'm going to have to make small talk with some stranger taking up residence in the pig room, which is entirely too close to the sheep room, the one I rent from Doug.

Case in point: a dude I've never met is standing in Doug's house, looking at me with an expression of horrified disgust, as if I just spat on the creaky hardwood floor.

"Zeke!" Doug beams at me. "Look, it's our first Airbnb guest! And did I tell you? He's here to write about me and the Holiday-Off!"

I'm immediately wary. Doug was really rattled when Barton Asterstop, the editor of our town newspaper, wrote a long editorial basically accusing Doug of setting out to destroy La Fierte's annual budget and reputation by participating in the Holiday-Off with Atherton. Doug had to tackle me at the firehouse door before I went straight to Barton's office and gave him a piece of my mind.

He had the nerve to call Doug "thoughtless and without critical thinking skills." For the first time in the fifteen-plus years I've known Doug, I actually saw him *frown* when he read that line. My best friend doesn't fucking frown. Fucking ever. I sure as fuck didn't fucking like it when he did.

It's bad enough Doug already had to talk me out of confronting Barton. Now he's *invited* a journalist to live with us? How the hell am I supposed to protect Doug from asshole investigators when he's ushering them straight into our home?

I close my eyes and force myself to count to ten. When Doug announced that he was going to start renting rooms to Airbnb guests, I couldn't argue. For one thing, I don't own the place, and for another, it wasn't a bad idea. Doug and I rattle around together in this giant-ass house. He and his grandma might as well make some money off all the extra space. But living with a reporter who's watching Doug's every move? I'm not here for that.

Still, none of that may matter anyway, given our guest's expression. Maybe he doesn't like cross-stitch or lace doilies? He's eyeing the door behind me like he's ready to bolt.

"You—I—" The guy's staring at me as he stutters, his eyes wide behind trendy glasses and his hands balled into fists.

What the fuck is going on here? I'm not exactly known for my congeniality, and maybe I've been accused of having a Resting Fuck-Off Face more than once, but Doug's guest is looking at me like I'm truly scary.

This guy might be a serious threat to me too, I realize, the longer I look at him. Not only is he a stranger up in my space, he's a *hot* stranger up in my space. Gorgeous deep blue eyes, lithe body, pouty lips. Fair skin nicely complemented by his dark-blond hair. The kind of guy I jerk off to late at night.

Why is that a problem? Well, moving in someone who could have walked out of my sexual fantasies won't help with my Doug situation. The only thing worse than living with *one* off-limits fantasy is living with *two* off-limits fantasies.

Not to mention that it's got to be frowned upon to proposition your hot short-term roommate for sex when your landlord, roommate, and best friend doesn't even know you're into guys.

Shitfuckdamn to everything about this situation.

My impure thoughts aside, why is Blue Eyes creeping slowly toward the window, farther and farther away from me? What's he going to do, jump out? We're only on the first floor, but Doug won't let his grandma's rose bushes take that hit. Doug sends me a quick glance, lips pursed, and I know right away what he's asking: *Something's wrong, right? Do you know what's going on here?*

I tilt my head and arch an eyebrow. *No fucking clue.*

You spend enough years passing hockey pucks and responding to emergency situations with a guy—oh, and being secretly in love with him, I guess—and you really nail your silent communication.

"Max?" Doug says tentatively. "Is the room okay? Because there's another one down the hall you could take! Lots of horses in that one. Do you like horses?"

Max shakes his head. "This isn't going to work. Hell, no. I can't stay with *him*." He shoots me a glare that leaves no mistaking which one of us he's referring to.

"You two know each other?" Doug asks curiously. Doug and I went to junior high, high school, and college together, and we've both lived in La Fierte since I moved here when I was twelve. Almost anyone I know in life, Doug knows.

Max snorts. "I can't believe I landed in an Airbnb with Jonah James, for fuck's sake," he mutters under his breath.

Oh shit. Now I know what's going on. People mistake me and Jonah for each other just often enough to remind me how much I hate being the spitting image of that dick.

"Oh!" Doug cocks his head like a labrador retriever that's just found its misplaced bone. Usually I love that expression on him— it's so Doug. All sweet, curious innocence. But right now even Doug being cute can't make me feel better, because I'm too pissed about everything happening in this room. "I see what's going on here!" Doug continues. "You think Zeke is Jonah! Max, that's not *Jonah* James. That's *Zeke* James! They're twins!"

I've spent years trying to end the top-secret and highly unrequited crush I've got on my best friend. Dating Lydia Forsythe was only the most recent failed attempt at getting him the fuck out of my head. It was worth a shot with Lydia. She and I have been friends for a long time, and she knew exactly what baggage she was picking up at the airport the first night she kissed me.

But in moments like this, I have to admit that getting over Doug might be the lost cause Lydia told me it was last weekend. He's rushing across the room to pat Max on the shoulder, using the Firefighter Soothing Voice he generally saves for crying kids and animals stuck up in haymows. "Hey, I'm really sorry we didn't clear that up right away. You're local, right? Was Jonah mean to you in school or something? He can be a real butthead."

Calling Jonah "butthead" has got to be the understatement of the goddamn year. But Doug's gone twenty-eight years without swearing, and I don't think even Jonah's going to break his perfect streak.

"You're not Jonah?" Max asks me incredulously.

"No," I tell him. "I'm not Jonah."

"But how? In high school, there was only one of you!" Max stares at me, and I think I'm starting to understand the expression "looked like he'd seen a ghost."

How does my brother manage to inflict so much damage across time and space? The fucker leaves a path of burnt earth wherever he goes. Ask his twelve thousand ex-girlfriends. Ask anyone who's ever tried to be friends with him.

Ask Max, apparently.

"Our parents divorced when we were in the sixth grade," I explain. "Mom and I moved to La Fierte, and Jonah and Dad moved to Atherton. Jonah went to high school there, but Doug and I went to high school in Devon Falls."

"Real-life *Parent Trap* twin split-up," Doug interjects. "Me and Zeke watched both versions of that movie after Jeb told me that he parent-trapped Adam and Embry into dating him."

"Wait, are you talking about Adam O'Connor?" Max asks Doug excitedly. All the hostility drains from his face at once and his eyes somehow get even brighter than they were a moment before. I clear my throat and try not to stare.

"Yeah!" Doug says. "Do you know him?"

Max shakes his head. "No. But I love Adam's Instagram account about the Stock Tree Farm."

Doug's happy expression fades to a more somber one. "Oh. So, you've probably seen what he said about the story in the local paper."

I wince. I knew immediately that any out-of-town reporter who showed up wanting to interview Doug had to know about Adam's viral social media post and the resulting shitstorm of interest in our town, but of course that didn't occur to Doug. He has no space in his mind for negativity, and I've watched him do his best to forget that Barton's article was ever fucking written, much less shared a few million times online.

"Yes," Max says, and I appreciate his honesty. "But I was already a fan of Adam's," he goes on cheerfully. "Adam, Embry, and Jeb's life on their farm and the way they're such a part of the community really shows off all the best things about living around here. I had a different experience as a kid, but it shows me what I *wish* growing up here had been like. If that makes sense?"

Yeah, what he's saying makes sense. Now, I want to choke Jonah. Our friends Jeb, Adam, and Embry, who run the Stock Tree Farm, are in a relationship together. Their farm is probably the most inclusive, welcoming, and happy place I've ever visited.

I'm sure attending high school with my brother was the exact opposite of inclusive, welcoming, and happy.

"That was probably a little too much sharing," Max mutters shyly, skimming a hand over his hair.

"No way," Doug says warmly. "Thank you for opening up to us." He glances pointedly at me, and I clear my throat.

"Yeah," I say gruffly.

Doug gives me a fond, long-suffering look, and then announces to Max, "We'll take you to the 3way tomorrow!"

Max does a double-take, and the way his big blue eyes get even wider is so cute, I almost smile. Instead I clarify, "Sometimes that's what the guys call their farm. But they mean it in a—uh, clean way."

Doug studies me with the little confused wrinkle in his nose that always makes me want to—ugh, focus, Zeke. "What do you mean, a 'clean' way?" he asks.

I lower my voice. "You know, *clean*. Like, *not* in a sex way."

Doug looks even more confused. "Why wouldn't sex be clean?"

I shoot a glance at Max. This is *exactly* why no heartless, soul-sucking journalist should be living with Doug twenty-four-seven. Doug is—well, Doug. For all the people with enough brain cells to recognize his selfless heart and relentless optimism for the fucking miracle they are, there are always a few assholes who want to laugh at him. Like Barton. I'm always ready to *end* those few people, by the way.

But to my relief, Max is smiling at Doug with no trace of mockery. "I'm glad to know that Mayor McEmbirk has a sex-positive attitude."

"So does Zeke," Doug assures Max. "He's the one who had the idea to buy up every book on the 'Most Banned in Florida' list and donate them to the school library." While I try to ignore the mystified look that earns me from Max, Doug keeps talking. "You said you wanted to follow me around for a few days, right? Zeke and I do part-time work for Stock Tree Farm, and we're helping them this week with the holiday rush. Oh, maybe we can even go over there tonight! We can start the interview at the farm if you want!"

"You have an event this evening," I remind him. Doug's

mayoral calendar lives entirely on my phone *and* almost entirely in my head—a detail Lydia definitely dropped in our conversation this past weekend.

Never get dumped by a lawyer. They come to the conversation with evidence.

"Oh yeah." Doug tilts his head. "Tomorrow, then. Is this the goat-herder dinner? Or the thing for the school?"

"It's the elementary school's play," I remind him patiently. "Remember? They always do it the week after Thanksgiving."

Max, meanwhile, is looking back and forth between us, his expression confused but interspersed with quick moments of horror whenever his eyes graze across me. Because I remind him of Jonah. Fucking fantastic.

"Anyway," Doug goes on, "tonight I'll cheer on the kids, and *tomorrow* we'll take you to the farm. You can come to the play and the farm with me—or just the farm. Whatever you want! How's that sound?"

Max frowns. His eyes dart back to me again. No surprise there, and I definitely don't blame him. I sure as hell wouldn't want to live in the same house as the doppelgänger of my high school bully. What a mind fuck.

Honestly, the whole identical twin thing is bullshit. I'd take the damn DNA back if I could, but I already tried that when I was eight. The doctors told me in no uncertain terms that Jonah and I were going to be twins forever, whether I liked it or not.

I still think if science can put a man on the moon they should be able to fix shitty genetics, but whatever.

"Okay," Max finally says. Slowly. Carefully. "I'll stay. That's what will be best for my article."

"Excellent!" Doug beams at him. "It'll be so much easier to tell you all about why the Holiday-Off is really a great idea if you're staying here." He claps his hands excitedly in a classic Doug motion, and my stomach clenches slightly as I process the scene in front of me.

Best friend who doesn't know that I'm bi or in love with him: check.

Brand-new crush who can't stop looking at me like I'm the devil incarnate: check.

Happy fucking holidays to me.

While we've got this chat going, I noticed the Airbnb listing specifies "no ritual sacrifices or unauthorized fires." Has this been a problem for you?

DOUG

When I set up the Airbnb listing, Zeke was worried about having strangers come, and he said those things could happen, so I edited our description.

ZEKE

That wasn't EXACTLY what I said.

DOUG

You had concerns, though.

ZEKE

I think what I said was, "if they want to commit a ritual sacrifice or set fire to the curtains, what are you going to do about it?"

I promise not to hold any ritual sacrifices or set any unauthorized fires.

DOUG

Excellent. Really glad you're our first guest, Max!

CHAPTER 3
DOUG

I'm used to people not warming up to Zeke right away. He has that growly face. And then there's the actual growling. And the swearing. He works pretty hard to keep it a secret, but Zeke is the nicest and most thoughtlessly generous and awesome person in the world.

We met on the first day of sixth-grade hockey practice. Torrance Perkins scored an own goal and while other kids laughed, Zeke picked up his stick for him and then carefully fed him the scrimmage-winning shot at the end of the match.

At school, everyone thought Zeke was scary at first. But I remembered that hockey practice and I knew Zeke's secret. So when kids dodged him in the halls and the teachers brought out their careful voices, the ones they used with troublemakers, I grabbed his arm and hauled him into conversations so that other people could see how great he was.

The day we moved into the dorms for our freshman year of college, Zeke rounded a corner with his growly face on and scared our across-the-hall neighbors so bad that one of them dropped the futon he was carrying. Eventually I tempted those guys into our room with a case of beer I smuggled into the building, and then I helped them see through Zeke's grouchy shell with a couple rounds of beer pong.

You can't play a drinking game together without bonding. I'm pretty sure that's science.

Too bad busting out a six-pack at the moment is probably inappropriate. It's 10 a.m., and Zeke tells me we're too old for day drinking.

"Hey," I tell Max solemnly, "I get that you were surprised to see Zeke. But he's actually the best. I can tell you're doubting me right now, but I promise you, he's *so* much nicer than he looks."

Zeke's contribution is one of his grunts. It's his agreement grunt, but Max probably doesn't know that, so he's not really helping my case.

"So, what do you like to eat for breakfast? Are you allergic to any of the standard ingredients in bath salts? Oh, do you like cats? We've got a whole feral colony living in the town square park right now."

"Doug," Zeke says gruffly, grabbing my elbow. "Just let the guy get settled in, huh?"

"Yeah, that would be good," Max agrees. "I'll text if I need something."

I nod. "Of course! Do you—" Zeke squeezes my elbow pointedly, and I cut myself off and swallow. "I'll keep an eye on my phone, then."

With a tiny, tense smile, Max closes the door between us.

Only then does Zeke let go of me, like he was holding me back from a fight instead of a friendly conversation.

I turn to him. "That was a close call. At least he decided to stay… no thanks to you." I shove him in the middle of his chest, which is kind of like tapping a boulder. He doesn't so much as lean away from me. He *does* frown hard and cross his arms.

"I think talking a guest into staying here against his will is a form of kidnapping."

"Oh my gosh, 'against his will,' really? He walked into the pig room all by himself! Anyway, don't distract me. Why didn't you want him to stay?"

"We shouldn't talk right here," Zeke mutters, grabbing my arm again. "He could hear us."

That's a good point. I let Zeke drag me out to the front porch. When we're facing each other, I raise my eyebrows, silently repeating my question.

"I don't care if he stays," Zeke says shortly. "It's your house, not mine."

"It's Grandma's house," I remind him automatically.

"She literally gave you the deed."

"But I haven't recorded it yet."

A look of deep frustration passes over Zeke's face. "Whatever. Anyway, I don't care. It's up to you—and your grandma, fine—to do what you want with the house. I'm just your roommate."

Zeke is my best friend. My teammate. He's family. He's definitely not *just* anything, and definitely not *just* a roommate. But when I tell him things like this he gets even more grumbly and scowly than usual, and I know when to pick my battles.

"You are so full of crud," I tell him instead. "Just try to be nice. Okay?"

"I won't have to be nice. I'm not going to be around that guy at all. I'll be in my room, he'll be in his."

"It's not like I'm gonna lock him in, Zeke, jeez. He has exclusive access to the pig room, but shared access to the common areas. It's all right there in the listing. Remember?" I guess I'm pretty mad, because I say the next thing without thinking. "If you have such a huge problem with having a stranger here, you could always stay at Lydia's."

His eyebrows climb practically to his hairline. "You're *telling* me to stay at Lydia's?"

"I mean, she *is* your girlfriend." *Practically your fianceé,* a voice whispers in the back of my head. He's been carrying around the ring for so long now, waiting for the right time or whatever. I try not to think about it. "You stay over there sometimes."

"Yeah, and whenever I do, you sulk because I miss chicken-fried-steak night, or movie night, or day-ending-in-y night."

"You know, *you* were the one who started our day-ending-in-y night traditions, so don't even start with me!"

Oops, I shouted a little. I only notice because Zeke gives a pointed glance toward the sidewalk, and I turn my head to find our neighbor pausing to look at us in surprise while her little dog jumps around excitedly at the end of his leash.

"Um, sorry about that, Mrs. Dobrow," I call apologetically, with a smile and a wave. "I hope our argument didn't disturb Cosmo."

She waves back. "Oh, no. It's all very exciting for him. No worries!" She walks on, tugging on Cosmo's leash so he'll follow her. I take a deep breath and turn back to Zeke.

"What is up with you? You were acting weird even before Max got here."

There's a wrinkle between his eyebrows, which tells me something is definitely up, even as he shakes his head. "I don't know what you're talking about."

"Did Lydia do something?"

The wrinkle again. "What? No. Why would you think that?"

I shrug. Everyone thinks Lydia is so great, and maybe she and Zeke have never had an actual fight that I've personally observed or been told about, but I'm sure they'll break up eventually. She's not right for him. I can't explain exactly why I know that. I just do.

"Well, if you're really opposed to the Airbnb thing, we can talk about it, but *after* Max leaves, okay? I really want him to stay."

"Of course he should stay," Zeke says gruffly. "What else is he going to do? Driving back and forth from Atherton every day is a waste of damn time."

"And the Full Moon Inn is not an option," I add darkly, thinking of the last time we performed a fire inspection of the only motel within fifteen miles of La Fierte.

"Fuck no," Zeke agrees immediately, rubbing his forehead. "God, now I'm picturing it all again."

"The seven extension cords running from the kitchen to the vending machine?" I shudder. "*Under* the rug?"

"Don't remind me." Zeke rubs his jaw and gazes toward the house like he's suspicious about what Max might be doing inside. "It just seems over the top for the reporter who's here to write about you to also be *living* with you."

"I think it makes perfect sense. What better way to get to know me?"

"Maybe your personal life should be off the record."

Sometimes, I honestly don't know what Zeke is talking about. "When he first called me, I told him nothing is off the record."

"Seriously? Doug, that's not—" Zeke stops himself and scowls. "I mean, haven't we learned that we can't trust journalists?"

My head feels fuzzy and I hear a faint ringing sound, like I'm on an airplane and the altitude made my ears pop. I blink and reach for the porch post.

"Fuck," Zeke mutters. "I'm sorry."

I frown at him. "Why are you sorry?"

"For bringing up the article. And for bringing it up… *like that.* I'm an asshole, and now you're upset."

"I'm not upset," I say quickly. "I'm just feeling a little funny."

Now Zeke looks worried. He puts his hand on my shoulder. "You look pale. Do you need to sit down?"

"Maybe I ate something weird," I say, letting him guide me down to the porch step even though I don't need his help. "You told me to throw out the Thanksgiving leftovers, but Grandma said the cranberry sauce would be fine for ten days."

"I don't think it was the cranberry sauce." Zeke sits beside me and leans his elbows against his knees. "Maybe we should actually talk about the article. I know it got under your skin."

I rub my forehead. "I ate some of the Jell-O salad too. And there was a tiny slice of pumpkin pie left that I couldn't just put in the trash."

"It's okay to be pissed off at Barton. He pisses people off all the time. He pissed me off last year. I know you remember. His coverage of my under-eights league championship game was a fucking joke. And I still think it was unethical of him to report on a game that his granddaughter played in."

"She's his great-granddaughter actually," I remind him. "Barton is *old*. He calls Grandma 'young lady.'"

I feel a little mean for calling Barton old, but I get a soft laugh out of Zeke, and I can't help but smile.

Zeke studies me for a moment, then nods decisively. "Max is going to write a great story about you," he declares.

"It's about the Holiday-Off. Not just *me*."

"Sure. But you're going to be in it too, and you're going to get the recognition you deserve."

I frown. "Zeke, I don't think Max is going to let you write the article for him."

"Obviously not, wiseass. But he seems like a smart guy. He'll see exactly how hard you're working and how much you care." He sighs. "I'm not going to get in the way of that, is what I meant. I'm sorry I got caught up in my stupid bullshit. It's just a gut-punch to see somebody look at *me* and see Jonah."

"Oh, yeah." I hesitate. I always try to be careful when this subject comes up. I don't know all that much about Zeke's early childhood. We've been best friends for most of our lives, but Zeke doesn't like to talk about the years before he and his mom moved to La Fierte.

The first time I met Jonah, I was excited. My best friend had a twin! I imagined an exact copy of Zeke. But the guy I met quickly disappointed me. How they look is pretty much the only thing that Zeke and Jonah have in common.

"Well," I tell Zeke, "Max just needs to get to know you. You're nothing like Jonah. Personally, I can't believe you two are even brothers."

Zeke was looking down, and now he glances up at me without raising his head, so I'm seeing his eyes through his dark lashes. Nothing about Zeke is really soft or gentle, *except* for his eyelashes, which are super long and curl up at the ends. He looks amused. "Oh yeah?"

"Yeah," I say, nodding. "I mean, you do look alike, which is kind of a trip. But he's all…" I pause and search for words. "He's one of those people you can tell is putting on an act. And you're completely real."

Zeke almost smiles, which is basically a full-on grin from someone else. I smile back and give him a quick hug, because even though he's always stiff and weird when I give him one, my grandma says sometimes you have to hug people for their own good. As long as they consent to it, of course.

Also, I like hugging him. It always makes *me* feel better after we fight.

"You're going to feel better after we work at the Stock farm tomorrow," I tell him, pulling away and clapping him on the shoulder.

"I do love cutting shit up with a chainsaw," Zeke agrees. "Are you sure you're all right?"

"I'm great," I say immediately, but there's a tiny itch in the back of my mind. Did I just lie to my best friend?

Doug named the group chat "The Men of Grandma's House"

DOUG

Are you sure you're okay, Max? You've been in
your room a while. Zeke isn't a bully, I promise.

ZEKE

Pretty sure telling him I'm not a bad person isn't
going to convince him.

DOUG

But I don't know how else to tell him that you're
not a butthead like your brother.

MAX

OMG GIRL, they are so fucking hot. Holy crap.
I'm in so much trouble.

Oh no. No NO NO NO. DAMMIT I did it again.
Sorry. That text was not intended for this thread.
SHIT.

I was texting my best friend about something or
someone that is most definitely not you two.

It was about this hot sauce that's a 500k on the
Scoville scale.

Nothing else that was hot. Just a mistake. Sorry.

DOUG

No problem! I've texted people by mistake, too!

MAX

And yes, I'm fine. Perfectly fine. Thank you.

CHAPTER 4

MAX

I sit on the bed under the watchful, cross-stitched eyes of a dozen cheerful pigs and put my head in my hands.

What am I going to do? I know that *Zeke* does not equal *Jonah*, and the guy I'm sharing a roof with had no part of the routine torture his brother put me through for years.

Jonah was relentless in every way—from how he called me "Maxi Pad" to making fun of my clothing to the way he made me feel like I was less than because I was out and attempting to be proud in high school. And then there was the Kool-Aid incident.

Staying here could *really* reopen wounds, because when I look at Zeke, I reflexively cringe, girding up for an assault.

Except…

Except a part of me is *really* attracted to Zeke. I thought Doug had muscles, but this guy? He's so ripped he looks like he's descended from Vikings. Or pirates. Or maybe Viking pirates.

It's really, really annoying that Zeke-slash-Jonah's face is such a fucking *gorgeous* face. And don't get me started on that dark hair. Those thick eyelashes. Those intense, dark eyes.

It's a very, very unfortunate reminder that I used to occasionally have *highly inappropriate* thoughts about my high school bully. I mean, who has the occasional sex dream about the guy who's low-key torturing him with verbal attacks and pranks? I've never even been able to talk about that with my therapist. It's waaay too embarrassing.

The best-case scenario here is that I completely forget who Zeke's twin brother is and just focus on the article I came to write. But even if I could wipe Jonah out of my memory, this living situation would not be ideal.

Why? Because one gorgeous, happy man, plus one gorgeous, grumpy man equals masturbation material for me for weeks. And I was already horny before I got here.

I can tough it out, I tell myself. I can do this. Having twenty-four-hour access to Doug will help me to write a much better article—I'm sure of that.

I make it through the afternoon by researching the hell out of Vermont local politics on my laptop. I count the number of pigs scattered through the decor in my bedroom (twenty-three). I check in with my mom and then my best friend, Reyna. I draft notes for my article. I update my social media.

There's a knock at the door in the late afternoon, and I find Doug in the doorway, wearing a suit and tie. Oh good gracious me. A buff guy dressing up is extra hot.

He rubs the back of his neck. "Want to go to the school play at La Fierte Elementary?"

I look down at my jeans and T-shirt. "Do I need to change?"

Doug smiles, and it's the kind of smile that makes everything in the world seem better. "Nah. I dress up because I'm the mayor and get my photo taken and stuff."

Zeke comes up behind him, and the sight of his face has the same effect on me it did earlier. But this time it eases more quickly, maybe because I'm distracted by the fact that he's also in a dress shirt, and, okay, yes. Viking pirate cleans up nice, too.

"I'd love to come along," I say. "Let me grab my camera and notebook." I point at them. "And I think I should change into some slacks too. Give me a minute, and I'll join you." I'm here to write an article, but my new roommates are stirring up more sinful thoughts than journalistic ones.

Watching them cross the La Fierte Elementary School parking lot side-by-side, I can't help but stare. Doug's hair is medium brown and Zeke's is dark, but they're both suntanned, almost the same height. They seem to be in lockstep as they make their way to the school cafeteria, which apparently for tonight will double as an auditorium. Zeke has a grumpy look on his face, but when he says something that makes Doug laugh, I catch a fleeting smile that curls one side of his mouth. His eyes lighten when he glances at his friend.

Holy balls, they are both so attractive. I don't know how they go anywhere together without stopping traffic. Then a Subaru rolls to a halt so that someone in the back can lean out the window and call out, "Fireman Doug! Fireman Zeke!"

I guess they *do* stop traffic. The guys wave enthusiastically until the car moves along.

When they enter the auditorium, Doug is greeted by a ton of young parents—no surprise there—and he shakes hands all around. The three of us are seated toward the front, but on the side so that the towering firefighters aren't blocking the view of everyone seated behind them.

The lights dim, and the play begins.

I don't know what it is about children performing songs that brings a lump to my throat. Something about the sweet voices makes me feel like I'm that age again, innocent and vulnerable. It makes me long for a kinder experience than I had.

Maybe I'm getting a small chance to redo my experience, being here with Zeke.

Doug claps for every scene, and I get some good shots of him when he has no idea I'm taking pictures of him. He's totally engrossed in the story.

A few kids flub memorized lines, some are reading them from little scraps of paper, and the girl who plays a bear stands there picking her nose, but overall, it's a sweet play about solving problems by working together.

As soon as the kids take their bows and receive their standing ovation, pandemonium ensues. The cutest pandemonium I've ever experienced. Doug and Zeke are swarmed by kids. *Swarmed.*

While I understand why they may know Mayor Doug, I'm rather confused as to why so many of the children are hanging on Zeke. I can't blame them—he's less growly and more adorable around them.

When we're finished, we join the families in the rec room for a potluck.

If this kind of thing makes up all of Doug's mayoral duties, they're charming, but I wonder what motivated him to run for the office. Does he just like to be the center of attention, or does he have some deeper agenda? Is Doug *capable* of having an agenda? He seems so guileless. But I wouldn't be a reporter if I didn't investigate, and investigate I shall continue to do—tomorrow, at a tree farm run by a queer throuple.

Growing up, I couldn't have imagined that members of a polyamorous relationship could live openly in small-town Vermont and be met with not just acceptance, but celebration. Maybe my old stomping grounds have changed more than I realized in the past decade.

"Who are you?" An older man with gray hair and fading khakis held up by argyle-print suspenders appears next to me, carrying a plate of cookies and scowling.

I blink back my surprise at his abrupt introduction. "Hello. I'm, uh, Max Rivers. I'm a freelance journalist from DC. I'm in town to interview Mayor Doug McEmbirk."

He scowls even harder. "Son, I'm in charge of all newspaper reporting in this town. We don't need no flatlanders encroaching on our business here in La Fierte and writing nonsense about matters that are none of their concern."

I almost choke on the sip of punch I just took. I forgot about the penchant some Vermonters have for referring to non-Vermonters as "flatlanders." I kind of wonder: would they call someone from Colorado or Montana a flatlander? I mean, those mountains could eat up the sweet little baby mountains in Vermont.

"Well, sir," I say, doing my best to hang onto my most polite voice, "I'm from Vermont originally. I grew up in Atherton."

He doesn't recoil when he discovers that I'm from La Fierte's rival town, but my local ties also clearly do not impress him. He gestures at me sharply with his cookie plate, which is fortunately bundled in cellophane. I glance at the delicious-looking sugar cookies with rainbow sprinkles heaped on the plate as he demands, "You're here about that ridiculous Holiday-Off, aren't you?"

It's pretty clear to me at this point that I'm face-to-face with Barton Asterstop, editor of *The Pigeon* and sworn enemy of Doug.

"Yes," I tell him honestly. "I guess I am."

"Hey there, Barton." Doug swoops in next to me, smiling broadly. "Good to see you, as always, sir."

Now Barton jerks the cookie plate toward Doug. "Mister Mayor, I already told that secretary of yours over at the town hall: I ain't retracting my editorial. That fool Holiday-Off you got us embroiled in is a silly waste of money. Money that could be better spent!" He shakes his head. "I've said it before and I'll say it again: you had no business running for this job."

To Doug's credit, his smile never breaks during any moment of Barton's speech. He's opening his mouth to reply when Zeke appears on the other side of me, arms crossed.

And the scowl on his face? In the scowling Olympics, it would take gold over Barton's scowl, no contest.

"Mr. Asterstop," says Zeke, his glare never wavering. "I don't like to get into arguments with angry newspaper editors who bully town mayors in front of small children. Perhaps it's time you left."

Barton tilts his head up. Zeke might be a third of his age, twice his size, and the better scowler, but I have to be impressed by the older man's nerve. The look in his eye is challenging. "I've got more of a right to be here than either of *you*. I'll have you know my great-granddaughter's in this play. You know, the one who led the butt-kicking against your team in last year's championship?"

Your team? What team is he talking about?

Zeke's eyebrows go up, and now his expression can only be described as *murderous*. Doug steps between him and Barton, his bright smile still in place—even if it does look a little forced.

"Okay, everyone," he says. "I think we can all agree this isn't the time or place for this conversation. Casey was excellent in the play, Mr. Asterstop. She really brought the grizzly energy! Zeke and Max, let's head out. Okay?"

Zeke growls, bringing *much* more grizzly energy than the little nose-picker who must be Asterstop's great-granddaughter. For a moment, I think he's going to ignore Doug and hold his ground. But then he nods and strides for the door.

Doug extends his hand to Barton, the portrait of manners. "Good to see you again, sir."

Ignoring Doug's offer of a handshake, Barton grunts and turns away, and finally, Doug's smile wavers ever so slightly. Only for a moment, of course—and then it's right back in place.

Wow, am I having a hard time keeping up with my copious mental notes. So much just happened.

The way Zeke swooped in for Doug like that—if I didn't know better, I'd think the two of them were a couple. The other part of my surprise stems from seeing someone with Zeke's face taking the role of a protector, not a predator. I feel like I'm staring at one of those funhouse mirrors that distorts images in front of you until you're not sure what you're seeing anymore.

When I booked this trip, I had a feeling that returning to Vermont would mess with my head. Still, the reality is more bizarre than anything I could have dreamed up.

DOUG

Max, don't forget we're heading over to Stock
Tree Farm first thing in the morning. Still want to
join us?

MAX

Fuck wait until i tell you about the suits. SO HOT.

SHOOT, sorry, Doug and Zeke. Texted the wrong
number again. Um, I was still talking about the
hot sauce.

ZEKE

Hot sauce wears suits?

MAX

It's a term. You know, for the relative hotness of
sauce.

DOUG

Really? I've never heard of that before.

MAX

Yeah. Like three suits mean the sauce is very hot.

DOUG

Oh neat. Zeke, we've gotta tell Charlie Pendri to
start rating their sauces like that. Makes a lot
more sense to me than the Scoville scale.

ZEKE

I'm glad it makes sense to someone.

CHAPTER 5

MAX

The following morning, I stumble out into the living room, hoping these guys are the kind who drink coffee, rather than sociopaths who drink tea in the morning. Tea is for after I'm awake.

Okay, kidding. I take my caffeine seriously, though.

Zeke is sitting on the couch glaring at his phone while Doug is in the kitchen.

"Hi, Max!" Doug calls. "Did you sleep well? Want some breakfast? And how do you take your coffee?"

I head toward the kitchen so I don't have to shout my reply. Doug is in joggers, and his T-shirt is well-worn and molded to his body. I can see every muscle in his shoulders, biceps, and pecs. I want to bite my knuckle.

"Hey!" he says as I come into the kitchen. "I'm making sandwiches to take to the tree farm. Did you sleep okay? Do you need anything to help you feel more at home?"

I'm going to have to get used to Doug's aggressive and energetic affection.

"Everything is great," I tell him, which is mostly true. "Did I hear you say something about coffee?" I add hopefully.

He hands me a mug that says "Grandmas never run out of

cookies or hugs," and then he turns back to whatever he's got spread across the kitchen counter.

"Do you like turkey or ham? And what about mustard?"

I watch him, trying to catch up. "You're making me a sandwich?"

"Yep! For lunch at the tree farm. Embry's a good cook, but we don't want to impose. So we brown bag it."

"Turkey, please. No mustard. I can pay you for groceries—"

Doug holds up a hand. "No. I insist," he says. "Grandma always said everyone's welcome for a meal."

A grin overtakes my face as I head to the coffeemaker. "Okay, well, thank you, Grandma and Doug."

"You're welcome. Do you want cereal or toast or a bagel or eggs or yogurt for breakfast?"

"Maybe just coffee for starters?"

"You got it." Doug tilts his head. "I know I assume stuff and Zeke says that makes a donkey out of you and me—"

"I said ass, Doug," Zeke calls, grumpily.

"But dang it, Zeke. I don't say that word," Doug calls back, then continues to address me. "So I don't want to assume, but you still want to come with us, right?"

"Absolutely. I want to learn more about you."

Doug hands me cream and sugar. I doctor my coffee, then gulp it down while Doug finishes packing the lunches. A few minutes later, we file toward the door.

Zeke and Doug have a fascinating, instinctive way of working together in even small ways, like how Zeke loops a scarf around his neck and hands a second one over to Doug, who takes it without looking up as he's stepping into his boots, like he just knows that when he reaches out Zeke will be ready to hand him what he needs.

And I'm swept up in it too, surprised when Zeke fingers the collar of my light jacket, frowns, and then wordlessly drapes a second coat over my shoulders. I drown in it even with my other coat on, but before I can make a joke about it, each one of them has taken a sleeve to deftly roll back the cuffs.

"You two really know how to work together," I say, feeling a little faint as I follow them out onto the porch toward the truck.

"Well," Doug says, shooting me one of his constant smiles, "we played hockey on the same team for six years of youth and high school leagues and four in college."

"And you work together now, at the fire station," I add.

"Firehouse," Zeke corrects, opening the truck door for me. It's Zeke's truck, not Doug's. It's a little rougher around the edges, with a band of rust in the rear wheel well and some chipped paint on the fender.

I scramble onto the running board then feel the light touch of Zeke's hand on my back, balancing me. My skin flames at the pressure, even though there's several layers of bulky fabric between us.

"Right, firehouse," I amend, flustered. Zeke catches my eye as he climbs in beside me, and I blink in surprise because his expression is almost playful.

Doug swings the igloo cooler with our packed lunches into the back of the truck, then gets in the driver's side. Because of course they also drive each other's vehicles.

The truck has a single bench seat. Since I'm half the size of one of them, I'm strapped in the middle, and I have all the feels being between these amazingly beautiful, strong men. I guess I feel kind of sheltered in a way. While I don't know them well, I don't think Doug could hurt anyone. He's too pure. Zeke? Well. I'll just wait and see. He seems like he should be defending a castle from invaders. Lucky castle inhabitants.

"So," I ask, my journalist training coming back to me. "How do you balance being a mayor and a firefighter? I read some of your Insta posts about the importance of maintaining supervision while burning candles in the house." That's a neutral way of saying "I stalked you thoroughly on the internet," right?

Images run through my head on a fast-paced reel, imagining

Doug—and Zeke—in action as firefighters. Did I mention I have a thing for firefighters? I mean, who doesn't? I have so many fantasies, mostly involving a firehouse pole—and other types of poles.

Doug's hot enough to start a fire, and Zeke would burn the world to the ground.

My arms keep brushing theirs and occasionally Doug's hand brushes my knee when he reaches for the gear shift, and my whole body is on high alert. I swear I'm getting a vibe from them… *both* of them. I assumed they were straight and have no hard evidence to the contrary—but there was that scene after the play last night, where Zeke went all alpha-alpha male on the editor of *The Pigeon*. I'm still not sure what to make of all that.

"Doug's very committed to the town," Zeke says. "He just makes it all work."

I've been distracted by my horny thoughts, leaving me struggling for a moment to remember the question that I asked seconds ago and that Zeke is now answering. Oh, right: I wanted to know how Doug handles the different hats he wears around La Fierte.

"I couldn't do it without a lot of help from Zeke," Doug adds.

Zeke shrugs and grunts. It occurs to me that I never once heard Jonah James grunt the entire time we went to high school together. Jonah always knew what to say, whether he was ingratiating a teacher, impressing a cheerleader… or jabbing a knife made of words right where he knew it would hurt most.

I clear my throat. "It seems like a lot to have on your plate," I say to Doug. "And you're also a seasonal worker at a Christmas tree farm?"

Doug turns onto the route headed toward the outskirts of La Fierte. "We've always helped Jeb out when he needs it," Doug says.

"Which is less than he used to, when he was running the farm by himself," Zeke adds. "But even the three of them need all the help they can get during the winter holiday season. And this year they had a pumpkin crop, so we helped earlier this fall too."

"And last summer, at the first annual Goat Social," Doug interjects.

"Like an ice cream social, but with goats," Zeke explains, as if that clarifies things.

I'm starting to see Zeke has a habit of translating Doug's off-the-wall statements, but this time he's not making sense either. I scribble "goat social??" in my notes and shake my head, smiling. "So how did you become mayor?"

"I ran in an election," Doug says. "And won."

He really is too sweet for words. I know I'm supposed to be impartial, but after just a day with Doug, he's won me over with his earnestness. I want to protect him at all costs, and thinking back on the Barton Asterstop article that ultimately led me here, I can see why Zeke can't stand the guy. "What motivated you to run for mayor?" I ask Doug. I've done research on this, but I want to hear it in his words.

"We needed to save the fire department. We serve the whole county, and there's a good volunteer program. Based on that, Mayor Thistle thought the town was paying more than its share and was going to cut funding. But there was no room in the county budget to pick up the slack. That would mean we would have to cut back on services, but that would have been dangerous. When people need help, we need to be there for them." He shrugs. "Lots of people disagreed with the past mayor, but nobody wanted to run against him. So I signed up myself."

I believe that Doug's motivations really were that simple. I've never met anyone quite like him, but he's truly an open book. I turn my head toward the man on the other side of me, who's wearing a thoughtful frown as he gazes out the windshield. I think I've got Doug figured out. Zeke, however, is still a big mystery. My story isn't about Zeke, exactly, but clearly he's a huge part of Doug's life *and* his tenure as mayor.

"And what about you?" I ask Zeke. "Do you have a side gig when you're not fighting fires?"

Doug answers for him, and I notice these two do that for each other all the time. Answer one another's questions; finish each other's sentences. It seems to be part of their rhythm. "Zeke coaches hockey."

"For college?" I ask, scribbling in my notebook.

"No. Under-eights," Zeke says.

I blink. "Meaning kids?"

He nods.

"Zeke's a great coach," Doug says proudly. "Last year he had the youngest aged players on average in the league, and they still made it to the championship."

"Barton's great-granddaughter's on the team that beat us." Ah, that's what Barton was talking about last night. Zeke shakes his head. "I knew we should've done more speed drills."

Doug laughs. "Yeah, right. That's why half the time you let practice out early so the kids can build snow forts."

Zeke as a gentle giant, basically babysitting small children? This… doesn't compute. Except it kind of does, after seeing him at that play last night. I just can't get used to the idea that anyone with the last name "James" would be allowed within five feet of a kid. I have so many questions, but we're already pulling down a rutted windy driveway to a clearing. Doug stops the truck near a barn that has "3way Christmas Trees" painted on a banner and comes around to my side. Zeke gets out first, then holds out a hand to help me down.

It's like ten feet down to the ground. Okay, maybe more like three, but I'm not exactly leggy and the ground is uneven. I could use the help, but still I look at Zeke's hand dubiously for a moment before accepting it.

I take a deep breath before grabbing his rough, callused hand. A shiver runs down my spine at his touch, because if Zeke wasn't the exact image of my tormentor, I'd think that in addition to being smoking hot, he's a total gentleman.

Dealing with Zeke as not-Jonah scrambles my brain, but I need to remind myself that I don't know this person. I need to give Zeke a chance to make his own impression in my mind.

Releasing his hand as my feet hit the snow, I look up at his dark eyes. "Thanks," I mutter.

He grunts. Again.

Definitely grumpy, and definitely not Jonah.

I take a breath and challenge myself to try this: to try seeing Zeke as someone different from the brother who made it his life mission to destroy my teenage years.

Doug bounds around the back of the truck and heads toward a light-haired man with a beard who's strolling toward us. He's wearing snug jeans and a thick red winter coat, and he's the definition of sexy farm boy. I recognize him immediately from Adam's Instagram account, though he's even hotter in person. "Come on, Max! I'd like you to meet Jeb Stock!"

"Jeb, this is Max Rivers."

"Nice to meet you," I say, shaking Jeb's hand. Like Zeke, Jeb's rough skin doesn't hide the fact that he makes a living by doing things with his hands. Also, he's tall, too. I feel like a teacup Maltese surrounded by Saint Bernards and Newfoundlands.

"He's here to write an article about the Holiday-Off. And about me being mayor."

"That's so cool," Jeb says, beaming. "La Fierte needs more publicity."

"Does it, though?" asks a gruff voice behind me.

Spinning around, I come face to face with yet another tall and good-looking man. Jeb smiles at him. "Excuse my partner. He likes to forget that we actually need customers to stay in business. Max, this is Embry Matthews."

"Uh, I know," I say, trying not to stumble over my words. "I, um, follow Adam on social media." Embry has hair that's more gold than Jeb's dusty brown, a deep suntan, and a guarded expression. The guys look exactly as good in person as they do in Adam's posts, despite all the commenters who are convinced their collective hotness is unrealistic and that they must be heavy-handed with their use of filters.

Then Adam O'Connor himself walks up behind Embry and

loops an arm around his waist. I swallow the urge to cheer like a fan at a concert. Adam O'Connor is flat-out gorgeous, with light green eyes and dark hair, neatly dressed—of course—in a buttoned-up flannel and camel-colored corduroy pants.

"Hi," I squeak. "I'm Max."

Adam smiles at me, and it rearranges my insides. "I'm Adam. It's good to have you here, Max."

I try not to show my excitement, and judging by the look on Zeke's face, it doesn't work. Or maybe that's just Zeke's normal look.

Regardless, Jeb claps me on the back. I somehow manage not to fall over.

"Thanks for following the farm on our socials, man!" Jeb says. "Adam's done so much to build up our online presence. And I can't wait to read your article. Doug's really the best," he adds. "Have you tried his pies? Or eggnog? He's a great cook, too. It was surprising he ran for mayor, though, I gotta say. He's the last person I expected to take an interest in politics."

Doug frowns. "The last person?"

Jeb's face falls. "I didn't mean that in a bad way! It's just that politics are kind of stuffy, you know? Behind a desk instead of on skates or driving a fire truck? It was hard for me to picture."

"Right," Doug says, but I can tell Jeb brushed up against a sore subject. Which I can understand, particularly in light of Asterstop's scathing reporting.

I'm cynical enough to know that Asterstop probably isn't the first person to not take Doug seriously. Doug's young and good looking and a little naive—okay, a lot naive. But that doesn't mean he can't be a good mayor.

"Do you mind if I take photos?" I ask, pulling up the release form on my phone.

"No, not at all," Jeb says, as he takes my phone and signs the release, as does Adam. Embry does it too after Jeb elbows him.

"Thanks! So, what are we doing today?" I ask, looping my camera strap around my neck.

"Zeke and Doug were going to help out down at the far north stand of trees. That's our shuttle over there," Jeb says, pointing to a large tractor festooned with tinsel and hooked up to a wagon rowed with hay bales for bench seating. I recognize the set-up; I took a few hay-rack rides during my childhood in Atherton.

"Why don't you hop on the hay," Doug says, gesturing to the wagon. "We'll take you over to the part of the nursery that they're harvesting this year."

"Sounds good!" I say.

Doug fires up the old tractor while Zeke opens the back of the wagon and lets me up. A few other families walk over from the parking area to join us and get in with me, and then Zeke climbs up to sit right next to me, even closer than when we were in the truck. His side is against mine, and I like the way he feels, even though on some level it seems so wrong.

Not Jonah. He's not Jonah, I repeat to myself.

The scent of diesel and the noise of the tractor accompany us as we take off toward the rows of trees. I snap a few photos. The landscape is just so charming, with the barns and outbuildings, orderly Christmas trees, and neatly painted fences. My brain is already speeding toward potential article layouts.

As we near the end of the ride, there's a group of people standing next to a line of cut Christmas trees, waiting for their ride back to the parking lot.

Zeke stiffens his shoulders, and I look where he's staring.

Oh, for fuck's sake. Jonah James is here.

He's behind a small kid who's holding a candy cane. Jonah's expression is one of confusion when he sees his brother, but then his eyes latch onto mine, and he leers at me.

I never, ever should've returned to Vermont.

ZEKE

That's what everyone always says after a
breakup.

DOUG

Who broke up?

ZEKE

Shit. Wrong chat. Please fucking ignore that text.

DOUG

What's going on???

ZEKE

FFS, I was going to tell you. I just didn't get
around to it. Lydia and I broke up.

DOUG

What? You were going to propose!!!

ZEKE

Please don't make a big deal out of this.

MAX

Um guys? You know you're in this group chat,
right?

ZEKE

FOR FUCK'S SAKE.

CHAPTER 6

ZEKE

My brother is wearing a look of surprise, followed closely by a smile—but his smile always looks more like a sneer. My nephew, Shay, sees me and starts jumping up and down so excitedly that he drops his candy cane.

Well, this situation is about a million miles from ideal. Ideal is Mars, and we're stuck on planet fucking Earth on a Vermont tree farm.

When Jonah and I were kids and he was really being shitty, I used to imagine I was going to fly to Mars and leave him the fuck behind. I haven't thought about that daydream in a long time, but I'm sure as fuck thinking about it now as I look at Max's face. He looks at my brother like he's a combination of the Grim Reaper and Michael Myers.

"Uncle Zeke!" Shay comes running over to me. "I thought I wasn't seeing you until later!" He latches his arms around my waist. "I missed you."

"You just saw Uncle Zeke two days ago at hockey practice, Shay." Jonah stoops over to pick up the candy cane then saunters over to us, brows raised. "Zeke-o, I didn't know you knew Maxi Pad."

Max's face goes bright red, and his mouth freezes around words. "I—you—" he stutters out.

"What's a maxi-pad?" Shay asks as he loosens his grip on me to look up at his asshole of a father.

"It's a protective garment people wear to keep their underwear from getting dirty." Thankfully I have a ready, child-appropriate answer because I stumbled through answering the same question from one of the kids on my team last year.

"Oh, cool." Shay's eyes are bright. "Like underwear armor! Dad, can I get a maxi-pad for Christmas?"

"Oh, for crying out loud." Jonah rubs his hands over his face. "Now I'll never get him to stop asking, Zeke. Thanks a lot."

"Serves you right for calling someone names," I reply smoothly. "And *Max*, for the record, is staying at Doug's with us."

"Max is interviewing me!" Doug hops off the tractor behind me and settles a hand on Max's shoulder. "I certainly hope I didn't just hear you call our friend some ridiculous nickname and wreck shop on our La Fierte hospitality."

"It was definitely misogynistic, too," I add.

"Like when that coach from up north told his player he was acting like a little girl," Shay tells his father somberly. "That's really disrespectful, Dad."

"Maybe we misheard you, Jonah?" Doug asks calmly. "Since I know how much you value teaching Shay kindness in your house."

"Oh, for fu—for goodness' sake!" Jonah rolls his eyes. "Maxi— I mean, Max, I was just surprised to see you back here in Vermont. Thought I'd bring out your old nickname as a fun reminder. *Sorry.* Didn't mean to start a whole federal case."

Max still looks completely bewildered and horrified by the situation. I can't say I blame him. If I'd just run into my childhood archnemesis for the first time in years, I'd probably be that exact same shade of pale. But my childhood archnemesis is Elias Tucker, who earned the title in the eighth grade when Doug started sharing sandwiches with him at lunch instead of me. Fortunately, Elias moved to Rome last year.

Not that it's fair to compare sandwich-sharing to bullying.

Maybe Doug and I should have let Max speak for himself there. Dammit, I hope he doesn't mind that we jumped all over Jonah without letting him get a word in edgewise. But I've never been very good at just standing around and watching Jonah—or our father, or Barton Asterstop—treat people like shit. If my parents hadn't gotten divorced and split us up when they did, Jonah and I would probably have spent all six years of junior high and high school giving each other black eyes.

"No problem," Max mutters to Jonah, but there's a quiver in his voice that tells me he's got plenty of problems with how this entire interaction just played out.

"We've got practice this week, right, Uncle Zeke?" Shay grips my arm and bends his knees so he's dangling there. Kids are like monkeys, I swear.

"Of course, little man." I hoist him up and hug him. He giggles and loops his skinny arms around my neck. I can't keep from smiling. I love how open and affectionate Shay is. My dad gives him hell for it, but I have to allow Jonah some credit for letting Shay be a happy, loving little boy despite our own father figure's example. Jonah's heart is in the right place when it comes to Shay, and he'd do anything for him.

Well, anything except let Shay quit hockey and take dance lessons instead. But that's a problem we're currently working around. Or at least I'm working around it.

"Yay!" Shay calls out as I set him down. He peers over at Max. "So your name isn't Maxi Pad?"

"Just Max," Max tells him meekly.

"Cool. Are you coming to our hockey practice tomorrow?"

Jonah ruffles Shay's hair. "Shay, bud, we gotta get onto the wagon or we're going to miss our ride back to the car."

"But I want to stay here with Uncle Zeke!" Shay whines.

Max's face moves from pale to a shade of eggplant—the color

of   please-don't-make-me-stand-around-making-small-talk-with-Jonah-James. "I'll see you tomorrow, Shay," I remind my nephew again. "Looks like you've got to get home to decorate a tree."

"Oh yeah!" His face lights up with excitement. "I picked out orange lights! And Dad said you're coming to dinner at Grand-pa's next week. That'll be great!"

I scowl at Jonah as Shay sprints to the wagon. "I never said I was coming to dinner," I remind him darkly.

"Oh, for fu—fudge's sake," Jonah hisses. "Grow a pair and just come over, Z. I don't know what the hell your problem is. Dad's been asking for you ever since he heard you and Lydia broke up."

Doug's eyes snap to my face, and I do a mental round of *shit-fuckdamns* in my head. Doug's been asking me a lot of questions lately about my breakup with Lydia. I've been doing my best to dodge giving him any actual answers. But Doug's pretty fucking persistent when he wants to be. It won't be long before I run out of ways to avoid telling him the truth. *Hey, man, Lydia broke up with me because I'm hopelessly in love with you.*

Shitfuckdamn indeed.

"It's good to see you again, Maxi—I mean, *Max*. So many memories, am I right? Like that time you ended up locked in the computer lab? Who knew none of the teachers would be able to find the key for six hours?" Jonah snorts and claps Max on the shoulder so hard that he stumbles right into my side. An electric sensation fills my body when he crashes into me, and I grab hold of his side, pulling him up against me. His body fits perfectly against mine, and when he glances up at me, eyes wide and almost watery, I have this impossible urge to just pick him up and carry him away from Vermont and all the bullshit surrounding it. Away from my worthless brother and the memories I'm guessing Max is sorting through right now.

Jonah notices my arm going around Max and gives me a strange look. If we were still kids, I would have let Max go like he was on fire. But I'm not a fucking kid, and fuck Jonah. I squeeze Max's hip and glare at my brother.

"Dad!" Shay calls. Jonah gives me a final parting glance, eyes narrowed, then turns and jogs over to the wagon. Of course he avoids the steps welded to the wagon and instead awkwardly catapults himself over the side of it, nearly breaking his leg in the process.

Fucking Jonah.

The tractor fires up with Embry at the wheel, and the wagon lumbers off. The families we rode down with are scurrying around the orchard, examining trees and calling out in excitement when they find their favorite ones.

Meanwhile, Doug, Max, and I stand together in a tight circle. Max is still latched to my side, and I'm not finding the will to loosen my hold on him either.

"Well," says Doug. "That was…"

"A disaster?" Max finishes.

"A fuckhole of a trainwreck?" I try.

"I was thinking of something more along the lines of *not so great.* But okay, we'll take *disaster* instead." Doug shakes his head at me. "You owe another dollar to the swear jar, Zeke."

Max bursts out laughing. "You have a swear jar?"

I roll my eyes. "I'm allowed regular swear words, but compound swear words get taxed." It's a rule Doug instituted after I said *shitfuckdamn* one too many times in our house.

"No way." Max wipes at tears in the corner of his eyes. "You two are something else. Hey, listen. Thanks for saying what you both just said to Jonah. I appreciated it. Nobody's ever done that for me before—especially with him." He still hasn't moved away from me, and I take the opportunity to gently squeeze his shoulder.

"If we'd been with you in high school," I tell him solemnly, "we would have stood up for you then, too." Doug nods in agreement, his face locked with determination, and Max just shakes his head as he looks back and forth between us.

"I think I believe you." He pulls away from me, finally, and I carefully ignore the twinge that runs through my body as his warmth disappears. He's here to write a story about Doug, for fuck's sake. Not to mention that if I did decide to be into him in any kind of way, I'd have to actually say the damn words out loud that I haven't really said to anyone but Lydia my entire life.

Hi. I'm bisexual.

And even scarier, I'd probably have to say those words out loud in front of Doug.

Max starts exploring the rows of trees, and Doug sends me a long, searching look. I don't think I'm going to be able to keep *all* my secrets from Doug much longer.

Fucking Jonah. He just had to mention my breakup.

MAX

I know Vermont is weird, but since when do we have a state cow? I thought Marty was messing with me during our interview this morning, but I looked it up. What kind of name is Vermonica? SMH

DOUG

It's the PERFECT name! Didn't you see the spot on her forehead? Isn't it the EXACT shape of Vermont?

ZEKE

Debatable. I like the leaf though

MAX

Leaf??

DOUG

She was born with a maple leaf on her side!

MAX

Okay, I see it now. That is actually kinda cute

DOUG

And some people say that if you look real close, the spot on her haunches looks like the outline of Lake Champlain

If we could get Vermonica for the Holiday-Off judging, Atherton would never have a chance.

MAX

Is that a possibility?

DOUG

Marty's brother works at the Capitol! Marty thought he might be able to help squeeze us into the Christmas Eve appearance schedule. So far, no luck. She's at a governor's event the whole evening. [string of sad face emojis]

MAX

I swear, Vermont has somehow gotten MORE weird since I left.

CHAPTER 7

DOUG

"Okay," I tell the crowd, as Marty, the town secretary, pokes at the projection screen with a large stick he grabbed off of one of the trees outside. Our town hall meeting area isn't large—it's maybe twice the size of my living room, and half the space is taken up with overflowing boxes of holiday decorations—and it's packed to the gills tonight. Everyone's come out to hear about the Holiday-Off and where we stand against Atherton.

Max and Zeke are leaning against the wall at the back of the room. Zeke's arms are crossed and his face is locked in a wary expression as he scans the crowd. I know he's on the lookout for Barton, but so far Barton's a no-show.

Not that it matters. He's in the same knitting circle with half the people here. He'll know about everything we discuss tonight even if he doesn't see one minute of the meeting.

Max has a tablet balanced on his left arm and he's using a stylus to take frantic notes. And I'm determined not to worry whether his notes about me are positive.

"Okay," I repeat. "So, we're on budget for decorations. Now, about the twelve-foot menorah—"

"Already ordered!" Dellie Vranos calls out. "My cousin's bringing it over from New Hampshire next week."

The crowd murmurs approvingly.

"Great," I tell her. "So, that leaves entertainment. The choir's got a wonderful showcase planned."

Althea Lawson sighs from her seat in the front row. "Our choir's not going to cut the mustard, Douglas. I hear Atherton's got much bigger plans than that."

"Like what?" someone calls across the room.

"Well." Althea leans forward, like she's sharing a secret, and everyone in the room leans toward her. Heck, even I do. "This isn't official or nothing—*yet*. But my sister's boyfriend's hairdresser's cousin heard that… Atherton booked Vermonica."

The entire room gasps, but I barely notice.

My head feels light, like I've just been checked into the boards.

The clatter when Marty drops his stick breaks me out of my daze. "But she's not available!" he cries. "She was already booked for that governor's event!"

Althea shrugs. "I know. But my sister's boyfriend's hairdresser's cousin says that the booking got canceled, and someone in Atherton apparently knows the right people. They snatched her up before anyone else even got a chance." She shakes her head. "Like I said, it's not official. But my sister's boyfriend's hairdresser's cousin says that—"

"Right. Thank you, Althea." I gulp in some air as I scan the room. Everyone's faces have gone slack with shock, and my mind's blank.

What the heck am I going to say to them? Vermonica is a state *treasure*. She has more social media followers than our congresspeople. If Atherton got her, we're toast. We have no chance of winning.

I look at the screen, full of big dollar amounts for decorations, food, and music, and my vision blurs as a sick feeling floods my stomach. Is all that money I decided to spend going to go to waste? Zeke said that it could take years to recover what we took out of budget reserves to cover everything we've purchased for the Holiday-Off. And now Atherton is going to win, and everyone is going to be disappointed?

Without thinking, my fingers slide into the hip pocket of my jeans. There's a folded piece of paper there, and I toy with the weathered edges for a second before recalling myself and snatching my hand back, curling my fingers into a fist.

I try to focus on the present moment, where the meeting attendees are shouting at one another.

"We need to book Bowie! He's the only one who can upstage Vermonica!"

"Bowie's dead, remember? We held a memorial in the park, and Javier Munez cried for three days."

"Oh, right. Taylor Swift, then!"

"You think we can book *Taylor Swift?* Are you out of your mind? If I—"

"My aunt's got a cow named Taylor Swiss."

"Who cares what your aunt's cow's name is?"

"Adam!" I shout, and everyone in the room whirls around to look at me. "Adam O'Connor," I repeat.

Looking startled, Adam slowly stands up from his chair in the middle of the room between Jeb and Embry. "Um, yes?" he asks, one eyebrow raised.

"That ice sculpting team you hosted at the Stock Farm last winter—didn't they just get featured in a national magazine?"

There's a murmur of interest in the crowd. Okay, maybe I'm on the right track here.

"You mean the Icebreakers? Yeah." Adam's expression brightens. "They're huge right now."

"You're still in touch with them, right?"

He nods. "We've featured them on the farm's socials a few times. Nice folks."

"Would they be available on Christmas Eve?"

The crowd's murmurs grow louder, and my heart pounds.

You can do this, Doug. You can! You have good ideas! You can help the town!

Sometimes I like to talk to myself the way Zeke does. It helps in moments like these.

"I'm texting them now," Jeb calls out from his seat next to Adam. The whole room seems to be holding its breath as Jeb types. "Three dots… they're answering! Wait! Yes—the Icebreakers are available!"

A cheer echoes through the room.

"Oh." Jeb frowns. "But for Christmas Eve, their rates are triple." He grimaces. "They would be… not cheap."

There's another murmur through the room, and it's sad. Disappointed. I don't like that. I don't like it at all.

"Okay, okay." I hold my hands up, requesting silence. "Listen, everyone," I tell them. "We all know that winning doesn't really matter, right? Our town's celebration, this Holiday-Off, is about more than just competition. It's about community and togetherness and—"

"But we want to win!" Althea shouts. The town roars in agreement.

That cheer seals things for me, even as I see Zeke's frown fall into something more like a scowl. He's worried, I know. And I am too.

I promised La Fierte my leadership. And this Holiday-Off means so much to everyone. I can't let them down.

"Okay," I tell everyone. "We'll find the money. We'll book the Icebreakers. Whatever it takes to beat Atherton!"

The cheer that rolls through the room is so loud that the animals at the Stock Farm can probably hear it. Marty picks up his stick and waves it around, beaming.

I hope I haven't just made a promise I can't possibly keep.

Zeke and I are sitting at the kitchen table the next morning, our chairs crowded together so we can both look at the laptop. The columns of numbers on the screen are starting to look fuzzy. I don't know if it's because my eyes are tired, or because my brain wants to reject reality, or both.

"See?" Zeke asks, pointing at the scary red number at the bottom of the screen. "We're already way over budget. I suppose we can cut back on a few things. The choir did offer to perform without their usual fee, but that's not enough to offset the fee these ice artists want."

I watch him change the number in one of the spreadsheet cells and bite my lip.

"We have to make this work," I murmur.

He frowns and shakes his head as he does something else with the spreadsheet. Maybe because I really *don't* want to think about the Holiday-Off budget right now, my mind drifts back to another time Zeke and I sat at the kitchen table together like this. It was the night he told me he was thinking of proposing to Lydia.

"Zeke?"

"Hmm?" he says, still focused on the screen, eyes narrowed.

"We haven't really talked about Lydia."

His fingers freeze on the keys, then he snatches them back so he can scoot his chair a little bit away from mine. "Haven't we, though?"

"I mean *really* talked. You're acting like it isn't a big deal."

"Because it's not."

"How can it not be? You picked out a ring for her, for Pete's sake!"

Zeke presses his lips together tightly, still not looking at me.

In some ways, Zeke and I are incredibly close, and always have been. We tell each other almost everything.

Emphasis on *almost*.

We don't talk about the people we date. We never have. Since we were teenagers, Zeke would clam up if I brought up a girlfriend, and he never wanted to tell me anything about his own partners.

For the most part, I've tried to accept Zeke's boundaries in the past and not pushed him.

But this is different. How things are going with a girlfriend doesn't have the same gravity as a breakup in the most serious relationship that a person has ever had. I don't think it's healthy for him to keep his feelings all pent up.

And okay, I'm also really, really curious. Who could blame me?

"Actually, there is something I should tell you," Zeke says slowly, and I tense in my chair. Oh my gosh, is he *finally* going to open up?

He doesn't say more, so after holding my breath for a few seconds, I say encouragingly, "All right. I'm listening."

Zeke gives me a long, intense look that I'm not sure how to interpret. Usually I'm pretty good at parsing Zeke's expressions. He has fifty shades of scowls and frowns, and I know them all by heart. But there's something different about him in this moment, and I find that my heart is picking up speed in my chest.

Then he says, "Lydia and I broke up because she's not the one for me. And we both knew it."

Oh. That makes sense, and it *is* an answer to my question… sort of. But I feel like something is missing. Something is still unsaid. And so I nod and stay quiet, waiting for whatever *else* he is going to say.

Zeke wets his parted lips. He takes a deep breath. And then he wrinkles his nose and scowls. "So, can you explain why you told the town we'd find a way to book these ice people?" Zeke shakes his head. "We're never going to find the money for this."

It's clear we're done talking about Lydia. Back to that pressing problem I really don't want to think about. "But we have to," I tell him. "They're our only hope of beating Atherton."

"I couldn't agree more," Max says from behind us.

Zeke and I bump shoulders as we both twist around to see him walk into the kitchen. He looks great as always. He's a sharp dresser, as Grandma would say. Right now he's got on a blue sweater with such a fine knit that it clings to his lean torso. He's wearing it with a slim-fitting pair of khakis.

"See, Max agrees with me," I tell Zeke.

"I do," Max says. "And if you want to win this thing, it sounds like you need more money." He pulls up one of the other kitchen chairs and plops into it. "So maybe it's time to raise some funds. Have you thought about a silent auction? Maybe a holiday open house at the firehouse? Kids would love that, and you could keep the costs lower than what parents have to shell out for a day at the zoo or the waterpark."

I perk up. "That's a good idea. What do you think, Zeke?"

"I agree that people would be interested, but there's no way Jordy would allow it. Remember the whole ordeal with the barbecue?"

"Oh, that's true." I meet Max's confused eyes and explain. "Jordy is our union rep. And he's old school. He nixed Ross's plan to have a friends and family barbecue at the firehouse last year."

"Jordy and Ross are always butting heads. Maybe that's natural between the most senior guy and a rookie." Zeke shrugs.

"The whole thing got pretty bad," I tell Max. "But Jordy had a point. More than one, actually. Our insurance doesn't cover third parties in the building, plus there was the whole issue of what would happen if we got a call and all the visitors slowed our response time."

"Ross barely spoke to Jordy for six months," Zeke adds. "We don't want to pick at that scab."

"They're over it now though, thank goodness," I say. "Zeke, did you see the photo Jordy sent last weekend?"

"I don't think so," Zeke says, so I pull it up on my phone. He leans in to look, then almost smiles. "Those dorks."

I turn the phone toward Max, and he glances at the screen with a polite smile, then does a double take and stalks forward for a closer look. "Wait, *that's* old school Jordy and Ross the rookie?"

"Yeah," I say, confused. I look at the screen again to make sure I showed him the right picture, but I definitely did. There they are, both halfway out of their gear after a call. Ross must have jumped off the running board of the truck and straight onto Jordy's back, his arms looped around the older man's neck. They're both laughing, eyes bright.

"Does your whole fire department look like…" Max trails off. He gestures at the phone in my hand and then at me and Zeke.

"Like what?" Zeke asks, his brow furrowed.

"Like you're straight out of a porno!" Max bursts out.

My brows shoot up. Then I burst out laughing. Zeke coughs, and Max backs away from us and slumps against the counter.

"Sorry," he says miserably. "That was unprofessional." Then he perks up again. "Oh my God, I have a brilliant idea for your fundraiser."

Zeke and I exchange a look. "Um," I tell Max tentatively, "we can't record porn at the firehouse. Our insurance *definitely* wouldn't cover it."

"My brilliant idea is not porn!" Max laughs and shakes his head. "Definitely not porn," he repeats more seriously. "My brilliant idea *is*… a calendar! How many people work at the firehouse?"

"Four full-time, two part-time volunteers."

"Perfect. So two photographs of everyone equals twelve months. Plus a bonus group photo to cover December of this year. I saw the way people greeted the two of you at the school and the tree farm. You're local celebrities."

"We're not *celebrities*," I say. "It's just a small town. Everyone knows everyone." I glance at Zeke, but he has his thoughtful frown on, like he thinks Max has a point.

"What would it cost to produce, though?"

Max starts typing furiously into his phone. "My friend did something similar a few months ago. I can't remember what he said about the total printing cost, but I'll text him and ask. His project was a calendar too—only it was high fashion, and all the models were octogenarians. Fierce queens, each and every one of them. I'll show you later."

"People do take a lot of photos of us," I admit, the idea growing on me. Plus, I have eyes. I know my coworkers are all super attractive. "But we'd need a *real* photographer. And I doubt Barton would let us borrow any of his staff."

"He only has one staff photographer, anyway, and half the photos in that paper are out of focus," Zeke points out.

"Um, hello." Max raises his hand. "Professional photojournalist, here. And you can pay me with zero dollars and complimentary coffee." He winks.

"Really?" Now I'm getting excited. "You'd do that?"

"Of course. It'll be fun." Max smiles.

"I don't know." Zeke folds his arms. "Are you sure this isn't a conflict of interest, Max? And is it good for Doug's image for him to be naked in a calendar?"

"Naked?" I yelp.

"Only *half* naked," Max tells me soothingly, then turns back to Zeke. "I promise I won't make Doug out to be anyone he's not. But it's silly to try to hide who he *is*. And he's a young, hot firefighter." Max shrugs. "I'm not saying the Barton Asterstops of the world will approve, but who cares about them? Plus, the articles I'm writing are really human interest, not investigative, even if I joke about them being hard-hitting. I can write those fairly and still help the town out with a fundraiser."

Zeke nods. "Okay. Do you really think it will sell enough copies to make a difference? To get the money Doug needs to book the ice people?"

"Let me look into the printing costs, but I think so. And you should probably stop calling them the ice people."

Zeke snorts, then actually gives Max one of his tiny, rare smiles. "Thanks, Max. It's awesome that you want to help."

"You're welcome," Max says as he sends his own small, quiet smile back.

After a second, Zeke quickly turns away, closing his laptop and picking it up off the table. "I've gotta go to practice," he says. "Can't be late or the kids get grouchy."

"Are you ready to go into town?" I ask Max. "I'll give you the grand tour of town hall, then meet you back there after you make your other stops around town, right?"

"That's the plan," Max agrees, his eyes lingering on Zeke. Then he smiles at me. "Ready when you are."

Zeke leaves ahead of us, and I watch him go. When the door closes behind my best friend, my thoughts skip back to the conversation we were having right before Max joined us in the kitchen.

"Hey," I say to Max, who's tidying some dishes. "Remember that first wrong text you sent me? The one about your balls?"

Max lets out a startled laugh, his cup clattering in the sink. "Um, yeah. Super embarrassing."

"No, you shouldn't be embarrassed," I assure him. "I keep thinking about it though."

"You keep thinking about *my balls*?" Max clarifies, his voice a little squeaky, and shoots me a horrified look over his shoulder.

"I don't mean about your balls," I say quickly, my cheeks heating. "I mean the part where you said you meant to send the text to your best friend."

"Oh, right." Max nods. "Yeah, Reyna. I tell her almost everything." Still, I can tell he's confused.

"Zeke is my best friend," I explain, "but I'd never send a text like that to him. Not because it's bad! Just because… we don't talk about that stuff."

"Well, it can be hard to admit when you're going through a dry spell," Max says carefully, like he's still not sure what I'm trying to say.

"Yeah, but we don't talk about *any* of that stuff. Not about dating, not about sex." I suddenly remember that Max isn't just a friend, he's a *reporter*, and I grimace. "Um, this can be off the record, right?"

Max wrinkles his nose when he smiles. It's really cute. "Definitely off the record. I'm writing about the Holiday-Off and your mayorship, not how much you and your best friend discuss your respective sex lives."

"Okay." Relieved, I stand up and push in my chair, then turn to face Max. "Do you think it's weird that we don't talk about that stuff? I know other guys do. And we've been best friends since we were kids."

"I think that different people have different comfort levels with certain topics." Max tilts his head. "Have you ever talked to Zeke about this?"

I hesitate, then shake my head.

"Well, a conversation is probably a good idea. An important part of any relationship is sharing your feelings. Or in my case, oversharing."

I laugh. "I really like that about you." He rolls his eyes like he doesn't believe me, so I step forward and squeeze his shoulder to emphasize my point. "I mean it. You're amazing."

Max's eyes are wide and trained on mine as he looks up at me. His arm is warm and his sweater is incredibly soft. I freeze for a second, and then quickly let go of him and clear my throat. I need to stay *professional*, but there's something about Max that keeps tricking my brain into forgetting why he's here.

"Well," Max says briskly, "I still think you should talk to Zeke about why he needs some subjects to be off-limits. Just to understand where he's coming from. But in the meantime, if you ever need an outlet for your own oversharing, I volunteer as tribute."

I grin. "Are you saying I can text you about my blue balls?"

He laughs. "I find it hard to believe you're familiar with the condition. But yes, you can text me about the state of your balls. Consider this my blanket consent to assist any time you require a TMI moment. Off the record, of course."

DOUG

Z, so you know, Max and I might be a little late getting back to the house. The choir offered me an advance performance of their showcase for the holiday-off.

ZEKE

I hope Amos Fuentes warms up this time. Last choir concert he ended up with an injured hernia after he tried to Dougie.

DOUG

He always warms up now. And I still think it's cool there's a dance move named after me!

MAX

I have to say, La Fierte is a LOT different from Atherton. How did I not know this growing up?!

DOUG

Idk!!!! I wish we'd known you back then.

MAX

Me too. I think being openly gay in La Fierte would have been a lot more fun.

DOUG

Definitely!! Devon Falls High had a Gender-Sexuality Alliance. Remember when we played in the hockey match to help them raise money, Zeke?

ZEKE

Yup.

DOUG

Shoot, sorry. Shouldn't have mentioned it. I forgot how mad your dad got about that.

ZEKE

My dad's a fucking fuckhole.

Shit. Probably shouldn't have said that to a reporter, huh.

MAX

Consider it off the record.

DOUG

I'd make you put money in the swear jar, but your dad gets my blood going too sometimes. Hey, let's talk about something more fun. Max, did you know that Zeke and I once dressed up as Bert and Ernie for Halloween? I have pictures!

MAX

[gif of person sitting up and staring with interest]

ZEKE

[face palm emoji] It's a shame you can't fucking burn the cloud the way you can burn photo albums.

CHAPTER 8

ZEKE

"Third line, you're up!" I blow my whistle with a little more force than necessary, and the shrill noise echoes through the rink. A tug on my shirt alerts me that one of the munchkins has snuck up on me. I turn to find Shay there, his helmet crooked on his head and his hockey jersey on backwards.

"Uncle Zeke," he asks urgently, "when's dance time?"

I whip my head around to check that his father isn't anywhere nearby. Jonah usually drops Shay off for the first hour or so of hockey practice and then comes back to watch the scrimmage.

Which is why I've strategically arranged for "strength and flexibility instruction," aka dance, in the middle of practice.

"David's working with Group A," I remind Shay patiently. "You're Group B. You're supposed to be skating right now." My eyes drop to his feet. "Why aren't your skates on?"

"I don't like 'em." Shay wrinkles his nose. "They hurt my ankles! Can't I just stay in the training room with David?"

I should say no. I should absolutely, one hundred percent say no. We have a match next week, and Jonah will expect to see Shay on the ice. If Shay sucks, which tends to be what happens when a player spends hockey practice working on flexibility and dance moves instead of, you know, actual hockey, Jonah will bust my balls. And if Jonah ever finds out that Shay's spending all of his hockey practices not-hockeying, he'll try to rip my balls off altogether.

I'm not afraid of my brother. But Shay's a sensitive kid. I've got no desire to subject him to violent family conflict.

"Please, Uncle Zeke?" Shay drops his lower lip into a pout and pushes his helmet further across his forehead. "Please! I just wanna hang out with David. He says my fifth position is really good!"

"It's like we're in fu—um, flipping *Billy Elliot*," I mutter.

"Who's Billy Elliot? He can dance with us too!"

"Never mind." I shake my head. "You can go to the training room now. But next practice you gotta skate, okay?"

"I will. Thanks!" He beams and rushes off toward the practice room in sneakers with light-up heels, skipping and singing to himself.

The next thirty minutes follow the usual pattern of kids falling on top of each other and either giggling or crying, depending on how hungry and tired they are, while I pick them up and remind them which goal is theirs. Goals get intermittently scored, usually by Trina, our little hockey savant. She's the daughter of the local veterinarian, and my assistant coach, Samara, calls her "mini Sidney Crosby."

It's a strangely satisfying job, coaching peewee hockey. When I was a kid, the hockey rink was my favorite place in the world: the one spot where I was free of Jonah, who played for a different team, and my arguing parents. I thrived in programs like this, and every time a kid tells me how much they love hockey practice, my entire body lights up with excitement.

And if I have to bring the dance instructor from down the street into my practices to give my nephew the same kind of happiness I had as a kid? I've got no problem doing that.

"Why isn't Shay out on the ice?"

The gruff voice in my ear is so surprising I nearly jump. "Dad? What the hell—what are you doing here?"

Randall James, aka my asshole father, has appeared by my shoulder, looking ten years older than when I saw him a month or so ago. His skin is drooping around his mouth and eyes, and his hair, which used to be as dark as mine and Jonah's, has gone almost completely gray. He's huffing and wheezing as he barks the words out at me, just from walking up the five-foot ramp into the rink.

That's what happens when you spend fifty-something years smoking, drinking, and living on hamburgers and fries. Eventually, your body fights back.

"Jonah got called into the store," Dad explains impatiently. "So I said I'd pick up the squirt." He squints at the kids on the ice. "Now, where is he?"

"Shay's doing flexibility training." Fuck, I didn't plan on talking to Dad today. Normally I like to gear up for these conversations. Get in some light meditation first, or at least a shot of tequila.

"Flexibility training? Sounds like that new-age bullshit they got hockey players doing now. I saw on the news that the Habs do yoga. Yoga! Can you fucking believe that nonsense?" He shakes his head. "May as well have a bunch of women out on the ice."

"Dad, there's an entire league of female hockey players who could have skated circles around you, even in your prime. Not to mention the female hockey players right in front of you." I gesture at my players. "Keep your voice down and stop swearing with the kids around," I hiss. Normally, salty language is the one thing Dad and I have in common, but even I can keep a lid on it when I'm surrounded by elementary schoolers. "And so you know, I did yoga with my college hockey team. It is great for flexibility." I study him, increasingly worried he's going to collapse right in front of me. "Should you be on your feet?"

He sneers at me. "Everyone thinks they're gonna tell me how to live these days. You know that damn doctor I'm stuck with wants me to give up beer? Fucking women, son. I tell you."

I've got to get out of this conversation before I hit an old man. I fucking *told* Jonah not to send him to pick up Shay anymore. If it were up to me, Shay would never spend two minutes with this bastard.

"We're not going to be done for a while," I say sharply. "I'll bring Shay back. You can leave."

Dad sends me some side-eye that I know I inherited, and *fuck,* why the hell do I have to look so much like certain members of my family? "You got a problem or something? You been actin' awful weird lately. Not answering my calls. What's this I hear about you not coming to Sunday dinner? And why the hell did you break up with that Lydia girl?"

Great. Exactly the conversation I've been avoiding—and now we get to have it right in the middle of a public hockey rink. "People break up, Dad," I tell him carefully, breathing in between each word as I brace myself for the words that I'm sure are coming out of his mouth next.

"A real man knows how to keep a woman. You know, people are starting to talk, son. You spend all your time with that pansy mayor—what kind of man won't even swear?—and you hang around that farm where people are married to more than one person. How's that even work?" He snorts. "Now you've gone and broken up with one of the prettiest women in town? I'm telling you, if you ain't careful, people are going to get the wrong idea about you."

Unspoken words pile on top of each other in my throat like bile. Over the years, I've gotten pretty good at putting Jonah back in his place—or least trying to—whenever he spews bullshit like this. But whenever my dad says it, it's like my throat dries up around everything I know he needs to hear. Somehow I always end up feeling like I'm seven years old again, back in my bedroom, listening to my dad scream at my mom that she's too soft on me and Jonah while she tells him that he's emotionally stunted and she never should have married him in the first place.

I never had the words to say what I was thinking back then. I should have those words now. I know I should. But whenever my dad opens up his mouth, it's like they all disappear into a cloud of his old, stagnant cigarette smoke.

Poof.

"Can't even imagine if your mom had gotten custody of you both." Dad shakes his head and rolls his eyes, smiling at me with that same expression Jonah has—the one that always looks more like a sneer.

I do imagine that sometimes. I imagine all kinds of things. What if I'd had a different father? What if my mother hadn't taken me with her when she left? What if she had gotten custody of Jonah, and he hadn't spent his teenage years living with this bitter, hateful man?

And then there's the thing I imagine all the time: what would it be like if Dad ever found out that I'm in love with a man? What would he do? What would he say?

I shouldn't fucking care. It shouldn't matter. I *know* that. But the wondering still fucking haunts me anyway.

Dad waves his hand at me. "At least I got Jonah. This whole county knows what kind of man he is."

I think of Max, and the expression he had on his face when he saw Jonah at Stock Tree Farm, and my vision starts going a little dark around the edges. I open up my mouth, and all the words I want to say to my father sit there, ready to plummet over the edge and finally come out of me—

The whole county knows Jonah's always been a dick, because you raised him. And I think he wants to do better with Shay, but you keep stepping in. What if he ends up letting you fuck up Shay the way you fucked him up? Oh, and by the way, I'm bisexual, and I'm in love with Doug. And I always have been. But I never seem to be able to tell him that. Maybe it's because I'm afraid of ruining our friendship, but maybe it's also because I see your face in my head every time I try. And—

So many fucking words just keep piling up inside of me, burning bright until it feels like they might break through my skin.

I turn away from Dad to stare at the ice. The kids are busy

turning a scrimmage into a messy puppy pile, while Samara skates around them trying to make sense of the chaos. Usually this kind of shit makes me smile, but right now all I feel is the thrum of the anger that I sometimes worry might take over my entire body and swallow me whole if I'm not careful.

"Get out of here, Dad," I finally say, because those are the only words I can say to him right now. "I'll make sure Shay has a ride to the hardware store." I march away from him, fast, toward my giggling skaters and Samara, trying to figure out how the hell I'm going to calm myself down before I get to them. I pull my phone out of my pocket and look at the photo Jeb sent me earlier today. The one I've already stared at a dozen times.

It was taken at the Stock Farm. Doug and I are standing with Max in between us. We tower over him like fucking giants. Doug's got one hand on Max's shoulder and they're both staring off at something in the distance. I'm looking over at both of them.

And I'm smiling.

Jeb sent it with the caption: "Never seen you smile in a picture! Had to send it, man."

I work my finger gently back and forth over my phone screen's glass. I know I have to get out of this rink before my heart explodes out of my chest. "Samara," I call out. "I've got to run an errand. Finish up practice for me. Oh, and ask Trina's dad to bring Shay over to the hardware store."

I rush out, feeling my father's eyes on my back the whole time, the weight of his sneer stabbing through my spine and into my chest.

I end up outside of the town hall, standing next to an eight-foot light-up elf dressed in purple and green. Clearly, the decorations for the Holiday-Off have started to arrive.

"I hear its name is Sneezy," says Max from behind me. I turn and he smiles. "I didn't expect to see you here. Did something go wrong at hockey practice?"

I roll my eyes. "Yeah. My father showed up."

"Oh." Max's eyebrows draw together. "So, you two aren't close?"

I pull in a breath, trying to slow down my racing heart. I really hope I'm not having a fucking panic attack in front of the journalist I'm quasi crushing on and an eight-foot elf.

"No," I finally say. "We can't spend five seconds around each other without getting into a fight."

Max purses his lips and frowns as he sits down on the front steps of the town hall. "You don't have to tell me anything you don't want to, but if you need to talk, I'm here," he says.

Before I can think about it too hard, I sit down next to him. "Thanks," I mutter.

It's been a chilly, gray day. Snow's coming, I think. Right now the sky is beginning to fall through the gray toward evening's darkness, and the angry clouds plunging away from light feel like a perfect reflection of everything happening inside of me.

"Dad found out about my breakup. Said some nasty shit about it," I finally say.

"Ah." Max nods. "I'm sorry. That's really tough. Hey, so you know, I think Doug might also have some questions about your breakup. He seems worried there's something you're not telling him."

I watch one cloud swirl around another, so fast it could almost be dizzying if you stared at it too long. "There are too many things I haven't told him," I finally say.

We're both quiet for a long time. Then Max says, "For what it's worth, I bet Doug would rather you tell him whatever's bothering you. Especially if keeping it locked up inside is hurting you."

I frown, because all my words are stuck in my throat again.

"I want to be different from him," I finally say. "Different from my dad. Better. That's all I ever wanted. But sometimes I feel like too much of him is scratched into my skin. My DNA. I'm not very good at, well, emotional stuff, I guess."

Max nods. "Emotions are hard. Being vulnerable is hard." He sends me a small smile. "Being yourself is really, really hard sometimes."

I snort. "How'd you get so good at it? Especially with my brother breathing down your neck all of high school?"

He shrugs. "Maybe that's why I got good at it. I couldn't be anyone other than me, you know? I knew I never could. So I learned to love who I was, regardless of what anyone else thought." He smiles over at me. "But yeah, it's risky, being yourself. Vulnerability is always risky."

I grunt. I hope he knows I'm agreeing with him.

"I'll just say this," Max goes on. "We all know I'm the king of oversharing, so maybe take what I'm about to say with a grain of salt. But I only met you and Doug a few days ago, and I can already tell that your friendship is the most important thing in the world to both of you. And I think friendships can just as easily be ruined by what we *don't* say as by what we do say. If that makes sense."

It makes all the fucking sense in the world, actually. No one else in my life has ever mattered to me the way Doug matters. How much longer can I risk our friendship by not telling him the truth? What if Max is right? Is my friendship with Doug doomed to be just one more thing in my world that I let my father destroy?

And just like that, I know what I need to do.

"I need to talk to him," I tell Max.

He nods and pats my knee. "You've got this."

Warmed by Max's encouragement, I stand up and march through the door of the tiny town hall, my eyes trained on the door of Doug's small office at the end of the hallway. I charge inside without knocking, and Doug's eyes light up. "Hey! There you are! I thought Max and I would meet back up with you at home." He frowns and lowers his voice. "Is everything okay?

You've got that same look you had when we lost the state semifinals match."

Of course I remember that tournament. It plays on repeat in my head sometimes. We were in ninth grade, on our first run for the state championship. We lost in overtime. I cried in our hotel room that night, and Doug held me, rubbing my back and whispering soothing words as I sobbed against his shoulder. I don't think I'll ever forget how good his body felt against mine—how right.

I remember how much better I felt the next morning when we woke up together, our legs tangled around each other's in the hotel sheets.

I remember going back home and finding my father waiting in the driveway of my mother's house. I remember how he yelled at me for ten minutes straight for losing the game, calling me an embarrassment. Worthless.

A damn pussy.

"Did I do something?" Doug rolls his chair around the end of his desk to get closer to me. "I know I sent you a bunch of emails this morning, but you're the one who told me to forward you all meeting and appointment details. You know, I can keep track of my own schedule if you want. I've had a calendar before!"

I can't help my smile. "Doug, do you even know where the calendar app on your phone is?"

"No," he admits, "but I'm sure I can find it."

There's a buzz of voices behind me. I glance over my shoulder to see that the La Fierte United Congregational choir is right on time to demonstrate their showcase. And judging by their red and green robes, it's a dress rehearsal.

"Zeke," Doug says, his voice low but raised enough to be heard over the chatter of the choir members. I turn back to him, meeting his wide, worried eyes.

I love him so much. I always have. And if the past fifteen or so years are anything to go by, my feelings are only going to get stronger as more time passes.

Emotions are so fucking hard. But I can't imagine what I'm about to say will ever be as hard as it would be to lose my best friend because I couldn't be honest with him.

I take a deep breath and square my shoulders. "Doug," I announce, "I'm bisexual. And I've been in love with you since we were thirteen."

The hall falls silent at once, and I wince. I may have spoken a little louder than I intended to. As I back away from Doug's desk and dare a glance at the choir, the shocked expressions on their faces leave no doubt that they heard every word I just said.

Max is standing just inside the entrance too. He's grinning, and doesn't look shocked at all.

Looks like I dethroned Max as the TMI king.

PART TWO
WTF

From the group chat "The Men of Grandma's House"

MAX

I am so jazzed right now. Can't wait to start work on this calendar! Anything involving photography just makes me so happy.

I mean it's not better than sex, but definitely still really good. On par with a decent dry hump.

Sorry, that was unprofessional

I have no filter sometimes :(

...Zeke? Doug? I really am sorry.

DOUG

Don't worry, Max. I was just busy looking at a giant elf someone ordered. And Zeke can just be kind of uptight.

ZEKE

I'm not uptight!

DOUG

You're right, I'm sorry. It's like you said, some things are off-limits between friends. And that's ok!

ZEKE

Just for context, Max, I said that after Doug asked me to help him choose a DICK PIC to send to his girlfriend.

DOUG

And for additional context, Max, I was sixteen and it was my first dick pic. I was nervous.

MAX

Really appreciating all the context. And definitely feeling less self-conscious about mentioning dry humping now. Thanks, boys. ;)

CHAPTER 9
DOUG

Zeke is looking at me. I'm looking at Zeke.

My ears are ringing like that time I took a hit so hard, I cracked my helmet on the ice.

Zeke's words do feel like a hit. The kind that makes the world look a little unfocused in the aftermath. Zeke's face is so familiar. If I was an artist, I could draw it with my eyes closed. But right now he looks, I don't know, different. *New*.

I try to say something, because a silent stare is *not* the right play in this moment. But when I open my mouth, words don't come out.

Zeke's lips twist into a grimace. I'm hurting him right now, and I hate it, but I think I've literally lost the power of speech, like mermaids when you take them out of the water.

"You don't have to say anything," Zeke says, his voice like sandpaper. He shoves his hands in his pockets. "I just wanted you to know."

"Zeke," I finally manage. "It's not..." I push myself up from my chair and in the process, I knock a whole stack of files off my desk. They hit the floor and half of them burst open in a paper explosion.

Marty is *not* going to like that. I remember Marty and the

church choir and look past Zeke at our audience. Some of them are pretending not to have noticed Zeke's announcement but most of them are openly staring.

I grab Zeke's wrist and pull him after me, pausing to nod at the folks as we pass. "Excuse me, ma'am," I say politely to Jemima Ackerman, who's fully blocking the door.

"Oh, of course, pardon me," she says, jolting like my words broke a trance she was under. She gathers up her green robes and shuffles sideways. "Good for you, Zeke, honey," she adds to Zeke as we step past her. "You know, my daughter Niedre is a late-blooming lesbian," she tells us. "I'm a card-carrying member of PFLAG."

"That's... uh, good for you," Zeke mutters. I pull on his arm again and we continue out onto the town hall steps, then out onto the sidewalk.

I turn to face him and fold my arms. "Why thirteen?"

His nose wrinkles as he frowns at me. "What?"

"You said you've been"—I can hardly get the words out—"in love with me," I manage in a rush, "since we were thirteen. And I'm wondering—why thirteen?"

Zeke frowns and looks away, rubbing his chin. His stubble is a little longer than usual. For some reason, I stare at his blunt-tipped fingers.

"I don't know why. That's when I knew, though. Remember when you got that awful haircut?"

I do, actually. I groan. "Gosh, that was so embarrassing." Grandma's friend had a daughter who was fresh out of beauty school and needed the business.

Zeke's lips twitch toward a smile but don't quite get there. He glances at me. "How long did Carrie Ann's salon stay open? Six weeks?"

"Four," I mutter. "So, what about the haircut?"

He shrugs. "That's what did it. You showed up to school that morning, looking like a lawn mower had run you over. And by lunchtime, I knew."

Zeke doesn't do jokes. Especially not elaborate, complicated fakeouts. He hates that kind of joke, actually. Every time someone pranks him at the firehouse, he goes on a rant about how there's no such thing as a white lie.

I know Zeke better than I've ever known anyone, which is how I know that he's being honest right now. But my head is still rejecting everything that he's saying, like a vending machine spitting out a crumpled dollar.

"Maybe I shouldn't have told you," Zeke says into the silence that fell between us for a few seconds. "Not that I'm bisexual. I'm glad I told you that, and I should have done it sooner. I mean that maybe I shouldn't have told you about the other thing. It's just that I'm really tired of keeping shit to myself, you know?"

I nod. I don't know if I've ever wanted to hug him so much, but I don't move. It's like this nightmare I have, where I'm back in high school and cast in the school play, but I've forgotten all my lines and nobody has an extra script. What's the script for a moment like this?

"I'm glad you told me," I say. "I just don't know…"

He waves a hand at me to shush me. "I don't expect you to say anything." He rolls his shoulders. "I know you don't feel the same way, which is why it was probably unfair to put that on you."

The town hall doors squeak as someone pushes them open, and I glance up the steps to find Max peering out with a little, uncertain smile. He waves at us, then slips the rest of the way through the doors and trots down the steps. "Hey, I'm really sorry to interrupt. But there was a debate about whether somebody should come out here to check on you, so I volunteered. I figured you guys would want to avoid the additional gossip if you could."

Now I want to hug Max, but I remain stiffly planted in the spot on the sidewalk where I stand, only managing a smile and a "Thanks."

"Yeah, thanks," Zeke agrees, and touches Max's back with the palm of his hand. "There's no avoiding the gossip at this point, though. Fuck."

Zeke grimaces, and my chest is tight with the urge to say something, *anything*, to make him feel better. But I still have no clue what that would be.

Fortunately Max is here. He squeezes Zeke's arm. "That was really brave." He glances between us. "Are you two… okay?"

Now we both seem to have been struck silent. Zeke does grunt, but even I don't know what he means by it.

The town hall doors open again. This time Marty steps out. "Mayor?" he calls pointedly, then taps his wrist even though I have never seen the guy wear a watch.

I blow out a breath. "The showcase rehearsal."

"Yeah, I was supposed to remind you about that," Max says. "Some of the choir members have to get to a knitting circle."

"Okay," I say, unfolding and refolding my arms. "Well, I guess I'll—see you two back at home, then?"

Zeke doesn't even look at me; he just nods and walks away. Max hesitates, searching my face, then looks after Zeke.

"I'm glad you'll be with him," I murmur, squeezing his shoulder as Zeke strides toward his truck. "Max," I add, struck by a thought that hits the pit of my stomach like I swallowed a rock. "Is this—"

"Completely off the record," he assures me, smiles again, then turns and jogs after Zeke. I watch them go, hoping Zeke will look back at me, that our eyes will meet, that I will read something in his face that will stop this panic that's filling me up. But he doesn't look back, and by the time he pulls his truck onto the street and takes the turn at the end of the block, my heart's racing.

Nobody is more important to me than Zeke. How did I miss all of this?

Two hours later, I've seen the church choir's showcase. I politely applauded every number, even though all the notes went in one ear and right out the other. If somebody asked me to name one song from the performance, I would have to take a wild guess.

Marty can tell I'm distracted, so he tries to send me home right after the choir finishes up. But I feel another surge of panic at the thought of facing Zeke. I'm not ready yet.

So instead I get hyper-focused on the most mundane tasks I can find at town hall. First I carefully pick up the paperwork that I knocked on the floor. Next I clear my whole desk, putting away files that I've had out for weeks. Then I alphabetize the file cabinet because our office assistant's system has never made any sense. But then I worry that she'll get upset so I put them all back.

Finally, I volunteer to take a few packages to the nearest UPS drop-off in Devon Falls. Marty usually does it, but he's happy to let me run the errand instead.

Driving the familiar route to Devon Falls, my thoughts catch up to me like they were waiting to pounce. A bunch of questions that must have been brewing in my head all afternoon spring to mind.

How did I never know Zeke was bi?

How did I never know he was *in love with me*?

What made him tell me today, of all days?

What took him so long to tell me?

Why did he tell me at all?

Another question I'm sure is none of my business jumps into my head and sticks there.

Has Zeke ever been with other guys?

I've met his handful of girlfriends over the years. And we spend so much time together that I've known about a lot of his more casual hookups too—always women. But Zeke doesn't like to talk about dating or sex. That's always been a line in the sand between us. So it's totally possible that he's slept with guys and I just didn't know.

But Zeke with another guy? I can't even imagine it.

Except as soon as I have that thought, I *am* imagining it. Zeke pulling another man close, staring down with those intense, dark eyes, and then leaning in for a kiss like he does everything—focused, purposeful, determined to do the job right.

A horn blares from the road ahead of me, and I swerve hard back into my lane to get out of the way of an oncoming car.

"Dang it, Doug," I hiss to myself, hastily pulling my truck onto the shoulder and throwing it in park. Then I stare at myself in the rearview mirror. My eyes are wide and my hair is standing up because I've run my fingers through it a thousand times this afternoon. I probably look similar to the way I did when I was thirteen and one of Carrie Ann's first victims.

That day was almost fifteen years ago.

What took him so long to tell me?

Why did he tell me at all?

No, I'm not going to think about that.

I make it to the general store and leave the packages. And then I've got nothing else standing between me and home.

But there's still a whole wall of confusion between me and Zeke. I'm not ready to see him yet.

Which is why I end up in Luis's Café and Bar, home of excellent meatloaf that's nearly as good as Grandma's and plenty of local beer on tap. It's crowded, which I guess isn't that surprising for a Friday evening right after work.

I only see one open seat at the bar. As I grab it, the woman on the next stool turns, and I freeze.

Shoot. It's Lydia. As in, Zeke's ex.

She looks just as surprised to see me as I am to see her, but she recovers first. Lydia is really sharp. She's a lawyer, which isn't a bad thing, exactly, but she makes me nervous. "Doug. Wow. *Not* who I was expecting to see. I thought you and Zeke would be hanging out with your houseguest tonight."

I shouldn't be surprised that she and Zeke are still in touch. They were friends before they dated. But I *am* surprised. Unpleasantly surprised. "I had to come to Devon Falls," I say stiffly. Lydia has this weird effect on me I can't explain, and it makes me bad at talking.

"Right." Her brows are up again. "Well, are you going to have a seat, or what?"

I don't know how to say no without being rude, and there really isn't anywhere left for me to go. I get on the stool, and Lydia watches me with a smirk.

"Honestly, Doug, I won't stab you with a fork or throw my drink in your face. Relax."

"I didn't think you would do either of those things," I mutter.

She chuckles and signals the bartender. "What do you want?"

My eyes flick to her glass. "What are you having?"

"They have this new strawberry cider on tap. It's good."

"I'll try that."

She orders for me and puts it on her tab before I realize what's going on. Then she winks at me. "It's on me. I probably owe you one."

"What do you mean?"

"Come on, Doug. We both know you don't like me. *Everyone* knows you don't like me. Last year one of the hockey moms with my under-eights team asked me if I'd killed your dog."

"I don't have a dog!"

"The point is, everybody assumes I had to do something horrible to make *Doug McEmbirk*, of all people, dislike me."

"I don't dislike you," I insist, but lying isn't my best skill, and I kind of make a face as I say it.

She laughs. "It's okay. I came to terms with it years ago. And I might have used your aversion to me to amuse myself from time to time. As a coping mechanism, or some shit. So, like I said, I owe you a drink."

My glass arrives, and darn it, I've never tasted better hard cider in my life. I take a few gulps while I try to think about how the heck I got myself into this situation and how quickly I can get myself out of it. I'm so tense that I just blurt out, "You and Zeke broke up."

Lydia raises a brow at me and sips from her own glass. "We most certainly did."

I grasp for something else. "How's your team?"

"I don't want to share any details about our game that will get back to our primary competition," she says coolly. I can't tell if she's being serious. I mean, hockey is serious, but the coaches in the under-eights league have gotten a little too intense.

I'm almost out of material for small talk attempts with this woman. I've only got one more topic in my pocket, but I'm not sure how to phrase it. "And how's your… law stuff?"

"My *law stuff* is fine." She looks at me for a long second, then sighs. "Fuck it," she says, turning on her stool so she's facing me. "Why do you hate me, Doug?"

I stare at her. Her knee is digging into my thigh, and I wish I could shift away, but there's no room unless I get off my stool. I have a weird urge not to yield any territory to her. So I square my shoulders and give her an honest answer. "You never took Zeke as seriously as you should have. He's the best person in the world, and you were really lucky to have him. But you obviously didn't realize that."

Lydia's eyes widen, and she leans against the bar. "Wow. That's several more degrees of self-awareness than I was expecting. You're right, I didn't take dating Zeke seriously. That's because I knew our relationship wasn't serious. Zeke was not emotionally available when we got together or at any point while we dated. I knew that, and I was fine with it. I care about him, he cares about me, and we had fun. But that's all it was."

When she says the part about Zeke not being emotionally available, I bite the inside of my cheek. Zeke was going to propose to her. At least, he got a ring. But is Lydia right? Zeke said he's been in love with me since we were kids. Then again, I know that people can be in love with more than one other person. We have plenty of examples of that in La Fierte.

Lydia twists back around to pick up her drink. "This is actually nice. I like that we can be honest with each other. Finally." She clinks her glass against mine.

Hearing the word *honest* makes my stomach swoop. Lydia looks alarmed. "Doug, are you choking? You look terrible."

Before she can give me the Heimlich, I shake my head. "No. I just—okay, you said that we could be honest with each other, right? Because you don't care about hurting my feelings. Because we're not friends." It's weirdly freeing to say it out loud, because we *aren't* friends, and I really don't know if I would say the same about anyone else in my life who I've known as long as Lydia.

"That's overstating it a bit, I think. But as to the part about being honest even if it hurts your feelings, then my answer is yes, within reason."

I nod. "Okay. Yeah. So, did you ever think that maybe Zeke and I were… I don't know, more than just best friends?"

Lydia gives me another really long look. I wait her out uncomfortably, feeling like she's seeing through my skin. When she finally answers, it's with her own question. "Did *you* ever think that you and Zeke were more than just best friends?"

"No," I say immediately. But as soon as the word comes out of my mouth, I'm not sure if it's true.

"Really?" Lydia prods. "Think back. Never?"

I suck my lower lip between my teeth and do as she says.

"Maybe he did always act a little funny when I talked about women I was dating," I say slowly. That's sort of an understatement. If I went into too much detail, sometimes he actually turned green. "I thought he was kind of a prude, maybe, but…"

I trail off as a memory hits me, fast and hard. The night of our senior prom, I hadn't gotten my bow tie tied right, and I was still fussing with it when Zeke and I left his mom's, where we'd gotten dressed. I made a joke that I'd have to have Grandma tie it.

Zeke stopped right there in the driveway and turned to me and grabbed me by the collar. Suddenly, we were nose-to-nose.

For a second, I had the weirdest thought that he was going to kiss me. But his rough fingertips brushed my throat as he buttoned my collar and tied my bow tie for me.

He wasn't going to kiss me. Of course he wasn't. But in those heartbeats of time while Zeke frowned in concentration, his breath warm on my chin and his strong fingers knotting the silk tie, I wasn't relieved or amused by my silly mistake. I was *disappointed*, like when we were out on the ice and one of our plays didn't come together. A flash of possibility, gone in a second, like a shooting star.

I haven't thought about that moment in—well, maybe ever. What the heck is that about? Zeke and I talk about senior prom all the time, and Grandma loves to go through the pictures every spring. But it's like that moment is a photo that slipped out of the album, lost until now.

I rub my hands over my face. They're shaking like they were back on the side of the road. I can't believe I'm having this conversation with Lydia of all people, but she's here, and I feel like my insides are spilling out. I'm like an accident victim. I don't get to choose who shows up on the scene of my emergency.

I try different words. "Do you think it's normal for something to happen that makes you look back and see your whole life differently?" I part my fingers to stare into the mirrored wall behind the bar. "To see *yourself* differently?"

"Oh, boy." Lydia sighs and holds her hand up. "We're going to need something harder than cider."

MAX

Hi, Doug and Zeke.

I was just wondering if either of you are coming back to the house anytime soon? I think all the crochet pigs and cows and sheep and horses are starting to miss you.

I mean, it's okay if you're not. I know you both have a lot to think about!

Anyway, I just wanted to say

If either of you ever want to talk, just let me know, okay? I'm a really good listener! And I promise not to blurt out weird things that might make you uncomfortable.

Well, okay, I can't promise that. But I can TRY.

Okay, I'll stop babbling.

But I really am always happy to talk. If either of you want to.

And I hope you're both okay.

CHAPTER 10

MAX

"Oh! One more thing! I need to get Uncle Stewart a new pen set for his office," Mom says. We walk into the tiny gift shop in downtown Atherton, bells jingling as we open the door. "Wouldn't that be a good present for him?"

"Sure," I say absently, looking at the vast selection of maple candy. I was feeling rather guilty about how long I've been in Vermont now without seeing my mom, so I arranged for a rideshare to drive me to her house so I can surprise her. My decision to go to Atherton has nothing to do with me wanting to let things settle between Doug and Zeke. Or me feeling like I'm getting in the middle of them when they need to figure their shit out without me. I just wanted to see my mom. That's all.

Okay, yeah. I sound defensive even to my own ears. In reality, though, I don't think there's much I can do for them right now anyway. It's been a full day since Zeke made his announcement to Doug, and I've hardly seen either of them since. Right after Zeke and I came back to the house yesterday, he announced he was going to the rink to skate and disappeared. This morning he left early to coach a hockey practice. Doug didn't come home until almost eleven last night, even though I'm pretty sure La Fierte doesn't require his services that late in the evening. This morning

I asked him if he wanted to get started on the firefighter calendar soon, and he just muttered something about needing to check on an oversized menorah and then left the house without saying goodbye.

All in all, it seemed like a good time for a family visit. I've been needing some time with my mom, and I can also use some time to process all the thoughts I've been having about those two men.

I've been shopping with her for the last hour, and it's been somewhat successful. She's bought presents for her friends, and I found a new mug for my friend Reyna, who is an attorney in California. I met her in college, and we became super close, even if our relationship these days mostly consists of texting each other whenever we can. The mug says "LAWYERS NEVER LOSE THEIR APPEAL."

"You okay, hon?" Mom asks as she holds up a calendar of corgi butts. "You're awfully quiet. I thought you'd have all kinds of news from the enemy territory you're entrenched in." She winks and we both laugh. Mom isn't taking the Holiday-Off nearly as seriously as some other people in Atherton, but she likes to tease me about my affiliation with "the dirty competition," as she puts it.

"I'm okay," I tell her. "Just feeling a little… weird, I guess." I add a grunt to the end of the sentence, because I guess I've been hanging with Zeke too much. She studies me for a moment, then does that Mom Thing where she clearly decides not to press me. She goes back to talking about pen sets and my uncle's preference for gel ink while I nod along and get lost back in my thoughts.

Back in the scene at the town hall. Back in the memory of Zeke's face when he made his announcement. I was so proud of him, so proud of his honesty. The Viking pirate did good. But when Doug didn't respond to him right away, my heart broke into a thousand tiny pieces for both of them. I understood his reaction, of course, and I hope Zeke did too. Zeke's had a lot of time to get used to his identity and his feelings for Doug. Doug, on the other hand, was put face to face with them for the first time.

And I'd be lying if I didn't admit what I felt as I watched them stare at each other, both doing so much work to unravel the mess of string tying them both together.

Because that was very definitely the moment that confirmed what I've known basically since I laid eyes on the two of them together in the pig room: I'm attracted to *two* men at once.

Okay, that's not new. I mean, I've been attracted to *a lot* of men in my time, and I've definitely been attracted to more than one person before. But never with feelings so intense and both linked to the individual guys, but also their relationship to each other.

Doug gets me hot because he's so sexy and kind and unexpected in so many ways. Zeke because he's so… well, part of my twisted teenage fantasies, if I'm being honest. And kind and good.

But most of all, I like how they make me feel. With them, I'm completely me. Not the version of myself I am when I type my name to a byline, or the version who can't resist a shirtless dance floor moment at a club. I'm all of those things and more. And I *like* the guy I am.

Zeke being bisexual is almost unfair. How am I supposed to protect my heart knowing that he could actually be attracted to me too?

Of course, he's in love with Doug. But Doug's reaction to Zeke's declaration suggests he's never thought of himself as anything other than straight.

Yup. I appear to have become infatuated with two men I can never, ever have, just as they're in the middle of figuring out whether or not they can ever have each other.

"I heard that the mayor of La Fierte might have come out yesterday?" Mom says as she picks up a cow print-covered snow globe.

"Huh? What?" I snap back into the moment at the words "mayor of La Fierte."

"Could have just been a rumor, of course. I'm guessing you

would know more," Mom goes on. "But I saw Benny Gates over at Luis's cafe this morning, and she was all aflutter about Doug McEmbirk dating his long-time roommate. She said they announced it in front of an entire choir."

She pokes me with the base of the snow globe in her hand. "All I mean to say, sweetie, is that things here are a lot different than they were while you were growing up. I wish I could have done more for you back then," she adds wistfully.

"Oh, Mom." I lay my hand over hers so that they're linked together across the globe. "You always made me feel like I belonged with you."

She blinks back something that might look like a tear.

"Anyway," I tell her. "Try not to listen to people like Benny. Doug and Zeke deserve to be able to figure out whatever they want to figure out in their own time, without people gossiping about them."

"Absolutely," she agrees as she sets down the snow globe and squeezes my hand. "It sounds like they've been treating you well. I'm glad my baby is staying with two people who make him feel safe."

I think of Zeke and Doug, the way they tower over me—the way I feel so small and protected when I'm standing between the two of them. How all I want is to be wrapped up between them.

"You have no idea," I mutter under my breath as Mom examines a hand towel that says "WINE OR MILK? WHY NOT BOTH?"

"Oh! I forgot. I have something for you in the trunk," Mom says. "I found a shoebox of what looks like your old high school memorabilia when I was cleaning out a closet. Remind me to give it to you when we get back to the car. I figured you'd want it."

While *more* memories of high school are the last thing I need these days, I nod. When we get back to the car, I accept the Adidas box gingerly and slip it into one of the shopping bags.

Just because she gave it to me doesn't mean I have to look at it. Right?

When the same driver who had taken me to Atherton—Dante—pulls up to Mom's house to take me back to La Fierte, I open the back door of the sedan to find him staring at his phone, texting, just like every time I've ridden with him.

I am definitely not comfortable with how much time he spends looking at his phone while operating a motor vehicle. "Shouldn't you have that thing in the hands-free set?" I ask him as I get in with my purchases.

"Sorry," he mutters. "My girlfriend and I are having a fight." He shakes his head. "Don't worry, man. I know these roads better than I know my own house." He starts firing off another text as he pulls out of Mom's driveway.

That's not exactly reassuring, but I think he's fine. He puts the phone back down quickly and seems to be paying attention as he navigates us through the quiet streets of Atherton.

We're both silent. I'm staring out the window, thinking about too many things and nothing at all. Then we pass over a bridge, and Dante swears, getting my attention just in time to see his phone slip out of his hand and between the seats. He reaches for it just as I have the unmistakable sensation of riding in a car that hit a patch of ice.

Time slows down so I feel every second with perfect clarity. The rear wheels slip, and we slide left. I open my mouth to warn that we're headed into oncoming traffic, but Dante yells, "Shit," and after a second that feels way too long, he turns the steering wheel the other way.

There's loud honking from cars on, I assume, the other side of the road, but I don't see because we're rotating, and I'm throwing out my hands, barely able to process the overwhelming dread.

Is this my last moment? Am I going to die before I ever make a name for myself in journalism, or get a dog, or feel like I'm the most important person in the world to someone other than my mom or—

Dante's cranking on the wheel to the right, which I'm pretty sure is overcorrecting, and I yell, "No, the other way!" But it's too late and we're spinning in a full circle.

I'm jarred by a *bang* as the front bumper smashes into the guardrail. Then the windshield shatters and the airbags deploy.

I can't take a deep breath and my whole body is throbbing. But I'm definitely not dead.

When the airbags deflate, the car is facing the wrong direction. "Shit, shit, shit." Dante continues to chant as he guns the car, only we slip on ice again, and this time we head off past the guardrail at the end of the bridge and into a ditch.

The ground meets my window as the car rolls, and Dante wails, "Holy shit, we're going to die!"

DOUG

Hey, Zeke, don't forget that we promised to feed Sherbert when the 3way guys are gone in January.

ZEKE

Fuck, did we really?

DOUG

Yeah. All the other animals are covered. No one else will deal with Sherbert but us, though.

ZEKE

You mean YOU. Sherbert's a fucking nightmare.

DOUG

He's just misunderstood!

ZEKE

Sure. All goats stand up on their hindlegs and glare like that.

DOUG

I'm telling you—he's a total sweetheart!

CHAPTER 11
ZEKE

"Did you get the truck cleaned?" I ask.

"Sure did, buddy." Doug sends me one of his trademark smiles, but it's the same one he uses on Patrick, a rookie who's been stuck on dinner duty all week and had to be taught how to boil water for pasta. Doug's never used that smile on me. Well, not until this afternoon, less than twenty-four hours after my big announcement. We showed up for our shift at the firehouse and discovered we've lost the ability to communicate.

"Good," I tell him gruffly. "Good, that's good."

And then I run out of things to say. I stand in the doorway of the lounge, watching Doug from across the room. He's got his hands in his pockets, and he keeps looking back and forth between me and the floor.

I'm so fucking tempted to just leave this room and walk out into the kitchen. Nothing's ever been harder than wondering if I've ruined the most important friendship of my life just because I finally decided to stop hiding myself from Doug and the whole damn world. But at the same time, I can't seem to make myself leave this space. I can't take my eyes away from Doug's face, which is currently glued to the vinyl floor underneath us. His arms are wrapped uncomfortably around his torso, and I notice he's wearing the belt I gave him for his birthday last year.

Fuck it. I can't do this. I turn around to leave.

"So it sounds like the town's been really supportive," Doug says in a rush.

I turn around again. He's still wearing that Patrick-smile, but there's at least a little more of *him* in it now. "Say the fuck what?" I ask.

"Oh. There's a post on the online message board called 'We love you the way you are, Zeke.' You didn't see it?"

I smirk and roll my eyes, because Doug knows damn well that I never remember to follow the La Fierte pages on social media. They're usually just thread after thread of people complaining about rain during haying season or the lunch menu at the elementary school.

But it's kind of fucking nice to know people have my back. "Thanks," I tell Doug gruffly. "You're not getting any shit from the town? About what I, um, said about you?" I still wince when I think about how I managed to announce my feelings for Doug in front of an entire church choir. That probably wasn't fair to him at all. But he just shrugs and smiles.

"I don't think anyone knows how to ask me about that," he says. "Some people in the thread are wondering if we'll get together, but that's about it. How about you? No one's giving you a hard time, are they?"

"The hockey parents were really nice about it this morning," I tell him. Trina's dad actually wrapped me up in a giant hug I definitely didn't ask for. He might have even cried a little on my shoulder. He's interesting, that guy. A lot more emotional than I'd expect from someone whose kid causes at least one accidental bloody nose per season.

Doug's eyes widen. "Did you see Jonah? Or your dad?" he asks. "Shoot, Zeke. I wasn't even thinking about what they'd say if—"

"It's okay," I interrupt. "My dad sent me some shitty texts. I'm fucking ignoring them. Jonah was… weird."

Really weird, actually. He kept looking at me like he wasn't sure what to say, then opening his mouth, and then closing it again. It was pretty clear he heard what happened, and I'm honestly surprised he didn't say anything. I was fully prepared for him to lose his shit in the middle of the rink.

I mean, it would've been fun to fight him on the ice again. I would've kicked his ass. But I'm not sorry he decided to keep his mouth shut around Shay.

"He couldn't seem to talk to me about it at all," I tell Doug. And then something occurs to me that feels like the right thing to say. "And that's okay, you know? He's still getting used to this. He just heard about everything—about me. It's okay if he's not ready to talk to me right now. I'm not upset or mad about that."

Doug swallows hard and nods. Then he starts twisting his hands together.

Fuck. Doug gets nervous approximately two times a year. This is the guy who held his cool while he got two hundred heifers out of a barn just before it went fully up in flames.

"That sounds like good behavior for Jonah," he says. "I'm just glad he's not being a butthead to you." He takes a deep breath. "I think maybe you and I should talk. Want to go to the bunk room?"

Sure, I answer in my head. *Just as long as you're not about to tell me you never want to speak to me again.*

My heart pounds in my chest as I follow him through the winding halls of the firehouse and into the tiny room that holds two sets of bunk beds and not much else. Doug closes the door behind him and turns to look at me.

Fuck. This is it. I pushed too hard. I've ruined the friendship of a lifetime and destroyed a relationship that will keep me whole. I never should have told him. I never should have forced him to talk to me about what I told him. I should have just carried on, not saying anything. I could have lived with this secret, right? I could have kept it to myself. I could have—

"I'm not sure, but I think I might be in love with you too."

Doug's words are so unexpected that I actually trip backwards and start to crash into the post of one of the bunkbeds. Doug catches my arm and pulls me back toward him, and now we're face to face, our noses just inches from each other in the dim light of the room.

"Are you serious?" I ask him.

Doug squeezes my arm with one hand while he reaches up to place the other on my cheek. His palm is cold against my skin, because we keep the heat in the firehouse low, but the feel of his fingers against my face is still something like magic.

"I don't know," he murmurs. "I don't know what I feel. All I know is that you've always been the person I wanted to see every day. You've always been the person I wanted to come home to, ever since we started living together. No one on earth is more important to me than you, Zeke. And I always thought, sure, that's how best friends are supposed to be. But then I was talking to Lydia, and—"

"Excuse me, but what the fuck?" I interrupt.

"We ran into each other last night when I was out trying to figure out some stuff. We talked. She told me a lot about bisexuality and pansexuality and other stuff I didn't know much about. And I thought a lot about things that we've been through over the years together. Things I feel for you." He shakes his head. "I'm sorry I haven't been able to talk to you much since the town hall yesterday. There was just so much to think about, you know?"

I do know. I know that feeling all too well. "Don't apologize," I tell him gruffly. "And Doug, you don't owe me anything. What I sprung on you yesterday was huge. You get to have all the time in the world to think about it. And if you need some space from me, that's okay too. I can move out for a while, and we can—"

Doug shakes his head. "Zeke," he says, interrupting me. "Can I try something? Would it be okay if I tried to, um, kiss you?"

My heart's a rocket ship ready to beat out of my chest. I can't remember the last time I cried or vomited, but right now I feel like I'm on the verge of doing either or both. "Uh," I say. "I think so."

I'm not sure why the fuck I'm hesitating. All I've ever wanted for *fifteen years* is for Doug to ask me that question. But then he takes hold of my arms and starts to pull me toward him, and our faces are growing closer and closer. All the while I'm searching Doug's face for some clue that I might be fucking all this up. It's like I'm looking for a DANGER sign flashing somewhere.

Our noses touch, and we both stop. I jerk away from him, fast, just as he does the same. And now my body's frozen, stuck in place. I start to push back toward him, toward his perfect, slightly chapped lips—but I get stuck again, just as I'm centimeters away from touching two of the few body parts of ours that have never touched before.

I don't know why I can't just fucking put my lips against his. Our eyes are still locked. My body is hot all over and my jeans are getting tighter by the second. Every cell inside of me is thrumming on a rapid frequency, and I wonder if I'm in an alternate universe because this all feels so alien. I lean toward him, only to stop yet again. Doug blinks.

"I'm not sure what to do," he whispers. "It's like my mind keeps telling me to kiss you, but my body just…"

"Can't." I finish his sentence in a whisper, because I know exactly how it ends.

We both stand there, silent. The only sound in the room is the hum of the fluorescent light above us. "What the fuck?" I whisper.

The door to the room crashes open just then, and we pull away from each other fast as Samara rushes into the room. "Car accident. Some dumbass rideshare driver going from Atherton to La Fierte couldn't handle the ice. We gotta motor. We're probably looking at jaws of life."

Everyone in our firehouse is well-trained to go on autopilot when we get news like that, so the next few minutes are a blur of getting bodies into the truck and the truck on the road. We're almost at the scene—two minutes out—when the grip of the routine releases me enough for me to rethink Samara's summary of the dispatch call. I turn to look at Doug just as he turns to look at me.

"This morning Max said he was going to get a rideshare and go to—" I start to say.

"You don't think—" Doug says.

Shit. My lunch turns to lead in my stomach and I have to fight off the rising bile in my throat.

Doug's face has gone white. "It can't be him. It won't be him, right? But what if it is? I knew we should have arranged a ride for him. I told him the roads might be bad today. But I was thinking about… other things, and then I had to go to the firehouse, and—"

"Doug." I lay a hand on his arm and wait for him to make eye contact with me. "I'm scared too."

He swallows so hard I can track his Adam's apple moving. "I know he's supposed to just be a journalist working on an article," he says. "But he's more than that, already. You know?"

"He is," I agree gruffly. He's so much fucking more than that. He's *Max.* He's energy and light, full of a kind of individualized self-confidence that I can only ever imagine having. He hasn't been staying with us very long, and it already feels like he's changed our entire house. Changed us.

Without Max, I'm not sure I ever would have been able to do what I did at the town hall yesterday. I'm not sure I ever would have told Doug the truth.

I just hope that truth hasn't come at too high of a price.

DOUG

Max, you should try that maple taco stand
everyone in town keeps raving about.

ZEKE

Or maybe you shouldn't. Let's just say some
ideas work better in theory than in practice.

DOUG

Hey, I think they're delish!

ZEKE

You said the same thing about maple goulash. I
wouldn't stop anyone from trying it, though.

DOUG

Anyway, Max, let us know if you want a ride to
the taco stand later.

Max? Everything okay? You usually don't take
this long to answer our group texts.

ZEKE

Max? You there?

CHAPTER 12

ZEKE

As an emergency responder in a small town, there's no room for emotion when I'm out on a call. I know too many of the people I'm out here helping every day, so I've got to compartmentalize.

Dispatch has given us some additional information, including that no one has apparent, serious injuries, which is the only reason I can take a deep breath. But even if the worst hasn't happened yet, that doesn't mean that nobody's hurt at all. As we approach the accident, I do my best to take all the fears that are ratcheting up in one side of my brain and lock them up in a box I can't get to until later. Right now, I've got to be focused. In the zone.

When we get to the bend in the highway, I don't even need to check the mile markers because there's already a county patrol vehicle pulled up on the shoulder. It's Deputy Johnson's car, and I see Eric Johnson himself, standing in the ditch beside a smashed-up sedan, and speaking to someone through the backseat window.

Doug and I make eye contact, saying a lot without saying anything, the way we always do in moments like this after years of working together on and off the ice.

Samara stops the truck and kills the siren, and we all hop out.

From a side compartment on the truck, I grab the hydraulic spreader while Doug and Samara jog up to Eric. I glance over at where he's headed and see the face of the rear-seat passenger.

Fuck. It *is* Max.

"Where's the driver?" Samara asks Eric. Clearly he's not in the vehicle, but if he's hurt, Doug will provide emergency medical while Samara and I extract—fuck my life that I have to even think this—Max. In this part of the county, where the only ambulance services are privatized and take for-fucking-ever, every firefighter is also an EMT.

Dealing with Deputy Eric Johnson is never a picnic, but I'm so focused on seeing Max that I can barely spare a moment of exasperation for him. "He's in my patrol car."

"Is he injured?" Samara asks.

Eric shrugs. As usual, he's doing his best not to fully acknowledge our existence. Eric's commitment to acting like a child whenever he's around me and Doug would be almost funny if it didn't impede our ability to do our jobs at times. "He seems fine. Well, he's crying a lot, but I think it's just stress. Seems very worried he's going to get banned from being a Lyft driver. Something about a second offense?"

Samara rubs her forehead and sighs. I can practically *see* her trying not to snap at Eric for not waiting for an EMT to evaluate anyone involved in an accident this severe.

"We're going down there," Doug says. I nod, and we don't wait for Samara to acknowledge his statement before rushing to the car like it's on fire.

Doug winces as he squats beside the car. The window is lowered a couple of inches at the top, and Max is clinging to the top of the window, his long fingers white from gripping the tempered glass.

I slide my fingers over his and squeeze, staring him dead in the eye through the window. "Hey," I say, using my steadiest, most comforting voice, the same one I use with spooked animals. "It's going to be okay. We're going to get you out of there."

As our eyes lock, I realize just how pretty Max's are behind his glasses. I always knew I liked them, but now I see how many different shades of blue are floating through them, swirling and intermingling with one another like a painting that's not quite finished. His lips are parted, his face flushed with panic, and under my palm his fingers are long and cool.

He swallows hard, and then says, "Doug. Zeke. You're here."

"Of course we're here," Doug says soothingly.

Max swallows and nods. "I wasn't sure—I mean, I hoped—I wanted it to be you two..." He trails off, and Doug and I share a fast glance between us.

"We're going to make sure you're okay," Doug tells him soothingly. "I promise. We would never, ever let anything happen to you, Max. How are you doing? The deputy over there says you're not hurt. Is that right?"

"Yeah. I think I'm okay." Max takes a gasping breath while I rub his fingers.

"That's good," Doug says. "Then you just need to keep calm. We'll take care of the rest. Listen, babe, Zeke is going to engage the spreader now, and it's going to make a lot of noise. Do you want to cover your ears?"

The phrase *babe* hits my ears in a way that should probably be jolting—after all, Doug and I just shared a pretty fucking ill-fated almost-kiss together, and up until today, I've only ever heard him call his dates *babe*. But everything about the way Doug's talking to Max right now feels natural—not forced or strange at all. Max doesn't even bat an eyelash when he drops that word, and if Samara noticed, she doesn't show any hint of surprise. Max's hand twitches under mine, and then he shakes his head.

I give Max's hand one final squeeze before I'm forced to let go and move to the other side of the car.

It's fucking torture, keeping my eyes on what I'm doing and not on Max as the spreader engages and the squeal of bending metal cuts through the air. I spend plenty of time thinking about whether or not the victims I'm cutting out of a car are handling the stress and the fear okay, but this is *Max*. Max with the stylish clothing and the face that turns red every time he blurts out something he thinks he shouldn't have, and that sneaky, sparkly smile that sometimes make me wonder what it would be like to push him up against a wall and hold every part of his body against mine while I kiss the hell out of him...

Fuck. Is it morally acceptable to be crushing on my quasi-tenant at the same time that I'm trying and failing to start a maybe-relationship with my best friend?

Are the moral implications even worse if I'm doing it while cutting him out of a crushed vehicle?

I force myself to focus as I keep cutting. Max flinches at the sound of the spreader working but stays put, looking back and forth between me and Doug like we're his anchors in a bad storm on Lake Champlain. People have looked at us that way a lot since we became firefighters, but seeing the hope and faith in Max's expression hits different.

After minutes that feel like hours, I've opened the mangled car up enough that there's a safe way out for Max.

"You're doing so well," Doug tells Max soothingly. "Can you unbuckle your seatbelt?"

He shakes his head. "No," he says in a small voice. With the hand that's not under Doug's, Max pushes on the seat belt release and jerks on the strap, but it must be jammed from the impact.

"That's okay," Doug tells him. "You sit tight. I'll get in there and help you." He looks at me over the roof of the car and raises an eyebrow.

I nod. Doug should be the one to climb in the backseat. We're both fairly nimble for our size, but Doug is better at working in tight spaces.

Doug circles the car and slides past me, then halfway into the chasm created by the spreader. "I'm going to reach in and try to unfasten that seatbelt, okay?"

Bending down, I can see Max's face over Doug's shoulder. He nods hard, making the strand of hair that's arced up above his brow fall down into his eyes. "Okay." His eyes drift to mine, still bright with fear and worry.

"We are not going to let you get hurt," I tell him. "Ever," I add in a low tone.

Max nods, his eyes locked on mine. Meanwhile, Doug's working on the belt with a knife. It finally snaps open.

Max clings to Doug as he's pulled from the vehicle, and every tiny gasp and whimper he makes feels like it might just be ripping my chest in pieces. When he's finally out of the car, he tries to let go of Doug and stand, but he stumbles on his feet.

I instantly scoop him up, and he loops his arms around my neck. He can't weigh more than a hundred and fifty pounds soaking wet.

"I shouldn't have gone," he says into my shoulder. "Doug said the roads sucked. Should have stayed home. But I thought you two needed space. And shit! My gifts! They're in the car."

"We're just glad you're safe. That's all that matters. We'll make sure you get whatever you left behind," Doug tells Max, rubbing his shoulder and keeping pace with me as I carry Max away from the crash site. There've been no signs of danger, but procedures exist for a reason, and I'm not taking any chances.

We get to the extendable steps on the side of engine 22, where I carefully lower Max into a sitting position. "I knew you'd come." He gives us a shaky smile. "It isn't quite like I imagined it though."

I frown. "What do you mean?"

"Well, most of the times I've pictured getting rescued by hot firefighters, we end up naked," Max says, blinking dazedly. Then he groans and puts his hand on his forehead. "Sorry. That's over-sharing."

A laugh erupts from my chest, surprising the fuck out of me. It comes from a warm, full feeling that I'm starting to associate with being around Max. It's equal parts relief, affection, and… yeah, definitely attraction. I've noticed he was hot from the day I met him, but what I'm feeling right now… it's more than that, I think.

Somehow, some way, when I wasn't looking—maybe I was too wrapped up in my own secrets, too busy trying to find my way through the maze of my feelings for Doug—Max wormed his way into my heart. And as I watch Doug squat beside me in front of Max, grinning and running his hands over Max's hair, I feel like it's more than fair to say I'm not the only one with a big soft spot for Max.

Who knows? Maybe in another life Max and I would've hooked up. Been something together. Fuck, maybe he and Doug would have been something together.

But the only life I have is the one in the here and now—the one where my best friend and I just tried to kiss and miserably fucking failed at it.

Doug stands, and he and I exchange a quick glance. A real one. The kind we used to share all the time.

I know what he's thinking without having to ask.

What are we going to do?

From the group chat **"The Men of Grandma's House"**

ZEKE

Silicone dildo

MAX

Um, hi. You rang?

ZEKE

FUCKING FUCK

MAX

????

ZEKE

Fucking ignore that!!!

Just fucking pretend I never typed that here, okay?

MAX

Sorry, buddy, but some mental images get written with indelible ink. I will do my best, though.

CHAPTER 13
DOUG

Zeke and I walk on either side of Max, slowly guiding him through the front door.

"I feel like an old man," Max says, groaning as he steps over the threshold. "Like my bruises have bruises."

"Yeah, the body doesn't like those kinds of impacts," I tell him. "But don't worry. We'll ice down those bruises before we get you onto some heat packs. You'll feel better before you know it."

"We have some experience with coming back from body trauma," Zeke tells him. "Doug once got checked so hard his entire thigh was black and blue for four weeks."

"It's true," I say while Max's eyes widen. Zeke and I glance at each other, but then we both quickly look away. Nuts. While we were helping Max out of the car and getting him home, we were something like our old selves. But now that the emergency has passed I feel that weird barrier coming up between us again.

Zeke and I both have our arms around Max's tiny waist. Zeke's is a little higher than mine, and our hands have been grazing one another's sides as the three of us walk.

My heart jumps a little every time Zeke's body brushes against my arm. *That's* how weird things are. But I'm not going to let go of

Max, who I really wish had just taken Zeke up on his offer to carry him inside. He's awfully pale.

Eric told me that he ticketed Dante Fisher, the rideshare driver, for texting while driving. I could kill that little brat.

"I still think," Max mumbles as we both half-carry him to the stairs up to the biggest bathroom, "that this is about as close to my firefighter fantasy as I'm ever gonna get. Even if you two do have your clothes on." He snorts. "Sorry, there I go again. You'd think I was on painkillers or something. But nope, this is still just me being me."

"We like you the way you are," I tell him. Zeke grunts in agreement, and Max blushes.

"Hey," I say. "Hang on to Zeke, okay? I'm going to get the lights."

"He needs a—" Zeke starts to say.

"Bath," I finish for him. "I know." I flip on the lights in the stairwell, and Max leans harder against Zeke as they mount the stairs. There's not enough room for me to be on his other side, so I fall into step behind them, putting a hand on Max's back.

"A bath?" Max repeats. "That doesn't sound bad, actually."

"You'll feel a lot better if you spend some time in cold water," Zeke tells him.

"*Cold*?" Max squeaks. "I take it back. That sounds bad. Very bad."

"An accident is kind of like a rough hockey game," I explain. "You're better off if you get ahead of the bruises."

On the next stair, Max grasps the railing and hesitates. Zeke shoots him a look. "I could carry you."

Max laughs, his back vibrating under my hand. "I'm really fine."

We continue carefully up the stairs to the landing before I move ahead again to turn on the bathroom light. As Zeke and Max shuffle in, I crouch down to run water into the big clawfoot tub. Behind me, Zeke speaks softly to Max as he sits him down on the stool by the towel rack.

"There you go. Easy. Do you want another drink of water?"

"I'm—" Max's breath hitches and I quickly look over my shoulder, worried he's hurting, but instead I find him staring down at Zeke, who's kneeling on the tile floor in front of him, holding Max's calf in one gentle hand while he slips off his shoe with the other.

I quickly look away, feeling like I interrupted something, and fiddle with the temperature on the faucet to make the water a little less icy than I'd run it for myself or Zeke. Still, it should get the job done.

When I look over my shoulder again, I don't know why I'm surprised to find Max shirtless and thumbing the waistband of his jeans. It's not like he was going to get into the tub in his clothes. He looks between me and Zeke with his brows raised and a nervous laugh.

"I can do this part by myself."

Zeke clears his throat. "Right. Come on, Doug." He takes a step toward the door, then hesitates again. "If you need anything, we'll be right outside."

"I know," Max says with a little smile.

At the scene of the accident, he said he knew we'd come. The memory of his words make my chest tight, the ball of feelings growing painfully. I dig my knuckles into my sternum, like that'll help, and feel like I can't breathe right as I follow Zeke out into the hallway.

Avoiding eye contact the whole time, Zeke and I wordlessly go about arranging everything for Max. Zeke goes to find our collection of hot packs while I search for extra blankets, pausing by the linen closet in the hallway when I hear Max muttering through the closed bathroom door.

"Okay in there?" I call.

"Yes," he calls back, his voice muffled. "How long do I have to sit in this very fucking cold water?"

I grin to myself. Zeke is at the top of the stairs, waiting. I glance at him, and his lips twitch in an answering smile. I tilt my head in a silent question, and Zeke shrugs and nods.

"Go ahead and get out," I tell Max. "Do you need a hand?"

I'm reaching for the bathroom door handle when Max says sharply from inside, "*No.*" But then a second later, I hear a squeak, like his foot just slipped on the tiles, and a "Shit!"

I throw open the door and launch myself inside without thinking. Sure enough, Max is down on one knee on the bath mat where he obviously fell while levering himself out of the tub.

He stares at me with big blue eyes and fair, bare skin tight over his bones and pale from the cold and—

My body jolts in response, and I'm not sure how to feel. I've been in about a million locker rooms and seen plenty of naked guys. But Max is different. He's slight, almost delicate, and so *pretty.*

I'm pretty sure these thoughts are very bad to be having about my friend while Zeke, who I am probably in love with, is just down the hall. So I shove them aside and bundle Max in a towel, helping him up.

He looks up at me with an exasperated little smile and shivers. "Thanks. And so much for what's left of my dignity."

"What?" I frown down at him, rubbing the towel briskly over his upper arms.

"I'm not exactly at my best," he says, shivering some more. The ends of his hair are a little wet, maybe from splashing himself when he stumbled out of the tub.

"What are you talking about?" There's a blot of water on his nose. I wipe it off with my thumb.

He blinks at me. "I'm all... shriveled." His cheeks turn bright red.

I'm surprised into a laugh. "Don't worry, I didn't see anything," I say, which is true, but feels like a white lie.

He sniffs. "I'm a grower, not a shower, even at the best of times."

I laugh again, all the pressure in my chest eased, left with something light and warm instead. "Come on," I tell Max. "Let's get you warm."

Zeke is standing in the doorway when I turn around. He steps back so we can walk past him, and for the first time in our lives, the expression on his face is one I absolutely cannot read.

A half hour later, Max is situated in the pig room, surrounded by extra pillows, while Zeke plugs in the space heater he carted up from the basement and I layer heat packs around Max's body.

"This is some pretty impressive caretaking," Max tells us as he sips on the cup of lemon-ginger tea I just handed him. "Thank you," he adds.

Zeke frowns. "We should've grabbed your stuff from the car at the scene."

Max shakes his head. "It's not a big deal."

"I called and asked Deputy Johnson about bringing it by," I say.

"I'm sure he was eager to help." Zeke rolls his eyes.

I sigh. "He told me I can get it from the impound lot in Atherton during business hours." I catch Max's eye. "Eric Johnson is our age. He grew up in Atherton."

"Wait, did you say *Eric Johnson*? I remember that guy!" Max shudders. "He was a creep."

"Still is," Zeke says flatly. "He's lazy as fuck, too. Does just enough to keep his job and doesn't move one inch more." He shakes his head. "He finds plenty of time to be bitter about me and Doug making it to the college hockey leagues while he tapped out in high school, though."

"I can't believe he's in law enforcement," Max goes on. "I guess I was distracted given... well, everything. But I really didn't recognize him."

"He likes to pretend he doesn't recognize me and Zeke. Still salty about losing regionals to us our senior year."

"And that penalty shot he missed," Zeke mutters.

I laugh and look at Zeke. Our eyes meet, and for a second

everything is fine between us. Then the second splits, and Zeke quickly looks away.

"Okay, that's it." Max sits up, wincing. "I wasn't going to say anything because it's really none of my business. And honestly, I'm mostly just happy that the two of you seem to be speaking again—kind of? But something's clearly wrong here, and I'm not very good at butting out of other people's business. So, can we talk about whatever's going on with you two?"

Zeke makes a grumbling sound, and I make a decision. I cannot go one more second pretending things are fine with my best friend when they are very, very, very not fine.

"Zeke and I tried to kiss," I tell Max as I sit down on the end of the bed by his legs.

"That's—" Zeke growls.

"TMI," I interrupt, nodding. "But I'm starting to think that a little TMI is good for us." I pat Max's leg through the blankets.

"Hang on," Max says, pushing himself more upright with his elbows. "You kissed?"

"We *tried*," I clarify.

"And it was a fucking disaster," Zeke mutters, looking stubbornly out the window.

"Oh." Max's eyes widen. "Oh, I see. Well, what happened? Tell Uncle Max."

Zeke snorts. I'm used to speaking for Zeke when he's not in a "words" type of mood, so I figure I'll take things from here. But before I can say anything Zeke says, "We couldn't fucking do it." I can see his expression in the window. He's scowling, the scowl he has when he's sad. My instinct is to comfort him, but whatever wall has gone up between us is still there, stopping me from feeling like I can. "We couldn't even fucking try," Zeke says.

"Oh, well that makes sense," Max says cheerfully.

We both turn to stare at him. "Say fucking what?" Zeke asks.

Max shrugs and then squirms uncomfortably. I nudge one of the hot packs higher on his thigh. "Neither of you has ever been with a man before, right?"

Zeke bites his lip for a moment before he shakes his head, and I try to ignore the strange sense of relief that washes through me. I think it would have bothered me if his answer had been yes.

"Me neither," I tell Max.

"Okay. So it's new for both of you. And you've both known each other a certain way your whole lives. Now you're thinking about whether you want to know each other on a whole new level." Max smiles. "That's a whole lot of new things to try all at once. I don't think you should be stressing about it. Just keep practicing. You'll get there. And then you'll both know if it's something you want."

Zeke and I stare at him. "Well," I finally say. "That's, um, great. I think the problem is that we're not sure how to… ah, practice."

I glance over at Zeke, but his eyes are trained fully on Max.

"Oh, got it. Makes sense." Max nods and knits his eyebrows together. "Hey, how about this? I'll coach you!"

"Excuse me?" Zeke crosses his arms over his chest.

"I think you just need some encouragement and support," Max goes on. "And we're about to start working on the firefighter calendar, so we're going to be spending a lot of time together anyway. I'll coach you on how to try and be together!" He wiggles his eyebrows. "And if I get to bring to life some firefighter fantasies I have along the way, then all the better."

I start laughing, but Zeke's already shaking his head. "It's not a good idea," he says gruffly. "You're our tenant, and a journalist, and I'm not—it wouldn't—I mean—"

"Let's do it," I interrupt him.

"Really? Are you fucking serious?" Zeke turns to stare at me, and having him look me straight in the eye again is all the proof I need that I said the right thing. Nothing in the world is right when Zeke won't look at me.

"Yep. Zeke, listen, we've got things to figure out. I don't think we can do it on our own." I swallow the lump that's been in my throat since yesterday. "And I don't want to lose you, okay?"

"Hey now." Max reaches out to take my hand in one of his,

and he grabs for Zeke's with the other, like he's connecting us back together from the middle. "No one has to lose anyone, okay? Whatever happens, you two will figure all this out. I promise. And I'll help."

"Fine," Zeke mutters.

Max cheers, and I grin.

"First item on the agenda is safety," Max says. "Do we need to get you two tested for STIs?"

I look at Zeke and clear my throat. That question makes this thing between us feel more real. "Um, no. Zeke and I get regular physicals, and we're all good."

Zeke nods. "And what about you?" he asks Max.

"Me? I don't matter. But as I may have told the Airbnb hotline, I've had a lengthy dry spell and have been tested since I last was with anyone, so I'm good to go. Not that it's going to happen. I'm just the coach, not the starting lineup."

"For the record," Zeke adds darkly, "I've been told that I'm very difficult to coach."

Max dissolves into laughter, letting go of our hands to tug the quilt up over his body. "I've always liked a challenge," he tells Zeke, and winks.

For the first time in days, I see Zeke crack a smile.

From the group chat "The Men of Grandma's House"

DOUG

Now that we're all talking again for real, can I ask
about that whole silicone dildo thing?

ZEKE

I'd really rather you didn't.

MAX

ZEKE this is highly unfair. Especially after all the
TMI stuff I've shared with you.

ZEKE

Oh yeah? Suits to measure hot sauce, huh?

I've been meaning to follow up on those
firefighter fantasies you mentioned.

DOUG

SAME

MAX

We're at a TMI impasse

Doug changed the group chat name to "No Such Thing As TMI"

CHAPTER 14
DOUG

"This is it?" Max asks. He's standing on the sidewalk in front of the firehouse between me and Zeke.

"Yeah," Zeke says, drawing out the word and shooting me a questioning look. I shrug. I can't figure out what's up with Max, either.

I follow the direction of Max's stare and try to see through his eyes. The firehouse is—well, the firehouse. It was built three years ago after a big fundraising effort, and it's a long, steel-sided building. From where we're standing, we can see each of the rollup doors that lead to the apparatus room, where the trucks are parked.

Max is looking at the firehouse with what can only be disappointment. Can someone be disappointed in a building?

"What's wrong?" Zeke asks him, shoving his hands in his pockets.

"Oh, nothing," Max says quickly, sliding the strap on his camera bag over his head. "I'm sure I can work with the whole..." He gestures at the building and grimaces. "Industrial vibe. The calendar will still come out just fine if we use this space for the shoot."

Industrial vibe? Zeke mouths at me. I shrug again.

"I think I just pictured something with more character. You know, something that looks like a small-town firehouse and not a… um, really big garage?"

"Oh!" I say, relieved. "That makes sense. The old firehouse *does* look cool. I'm sure we could take the pictures over there." I glance at Zeke, who nods.

"Old firehouse?" Max repeats hopefully.

"Yeah." Zeke nods and points. "It's a block that way." He frowns at Max. "Should we drive?"

"Maybe," I say. "It's pretty cold." Max is wearing what could generously be described as a light jacket, even though Zeke and I both tried to get him to wear something heavier when we left the house.

He shrugged us off, called us overprotective, and reminded us it's been a full forty-eight hours since his accident. Personally, I still don't see how that's relevant. He may say he's feeling fine now, but the last thing he needs is to catch a chill.

"Guys, it's *one* block," Max says. "Show me the old firehouse!" He strides off.

Zeke and I fall into step behind Max, and our shoulders bump in the process. We jerk apart.

"Sorry," Zeke mutters, and falls back so that we're single-file behind Max.

Swallowing, I put one foot in front of the other, feeling so off-balance that I'm surprised I can walk. Even though it's been days since Zeke made his confession—and I made mine—I'm pretty sure the earth is spinning on a new axis. The easy rhythm of life at Zeke's side is completely messed up.

I'm still afraid I'm not going to get it back.

"Is that it?" Max exclaims from ahead of us, bouncing on his feet either because he's excited, or maybe because he's cold. His cheeks are *very* red, and it's a cute look on him. "That's perfect!"

"Well, not *perfect*," Zeke corrects. "The new one got built for a reason."

"There's only one bay, and it's almost too narrow for a modern truck," I explain to Max, who's practically skipping to the old fire-house's double front doors. The green paint on the doors is more chippy since the last time I came over here. The town uses the old firehouse for extra storage, and Marty sent me over with a partic-ularly heavy box a few months back.

"Can we look inside?" Max asks hopefully, peering through the grimy glass window panes in the carriage doors.

"I have a key," Zeke says, holding up the key ring that is tech-nically supposed to be mine, as mayor, but which Zeke has been carrying around after I misplaced it for three hours and almost had a panic attack. He squints at the keys until he finds the right one, then unlocks the doors and uses his shoulder to force them open.

"Reason number one thousand and one that we needed a new firehouse," Zeke explains over the squeal of the old hinges. "Get-ting out in a hurry was a huge pain in the ass."

"And kind of a big part of the job," I add, following Zeke and Max inside. Zeke flips on the lights, which flicker before they come on, and I smile as I look around, full of nostalgia. The new firehouse was built a few years after Zeke and I started, so coming through the doors always reminds me of when we were brand new to the job.

"Absolutely fucking perfect," Max says in a loud whisper, roaming into the apparatus room where the truck was once parked. Now it's mostly empty except for some old equipment and a stack of dusty gear.

"I bet you'll like the dining room," Zeke says, pointing over his shoulder with his thumb. He's smiling as he looks at Max, and Max grins back and follows Zeke through an open door. I feel a pang, wishing things were that easy between me and Zeke, and trail after them.

I look around the room, which is dusty and cluttered but otherwise pretty much how I remember it—one part dining room, one part gym, one part general hangout space. "Wait a second." I walk over and pull the sheet off of a bulky piece of furniture.

"Fuck, there it is," Zeke says, breathing out a laugh.

I beam down at the miraculous item that I just uncovered. "I can't believe it."

"Uh, guys?" Max asks, coming up beside me and tilting his head. "What am I missing? Isn't this just a hideous old couch?"

"Definitely fucking not," Zeke says firmly. "It's a hideous, old, *and* supremely comfortable couch."

"It's the most comfortable couch *ever*," I emphasize, tossing aside the sheet and launching myself onto one end. "It's still perfect," I announce happily. "Zeke, check it out."

He flops down at the other end and stretches his arms over the back of the couch with a happy sigh. "Perfect," he agrees.

Max shakes his head, setting down his camera bag on the old coffee table still stacked with dogeared fitness magazines and putting his hands on his hips. "I don't think this is sanitary."

"Don't knock it till you've tried it." Zeke pats the center cushion.

Max bites his lip, then shrugs. "Okay, but if I get hepatitis, you have to pay all my hospital bills." He hops into the space between us, and his eyes grow wide as he sinks into the cushions. "Oh, shit."

"Right?" I crow. "It's mystical, this couch."

"I can't believe it's still here. I thought Jordy was going to take it home."

"We had a tournament to figure out who got to keep it," I tell Max. "I still think he cheated."

"And then he didn't even fucking take it," Zeke grumbles.

"Yeah, what the heck?" We exchange a glance of mutual half-serious outrage, and then I grin and Zeke snorts. But that wall of awkwardness erupts between us a second later, and our eyes slide apart again.

"Hmm," Max says, and my eyes snap to his face. He's looking back and forth between me and Zeke, speculatively. "I think it's time for the first coaching session."

My heart speeds up, and I see Zeke stiffen, too.

Noticing our reactions, Max reaches out to both of us, putting his hand over mine on my knee, and squeezing Zeke's shoulder. "Relax, you guys. I'm not going to make you get naked or anything."

"Fuck," Zeke groans, his head falling back against the back of the couch. "This is so goddamn weird."

"I think the words you're looking for are 'This is a fascinating and impressively avant-garde method, Max,'" Max corrects, grinning. "Come on, trust me!"

Zeke looks back to Max. "We trust you," he says, tone serious. "There is literally no one else we would have dragged into the middle of our… complications."

I feel my eyebrows rise. *Complications* doesn't feel like the right word, but whatever. I agree with him anyway. "Yeah," I tell Max. "It's weird, because the three of us just met, but I do trust you more than anyone. Except Zeke, of course," I amend. "And Grandma," I add.

Max squeezes my hand. "That means a lot to me. I care about you guys too. And I want to help. So, I've been thinking a lot about how the two of you tried to kiss each other, and it didn't work like you wanted." He laughs a little self-consciously. "Thinking that through was *not* a hardship by the way. The two of you make a really hot couple."

I blink. "You think so?"

"Um, *yeah*. You're both gorgeous. And two big, ripped, masculine guys together is basically half of gay porn for good reason."

GAY PORN. The words flash in my head in all-caps like a giant neon sign. Of course gay porn exists, but I don't think I've ever seen any.

I note that I might have some homework to do tonight when I'm alone in my room.

"Obviously I don't have firsthand experience with the particular dynamic," Max continues, "but from what I've heard, it can be a little confusing at first. What do you do? What do you say?

Who goes first? That kind of thing. I think that might be part of the problem. What do you think? Am I way off base?"

"That does makes sense," Zeke says. He glances at me for a half-second. "Also, I'm used to…" He pauses and clears his throat. "I guess I'm used to pushing down those feelings about Doug when they come up. Letting them just *happen* feels… hard."

"Yeah," Max says softly. "I bet." He turns to me. "What do you think, Doug?"

I bite the inside of my cheek until it aches, then blow out a breath. "It's kind of different for me, maybe. I don't think that I was really aware of what I felt for Zeke until a couple of days ago. I know that sounds ridiculous, but it's true."

"It doesn't sound ridiculous," Max says.

"No, it doesn't," Zeke agrees. I dare a glance at him, and this time our eyes actually meet for a few seconds without either of us acting like we're allergic to eye contact.

"Anyway, it just feels so new. And, I don't know, big, I guess?" I feel foolish for not being able to use better words than "new" and "big," but Max and Zeke don't laugh. They just nod, and then Max folds his arms.

"Okay, team. Why don't you two show me what I'm working with?" Max asks playfully, jumping up off the couch and clapping his hands. "To start, could you sit a little closer?"

Zeke and I both shuffle a few inches toward the center of the couch, and Max rolls his eyes.

"Come on, boys. Share that center cushion."

Zeke chuckles and I smile, but my heart is pounding with nerves when Zeke and I meet in the middle of the couch, our thighs pressed together, his arm rigid against mine.

Studying us with his arms crossed, Max sighs. "Wow. This is somehow even worse than how you described it." He tilts his head. "*Definitely* not how I imagined it."

"How did you imagine it?" Zeke asks, his voice an octave deeper than its usual tone. And it has an effect on me. I feel heat rush through my body, and judging by the way Max's cheeks turn the same shade of bright pink they were when we were out in the December chill, I'm not the only one.

Max looks briefly surprised by the question, then thoughtful. "The two of you are so comfortable with each other. So natural. I imagined that your kissing would be the same way."

My tense shoulders feel a little more rigid. I could only wish this was as easy as everything else Zeke and I do together.

"I may have also imagined that you were wearing some fire-fighting clothes, surrounded by smoke from the fire you just put out," Max continues, grinning.

"Turnout gear," Zeke and I automatically correct him in unison.

Max rolls his eyes, grin unwavering. "It's a visual fantasy, okay? Not a textual one. And I have *so many* firefighter fantasies. Didn't I tell you?"

Zeke leans forward, his arm resting partially on my leg, and I'm very aware of his body heat, and the smooth skin on the back of his neck. But it's like my eyes don't know where to look because I also want to stare at Max—between his blushing cheeks and the words coming out of his mouth, he's contributing to the sudden tightness in my jeans just as much as Zeke.

"You mentioned some fantasies," Zeke says, still speaking in that tone of voice that seems to be full of sex magic. "But I didn't think you were serious."

Max nods hard, swallowing. "Dead serious. You have *no* idea."

Zeke licks his lower lip, and Max, watching him, makes a little noise, like the sight of Zeke's tongue did something to him. I get it. It did something to me, too.

"Will you tell us one of them?" I ask, then immediately worry I've gone too far. But though Max wrinkles his nose sheepishly, he doesn't seem uncomfortable.

"How about two big, strong firefighters, just back from saving lives. All hot and sweaty as they strip out of their gear, and their eyes lock across the locker room. Neither one of them have ever admitted an attraction before, but in that moment, it's too powerful to resist."

Holy crap, Max is good with words. I stare at him, mesmerized, and when I manage a glance at Zeke, I see he's staring, too.

"I have an idea," I say, my voice a little hoarse.

They both turn their heated eyes toward me, and the fire building inside me burns a little hotter.

"What if you two kiss?" I ask. "Because I can tell you want to."

The words coming out of my mouth shouldn't make any sense. I shouldn't want Zeke to kiss someone else. But I do. I really, really do.

Max's lips part in surprise. Zeke's breath hitches, and his hand slides over my knee. "Are you sure?"

I meet his stare, and I don't have to say anything. We're back in a place where we don't need words to communicate, a familiar affinity, even if we've never used it for a conversation anything like this one.

Zeke nods to me, then turns forward to face Max and leans back, his knee knocking against mine as his thighs spread. "Will you kiss me?" he asks Max.

"Please," I add.

Max stares at the two of us like he's not sure we're real, and then he nods. Soon it's like whatever is holding him back falls away, and he climbs straight into Zeke's lap, one knee nestled between Zeke's hip and mine.

Zeke grasps Max's waist in both hands and hauls him closer so that they're almost nose-to-nose. Max takes his glasses off and sets them on the couch.

I'm full of adrenaline and focus, that combination that kicks in when we get to a scene at work.

Seeing Max in Zeke's lap puts me on high alert.

My dick is aching and my jeans are now *very* tight. *That* is not a feeling I ever have at work.

"You're absolutely sure?" Zeke murmurs, staring into Max's

eyes. Max nods, and then Zeke turns to me, and I realize the question was for both of us.

"Absolutely," I say without hesitating. And I mean it.

Zeke cradles Max's face in his big paws, knifes up, and kisses him.

Hard.

And every part of my body is *singing*. Or something like that. Words aren't my thing. I'm so turned on I could explode. Max and Zeke aren't goofing around with this kiss—Zeke's hands are now gripping Max's butt like he wants to leave marks.

Before I realize what's happening, Max slides into my lap. My hands fly to his waist. Zeke is leaning toward us with a hand on Max's ass. I make a strangled noise in the back of my throat.

I'm so hard now that it hurts.

"Is this okay?" Max murmurs, looking at me with those gorgeous eyes of his.

I nod. *Yes.* Then I moan, because Max grinds against me before he raises himself on his knees to meet me. His mouth crashes into mine like thunder. If I'd imagined kissing Max, I would have expected it to be a sweet kiss. But this kiss is filthy. Perfect. My tongue swirls against his, and I taste a trace of cinnamon that can only be Zeke's familiar toothpaste. Then he sucks my lower lip between his teeth and bites down—soft, but firm. A statement. I gasp when our lips part. Max is wearing a very smug smile.

Zeke groans at our side, and Max reaches over and kisses him again while I hold him steady on my lap.

All three of us are breathing heavily, and I'm not the only one with a bulge in my jeans.

"Holy shit," Zeke breathes.

Max slumps against me, his forehead on my shoulder. "What Zeke said," he mutters, voice muffled by my shirt. I breathe out a ghost of a laugh and rub his back with my right hand. I look at Zeke. We're sitting as close to one another as we've ever been, and it's like Max joined us together by getting between us.

After a long moment where nobody moves, Max says, breath

tickling my neck, "Zeke, you've had feelings for Doug for a long time. You must have fantasies too. Fantasies about him."

Zeke nods, his breath hitching. "Yeah."

My eyes widen, and I can't look away from Zeke's face. He drags his teeth across his lower lip.

"Want to share? I told you mine, after all." Max's soft voice is playful. "You don't have to give any detail. Just some key words."

"I—um—thought about Doug jerking himself off. I've thought about it *a lot*."

I make a noise. I hear it, but I'm not conscious of it until it's coming out of my mouth. "Really?"

Zeke nods. He leans closer, his hand sliding into mine. I feel his breath against my face, and just as my eyes flutter closed—

Someone pounds on the firehouse door.

The three of us jerk upright.

"Are you fucking kidding me?" Zeke groans.

I can barely hear a voice that sounds like Marty from the town hall. "Doug, are you in there? This darn door is stuck!"

Max climbs out of my lap and puts his glasses back on, and I adjust my jeans. Fortunately the interruption has my erection fading fast. I can see Marty through the parted doors because Zeke didn't close them all the way, but he obviously can't get them opened wide enough to actually get inside.

"Thank God you're here," Marty says when he sees me. "I've been looking all over town. I thought you were at the firehouse! The *actual* firehouse. Oh, hi, Zeke."

I pull the doors open another several inches so Marty can slip through, and he leans against the wall, pale and panting, like he just ran a mile. Maybe he did, if he's been looking for me all over town.

"Jesus, Marty," Zeke mutters from behind me. "Did somebody die?"

"It's worse," Marty says flatly. "It's been confirmed. It's official. Althea's sister's boyfriend's hairdresser's cousin was right. Atherton got *her*! She's coming—for the Holiday-Off!" He holds up his phone. "Hashtag-belle-of-the-holiday-ball! Can you believe this? Atherton really booked Vermonica! Before we even knew she was available!"

"Hey," Max says, scooting between me and Zeke to pat Marty's shoulder. "I'm so sorry. Honestly," he adds. "But if this firefighter calendar idea works, we'll be able to book the Icebreakers. We've got a plan to fight back!"

Marty frowns and shakes his head. "We better," he says. "Because this post isn't just a rumor. Without those ice artists, there really is no hope now." He stomps out of the room, and we all listen as he slams the door to the firehouse behind him.

I stare at my boots. La Fierte is in so much trouble. If Max's calendar idea doesn't work and we can't raise the money we need for the ice sculptors, then the Holiday-Off judges won't even make note of our new decorations or our regionally renowned choir. The second the guest of honor steps onto the stage in Atherton's band shell, that'll seal the deal.

From the group chat "No Such Thing as TMI"

ZEKE

Max, I wanted to warn you: Jonah may stop by
the house later. Shay forgot his hat at practice.

MAX

Aww, thanks for the warning.

You know, it's weird. I'm not sure seeing him will
ever have the same effect on me now that I've
met you

It's like my brain's rewriting my unconscious
associations of your face or something lol

ZEKE

I guess I'm glad me looking like that fucker has
finally done something good in the world

DOUG

You know, Max, if you ever want to talk about
what happened to you back in high school, we're
always here to listen!

Sherbert's a good listener too, actually. Being
around him is really soothing.

ZEKE

You know you're the only person on the planet
who thinks that, right?

MAX

What's a Sherbert?

ZEKE

Jeb's demon goat

MAX

Of course it is.

CHAPTER 15
ZEKE

I'm not on cloud nine, exactly, but it has to be at least an eight and a half.

Sure, Marty's interruption—and his news—definitely sucked. I almost kissed Doug, and this time, the connection that has always been between us was sparking, instead of totally absent like when we tried to kiss in the new firehouse dormitory the other day.

And before *that*… well, I kissed Max.

And it was amazing.

Considering how I feel about Doug and how he *might* feel about me, I should probably be weirded out by kissing Max. But kissing Max with Doug there watching made me feel closer to Doug. Maybe I've had to rethink my definition of relationships, and the whole concept of monogamy, over the past few years. I mean, look at Jeb, Embry, and Adam. Or their neighbors on the Polyam and Proud farm.

Doug is driving us back home, and I know he's distracted by Marty's news, but he still keeps looking at Max in the passenger seat and smiling, then blushing, then looking at me and blushing harder.

It's so fucking cute that I want to drag him across the bench seat and kiss him.

He's driving, of course, so I don't. And by the time he parks the truck against the snowbank from the last time we cleared the driveway, the pathway between us that Max opened seems like it's closed again, and as close as he is, Doug feels out of reach.

Max was gazing out the windshield during the short drive, but when Doug kills the engine, he blinks like he's being stirred out of some deep thoughts. "So," Max says tentatively into the silence of the truck's cab. "How is everyone feeling about that extremely hot makeout session?"

I can't help a chuckle, and Doug is grinning. Max gets to the fucking point. It's one of my favorite things about him.

"'Extremely hot' sounds about right," I tell Max, leaning into his side. He presses his shoulder to mine and shoots me a grateful smile.

"That's a relief to hear. And… Doug?"

He leans against the steering wheel. "I don't like to hold a grudge, but I may never forgive Marty," he says. He sighs. "And honestly, I feel great about it. I'd like for there to be more of it, if you don't mind my saying. I could really use a distraction right now."

Max shakes his head. "I know I haven't lived in Vermont for a long time, but I still don't understand how one cow can have this much impact. You're really going to lose the Holiday-Off?"

"Yeah, Atherton fucking pipped us to the post," I tell him. "A cow who's born in Vermont with a maple leaf pattern on her stomach? That Holstein's fucking royalty around here. Doesn't matter what else happens now. We're done for."

"Done for." Doug drops his head against the headrest. "I guess Barton Asterstop was right about me after all. Maybe I really never should have run for this job."

"Oh, babe. Don't say that." Max nuzzles against Doug's shoulder, and I breathe a small sigh of relief. I've never been good at the hugging stuff, and Doug definitely needs a whole lot of hugging right now. I'm glad Max is here with us to help make him feel better.

"Yeah, that's fucking crap." I add. "Absolutely fuckasscrap."

"Swear jar," Doug says mildly.

Max laughs. "Well," he says, huffing out a breath. "At least neither of you have any regrets about today. If there were regrets, I was going to be deeply offended."

"No regrets," Doug says immediately.

"None," I agree, slipping my arm around Max's shoulder. He feels so good when he leans into me. It puts me instantly back to the moment when he was in my lap, my hands on his body, his hot mouth on mine. I swallow, feeling like a teenager who wants to fog up the fucking windows in this truck. But I'm a grown goddamn man, so I'd rather let this play out in the warm house if I had the choice.

"Maybe we can, uh, pick up where we left off," I suggest. "Preferably *indoors*."

Max makes a sound that is basically a pant, and my urge to maul him right-fucking-now immediately doubles. "Yes, *please*," he groans, and Doug nods, reaching for the truck's door handle.

We scramble out of the truck. I take Max's hand, like he might disappear if I don't keep track of him. He smiles at me as we follow Doug, who's practically running to the side door of the house. But then he pauses, looking toward the garage.

"Did you hear that?" he asks.

I can't hear much except the blood singing through my ears, but I try to focus. "Hear what?"

As soon as I ask the question, I hear it too. It's kind of a knocking sound. And then—was that a cowbell?

"Maybe a raccoon got in there," I suggest to Doug, who looks unsure. Like on the one hand, he wants to make sure an intruder isn't rummaging around on the property, and on the other, almost nothing can distract him from getting Max back into his arms.

I can sympathize.

Then there's a big crash, one much louder than a raccoon could likely create, and all three of us are rushing to the walk-through door of the detached two-car garage. The ceiling is too low for either of our trucks. Ever since Doug's grandma drove her Cadillac to Florida to take up permanent residence there, the garage has been empty except for the riding mower and several stacks of boxes and storage totes.

"Should I get the .22?" Doug whispers to me as he pauses at the door.

"A gun?" Max yelps, shuffling closer to me.

I squeeze Max's hand, about to tell Doug it might be better to be safe than sorry, when I hear the bell again and this time, a very distinct *moo*.

"What the heck?" Doug mutters, and he pulls open the door. I crowd in behind him to look over his shoulder.

The garage is a mess. But I hardly notice the overturned boxes, mostly containing Christmas decor, because there's a fucking Holstein standing in the corner, her head buried in one of the larger totes with its lid askew. Hearing us, she jerks up her head, making the bell on a leather collar around her neck clatter again. She has tinsel hanging out of her mouth, and a very distinctly shaped patch of black on her side.

Doug gasps as I study that spot and will it to be *any other fucking shape* than what it looks like.

"That's a maple leaf on her stomach," Max whispers.

It sure the fuck is. "It has to be a coincidence," I say, rubbing the back of my neck. "It can't be *her*."

"That's the shoreline of Lake Champlain on her haunches," Doug says breathlessly.

The cow turns her head so that we can clearly see the exact shape of the state of Vermont on her forehead, and we all gasp.

How did *Vermonica*, the state mascot of Vermont, show up in Doug's garage?

"Should she be eating that tinsel?" Max asks.

She definitely *should not*. Doug and I both rush to move her away from the box she's got her nose in and pull her away from the shiny green metal strings while she sends out a tragic bellow at the loss of her non-food.

"Why is she in the garage?" Doug asks, his eyes wide as he pushes back at his ski hat. "We don't have any hay! We need to get her some hay!"

Doug's not exactly the panicking type, and the last time I saw this much worry in his eyes was when we were down three goals in the conference championship our junior year of college with only four minutes left on the clock. "Okay, let's just take a beat," I say. "We can figure this out. Where did—"

"There's a note!" Max calls from across the garage. He tugs a brown envelope from where it's been taped to the garage door and holds it up triumphantly. "It's got Doug's name on the front."

Doug grabs hold of the bag of tinsel, eliciting another angry *moo* from Vermonica, and we both rush over to Max as he rips the envelope open.

Inside is a piece of notebook paper folded in half. Max flips it up, and we peer over his shoulders.

"Was that written on a typewriter?" I ask in disbelief.

"A *bad* typewriter," Max confirms. I can see what he means. The typesetting is slightly misaligned and the ink is uneven.

"Dear Mayor McEmbirk," Max reads aloud. "I heard Atherton procured their appointment on Vermonica's calendar by unscrupulous means. As a result, their advantage in the Holiday-Off is unfair. The playing field must be leveled. Therefore, I decided to assist you. Vermonica has no other appearances scheduled before Christmas Eve. If you can keep her secured in this garage and undiscovered by anyone but the members of your household, I will facilitate her return to the Capitol after the Holiday-Off festivities are over, and only the citizens of Atherton will be disappointed by her brief absence." Max stops and looks up, frowning.

"Wait," Doug says. "Does that mean the person who wrote this letter kidnapped her? Or, um, cow-napped her?"

"I don't think so," Max says slowly. "It says, 'Rest assured that

I have secured the necessary privileges to leave Vermonica with you. However, it is imperative that no one learns of her location prior to Christmas Day. Should she be discovered, there would no doubt be political ramifications. Tell no one of my interventions or your cooperation.'"

"Interventions?" I snort. "That's an understatement. This is a bovine conspiracy."

"Does it say anything else?" Doug asks.

Max reads the rest. "'I hope this gesture on my part will allow Atherton and La Fierte to engage in a more meaningful and honest competition. Best of luck, Mayor McEmbirk. Yours, a citizen.'"

The three of us stare at the letter in silence. Eventually, Vermonica lets out another low and tragic *moo*.

"We have to call the police," Max says. "Right?"

"We don't have any town police. Only the county sheriff." Doug grimaces.

I grunt. "Or more specifically, the only deputy they ever send to La Fierte. *Eric.*"

Doug rubs his face. "Yeah. Dang. He is *not* going to give us the benefit of the doubt in this situation. Not one bit."

"That's an understatement," I say darkly. "He'll probably accuse us of forging the note."

"Well, anyone would know that's ridiculous. There's no evidence that we brought her here! Plus, why would we call the sheriff if we're the ones who kidnapped her?"

I shake my head. "Even if we call *him,* he'll still find a way to make our lives miserable over this. Especially you. He hates that you're the mayor."

Max sighs. "You really don't trust that deputy?"

Doug and I shake our heads adamantly.

"How about contacting the owners directly?" Max suggests.

"The note said not to," Doug points out. "The note said that they had permission to have her here."

"Are we really going to trust the anonymous note-writer who

left the state mascot in your garage, Doug?" I ask. "What are people going to say if we get caught?"

"I don't know. They would probably think I was ridiculous for believing what the note said. They'll agree with Barton, that I'm 'a naive, C-student hockey player who is far out of his depth.'"

"Did you just quote Barton's shitfucktacular article?" I ask in disbelief. "How many times have you read that piece of trash?"

"Swear jar," Doug says weakly. Then he sighs. "A couple times. Maybe more like a few." He reaches into his pocket and pulls out a folded piece of newsprint. "Uh, no more than once a day?"

What the fuck? He's been carrying that angry little man's hateful, bullshit words around *in his pocket*?

"Doug." I walk across the garage and put my hands on his shoulders. "Barton's a fucking asshole, *and* he's wrong about pretty much everything he prints, including what he said about you. You don't need the town to win a contest to prove you're a great human being."

Doug's shoulders stay tense under my hands, and I can tell my words aren't getting any traction. His troubled expression remains, and he slips the article back in his pocket.

"You don't," Max adds from behind me. "But I understand why you want to." I look at him over my shoulder and he shrugs at me with a slight, wistful smile. "The words that hurt us the most are the ones that some part of us thinks could be true. That article also had a lot to say about the future of the town, too."

Oh, yeah. I forgot about those parts. Doug apparently hadn't. He nods at Max, still quiet and forlorn. "Yeah. In a town this small, there's always a lot to worry about. I learned that fast when we worked through the budget to keep the fire department running. Zeke, you know what I mean. You did most of the number stuff."

I grimace at the reminder of the "number stuff." I think the Microsoft Excel logo is going to be in my nightmares for the rest of my life after all the late nights we pulled, moving money around in the budget until everything lined up.

Doug goes on. "La Fierte needs to grow, and that means attracting new families and young farmers. But when our town gets a moment in the national spotlight, it's not about how great the community is. It's about what a loser its mayor is." His eyes meet mine before I can open my mouth. "I know you don't think it's true, Zeke, and I appreciate the way you see me more than I can even…" His voice cracks and he hangs his head, trailing off.

"Hey." I rub his shoulders, like we just lost a big game. Except the stakes are way higher at this moment than they've ever been in hockey, and the new territory is a little scary for me too. "It's okay, Doug."

Vermonica noisily chews her cud, apparently having given up on finding any edible Christmas decorations in Doug's grandma's stash. I look over at the cow. Her dopey brown eyes meet mine.

"For the record," Max says from behind me, "I think we should keep her. Fuck Atherton!"

"For fuck's sake," I mutter. "This is *not* a good idea." But when Doug raises his head, he has this hopeful look in his eyes, which are glossy with the threat of tears, and my resolve crumbles. "Okay," I say finally. "For now we'll hold onto her. Just while we think through the best course of action."

Max claps his hands. He's grinning like Christmas came early.

"We need to study the note," I tell him, trying to remain stern even though I really want to smile at the little troublemaker. "This doesn't mean we're committing to keeping her out of Atherton on Christmas Eve."

"We just need to get the Icebreakers booked," Doug says. "That will even the playing field and we can win, fair and square."

Alarm bells are ringing faintly in the back of my head, but I know I've lost control of this situation despite my best efforts. "And as far as *we* know, Vermonica's owners know exactly where she is." I know I'm leaning into a convenient story here, but who the fuck cares? "And all of us need to recognize that if this goes sideways, we could be in actual trouble," I remind them.

Doug's expression turns serious. "If someone takes the fall, it should be me. I don't want either of you to lie, but if someone finds her here, I'll take full responsibility and neither of you will contest it."

I roll my eyes. That's not going to happen. But I don't argue with Doug because I don't see a version of reality where we get caught. Who's going to come looking for a famous cow in Doug's garage?

Max squeals, and Doug pulls me into a long hug. "You've always got my back," he says into my neck. "Always, Zeke. Thank you."

I hold onto him, feeling the weight and warmth of him in my arms. "You've worked so hard to learn the ropes as mayor," I tell him. "You give it your all, like you always do. I'm so fucking proud of you. And you do deserve a fair judging that night. You deserve everything, Doug."

He starts to pull away, but now my body's responding like the magnet it's always been for him. He tilts his head until our noses are pressed together, our eyes locked, and the energy between us feels as palpable as the chill in the air surrounding us. I move slightly closer, and then so does he. Slowly, centimeter by centimeter, like the universe is reeling us in, until his lips are pressed to mine and mine are pressed to his. Every cell in my body is alive with wild, chaotic energy as Doug and I kiss for the very first time.

We break apart, both of us breathing hard, and Doug smiles as he traces a hand down my cheek.

"Are you okay?" I ask, searching Doug's face. He feels so right in my arms, and after all our years together I'm used to trusting my sense of his emotions and moods. But this time I need to know for sure. I need to hear him say the words.

"I'm—" There's a tremor in his voice, but he's smiling as he stops and swallows. "I'm perfect. That was perfect. Thank you."

He kisses me again and then puts his head on my shoulder. I lock my arms around him and never want to let go.

Behind us, Max breaks into applause, and Vermonica moos again.

Looks like I'm officially complicit in a cow-napping conspiracy.

MAX

I was thinking about something the other day

I've never actually seen you two fight a fire

Like, I wouldn't want to actually SEE that, bc that means something bad has probably happened, but THEN AGAIN

I bet you're both super hot when you're all decked out in that stuff you wear

ZEKE

It's called turnout gear, babe. Sometimes bunker gear.

DOUG

Yup. Or PPE.

MAX

OMG I'm getting hard just hearing you talk about PPE. Fair warning. You're going to be getting out of it in the photoshoot, though.

Guys?

CHAPTER 16

MAX

I grin and silently tell my dick to calm down. In addition to being hot as fuck, Doug and Zeke are so sweet with each other that my heart feels completely full as I watch them connect on a new level —one that is clearly so right.

When Doug and Zeke break apart, I can't contain myself.

"Okay, that was even better than I imagined." They both blink at me, and I throw up my hands. "What? You *have* to be used to my inappropriate outbursts by now."

Zeke's lips curve into one of his rare smiles, making me want to kiss him again. But kissing isn't the only thing I want to do, because every minute around these guys makes my imagination run wild and dirty. I've acknowledged and accepted my inner perv, thank you very much.

"I think we are, yeah," Zeke says. "It's part of your charm."

The guys have turned to face me, side-by-side with Doug's hand still on Zeke's waist. Zeke's arm slides around his shoulders. It makes my heart happy to see them acting so natural with each other.

"I mean, the only thing better than two firefighters going at it would be if I were in the middle."

Doug and Zeke look at each other, and though it's brief, I

recognize one of those moments where they are having a conversation with just their eyes. Their closeness amazes me.

"We like having you in the middle," Zeke says when he turns back to me. His smile is a little bit wicked. I groan.

"You cannot just go all Viking pirate and say those things to me," I protest, but I smile to make sure they know I'm *not* complaining.

Zeke's brow furrows in confusion. "Viking? Viking pirate? The fuck?"

I nod. "That's how I think of you."

Doug laughs and tilts his head back to study Zeke. "I think I can see it too."

Zeke snorts. "Aren't Vikings and pirates the same thing?"

"Eh." I shrug. "Maybe. They both raid, but one is by land and the other is by sea. Don't think about it too hard. I don't mean that you'd be a Viking pirate in reality, because Vikings and pirates did some bad shit. It's just more a vibe. You're a combo of Dracule Mihawk from *One Piece* and Rollo from *Vikings*. Here to ravage me with your fellow warrior at your side." I wink at Doug, then glance across the garage. "Although in my fantasy, this transpires without a cow watching us."

Zeke chuckles. "Yeah." He eyes Vermonica. "I guess she adds a certain ambiance. Don't—stop eating that!" He lunges across the garage to rescue a box of garland from Vermonica's seeking nose. "She's going to make herself sick."

"Yeah," Doug agrees. He steps behind me and absently palms the back of my neck, which makes me want to purr. Then he crosses his arms, surveying the disaster around us. "Clearly, we need to get some hay. Like, a *lot* of hay."

"And straw," Zeke adds, wrinkling his nose at a puddle on the concrete floor that my nose tells me is *not* melted snow.

"Yes," Doug says. "And a water trough. Without anyone in town figuring out that there's a cow in my garage. Somehow."

"And we definitely need to get all of this Christmas crap out of here." Zeke shoves a file box of lights across the floor. "We'll donate it to the Holiday-Off decorating committee. Perfect place to put all this shit before Hungry Heifer here eats it."

"Is she a heifer?" I ask with interest, then frown. "Wait, what's a heifer, again?"

"I think it's just a young, female cow. And she's not that young," Zeke says, then rubs Vermonica's head again. "Sorry, girl. You look great though."

"No, it's a cow who's never had a calf," says Doug, walking over to scratch Vermonica under her chin. His voice turns into a croon as he talks to her. "And you've had three babies, haven't you, good girl?"

Zeke rolls his eyes at Doug, but he's smiling. Vermonica's eyes get bright with happy surprise as Doug apparently finds an itchy spot. She *is* cute, I have to admit, though I've always preferred to keep a fence between myself and any and all livestock. Not every Vermonter is a farmer, okay?

"So," Zeke says, "I'll head over to the Stock place and see if we can borrow some feed and supplies. To, uh, help out a friend." He scratches his head. "Hopefully they don't ask too many questions."

I nod. "I'll help Doug carry the old decorations out to the truck, and we can take it to town hall?"

The guys nod. I clap my hands together again. "Good! And tomorrow we really need to work on this calendar photoshoot. We have the perfect location, and we have to move fast to have any chance of getting the calendar done in time to raise the kind of money those Icebreakers want. We *could* start advertising for presales now, *if* we had some example images. Preferably ones that show a lot of skin." I look them each up and down and wink.

Both men shift their weight uneasily. I can tell that getting them to strip down and pose for the camera may prove to be a challenge, but I think I'm up for it. At least a certain part of me is definitely up for it.

"Okay," Doug says, drawing himself up to his full height like

I'm suggesting he run into an actual fire or something. "I can do this. I'm ready."

Zeke looks much more skeptical. "You really think I have to be in this fucking thing?"

"Yes." I roll my eyes. "Have you ever even seen your abs? Trust me, you need to be in the calendar. Every potential calendar buyer on the planet agrees with me."

Zeke grunts. "Fine," he mumbles. Then he hastily sidesteps away from Vermonica as she lifts her tail and drops a pile of fragrant crap on the garage floor.

Twenty-four hours later, we've accomplished a remarkable amount in a short period of time. I set up a prototype website. Zeke got commitments from the other models with shocking efficiency—I guess I'm not surprised that people have a hard time telling him no. Meanwhile, Doug basically converted his garage into a barn, complete with mounds of golden straw that Vermonica can snuggle into, a feed trough, heated water tank, and a few portable fence panels to keep her contained on one side of the garage, away from the stack of hay and grain that she's allotted twice a day.

Next on the to-do list is to take the final photographs for the calendar, while channeling just how much I love Zeke's hidden kindness and caring nature.

Because he might be the worst photographic subject I've ever had.

Scratch that, I'm being generous. He is literally *the* worst.

"Babe," I tell him. "I know smiling for the camera isn't your thing, but do you think you could go for pensive, rather than 100% pissed off? I don't think your I Want to Kill You face is going to sell calendars."

Samara snorts loudly from the makeup chair, where she's getting set up for her own shoot.

"No one asked for your opinion, Ms. July," Zeke snaps. Then he takes a breath, moves the ax that I handed him earlier from one hand to another, and proceeds to display his scowliest scowl yet.

"Okay, this clearly isn't working." I lower the camera and shake my head, amused.

"What?" Zeke steps in front of the softbox lighting, next to the antique ladder truck. "I was fucking trying to be pensive."

"Well, then your pensive skews toward Viking-about-to-attack-and-ravage-a-new-land. And not in a good way, unfortunately." I'm trying really hard not to laugh. "Look, Zeke, you and Samara are the last shots we need to do to get this calendar out on the market. But at the rate this shoot is going we might not be able to start selling the thing until April."

"I told you he only has one look!" Samara calls across the room. "Every facial expression is just another iteration of pissed-off. It is his lot in life to be the hottest angry dude you ever met."

"I'm finding a new assistant coach," Zeke calls.

"I'm the best one you'll ever have," she calls back.

He grumbles under his breath that she's fucking right.

"I think we need to try a new tactic." I study him. "Okay, I have an idea. Come with me." I grab his hand and drag him away from the set while Samara snickers.

"I'm fucking sorry, okay?" Zeke says as we walk through the halls of the old firehouse. "I really am trying. I just don't like having my picture taken, and I don't understand what I would be doing with the ax indoors, and I—"

I open up the door to one of the bunk rooms, shove Zeke into it, drop my camera onto the bed there, and then jump into his arms. He instinctively wraps his big biceps around me, and he feels so damn good.

Zeke grunts from my weight. "What the fuck?"

"Kiss me, you giant Viking." I plaster my lips against his. My kiss distracts him as he explores my mouth, holding me tightly against his body. When I finally pull away, Zeke is panting against me. And hard. I feel his erection against my belly. Also, the expression on his face is *perfect*. Focused, but pensive.

I pat his back and ignore my own hard cock. "Now we're getting somewhere." I hop out of his arms and open the door. "Doug?" I call down the hallway. "Get in here please?"

Doug's sitting with Samara, chatting. Of course, his shoot was a dream. I mean, he's basically a porn star in mayoral form, with natural charm and an easy, warm smile. "What's up?" he asks as he peeks his head into the room.

I pull him inside and slam the door. "The light in here is terrible, but I think I can make it work in edits," I mutter to myself as I walk around the small space, opening curtains and flicking on lamps. The room is small, barely big enough for two bunk beds and a tiny walkway in between, but the weathered brick wall and the industrial steel windows will keep us nicely on theme. I finally stop in the center of the room and pick my camera back up off the bed, looping the strap around my neck.

"Zeke, we need to get your mind *off* the camera. So, Doug, I need you to take off your shirt."

Doug, angel that he is, strips off his shirt without hesitation. His obedience is giving me *ideas*. Distracting sex ideas, when I'm trying to think like a photojournalist. Okay, so a semi-unprofessional photojournalist, but hey. Sometimes you have to think outside of the box in a creative field, okay?

Zeke stares at Doug's unveiled pecs like someone just hit him in the back of the head. Which was not exactly the look I was going for, but at least he doesn't seem completely uncomfortable. But by the time I peer at him through the lens, he's stiff again. Except now instead of flinching away from the camera, he's flinching away from the sight of Doug's shirtless body.

"Hmm." I tap my chin. "I'm remembering a certain fantasy you shared with us, Zeke. One where you watched Doug jerk off." I look over my shoulder at Doug and raise an eyebrow. Maybe he and I aren't quite at the level of wordless communication that he and Zeke are on, but he still doesn't need me to spell it out. He bites his lip and unbuttons his fly.

"Are you fucking kidding?" Zeke hisses.

"It's kind of perfect," I say, a little distracted myself as I watch Doug's hand linger, uncertain, on the tab of his zipper. "Two birds, one stone. Sex coaching session *and* photography session in one." I smile at Zeke and step closer to him.

"Look, we don't have to," I say, adjusting the collar of Zeke's turnout coat so that it hangs open, framing his bare chest. "I'm not going to force you into anything. Doug, you can keep it over the underwear." I look at him over my shoulder, but it's obvious by the growing bulge behind his jeans—holy fuck, that's an impressive bulge, but focus, Rivers, focus—that he's into the idea.

I turn back to Zeke. He wets his lips, then nods slowly. "Okay. Yeah."

I grin, moving away and raising the camera. "Grab onto the top of that bunk bed for me." I hear Doug's zipper lower and my own blood runs a little hotter. Crap, I hadn't anticipated the challenge I was setting out for myself, here. *Focus, Rivers.* I get the camera on Zeke and start snapping, and every shot is gold. I go down on one knee to take some shots from below.

"This is perfect," I say into the air that's hot from the bodies of three extremely turned-on men, and shiver when I hear Doug groan behind me.

"Oh my fucking God," Zeke says, turning his head like he can barely look at Doug anymore.

And no wonder. Even in the loose trousers of his turnout gear, I can see his hard-on. And now I'm the one losing my cool and fumbling the camera.

"Sorry," I say, when Zeke's hazy eyes focus on me as I hold the camera firmly and sigh shakily. "It's just—holy shit, this is a top-ten fantasy for me." My filter is completely turned off, but I can't even begin to interrupt myself. "In the locker room of a firehouse with all the big sweaty men. On my knees, ready to be of service.

Because don't they deserve to use me to feel good, after all they do for the good of everyone else?"

Zeke's eyes are the size of saucers. "Max. Jesus fucking Christ."

I'm still on one knee on the floor, and now I drop to the other one, staring up at him. "Maybe I could…" I stare at his bulge, and then his abs, glistening with a sheen of sweat from the heat of the room and how worked up he's gotten watching Doug.

Doug.

Thinking about him, I look over my shoulder, and *fuck*. He's the golden angel to Zeke's dark one. Having one of them in front of me, and the other one behind me, makes my whole body burn like it could catch fire.

And then they could put me out.

I groan.

"Zeke," Doug says slowly, squeezing himself through his black briefs. "If Max made one of your fantasies come true, doesn't it seem like we should return the favor?"

I jerk my head around to see Zeke's eyes snap from looking down at me to over at Doug. His lips part. I've never seen him look shocked before. But a second later, the expression fades. He nods like he's hypnotized, then looks back down at me.

"You wanna suck my dick? 'Cause you're so civic-minded?" His voice is perfectly serious, and holy crap, if these two can stay in character this well, I am going to be putty in their big, callused hands.

I nod, totally unable to speak. Well, maybe I whimper a little. And I carefully set aside my camera.

Zeke steps forward, his gear rustling, and slides a hand through my hair. "I'm gonna need to hear you say the words."

My heart hammers in my chest but I manage to open my mouth and make words come out. The most honest ones I've ever said. "Yes, Fireman James. I want to suck your dick."

There's a long moment where I almost have time to wonder if

I've finally gone too far in my pursuit of unfiltered honesty and spontaneity.

Then Zeke silently undoes his button and pushes his turnout gear and underwear to his knees.

Oh, *yum.*

Zeke's big, hard, and like him, his cock is almost angry-looking. He's neatly manscaped and has that faint, musky, male scent I love. I stick my tongue out and lick the bead of precome from his slit. Then I take him in my mouth, sucking gently on the tip of his cock.

Our eyes meet, and I wink at him before swallowing him down deep.

Zeke gasps and thrusts upward into my throat. I'm barely registering the sexy sounds of Doug stroking himself. Concentrating on giving Zeke as much pleasure as I can, I work him up and down repeatedly. I want him to enjoy this, but I know that Doug and Zeke's colleagues are in the next room and it's only a matter of time before they wonder where we are. Guess that means I have to use my best moves.

"Doug," I murmur, popping off for a moment. "C'mere. I think Zeke needs to be kissed."

In an instant, Doug joins us, one strong hand behind Zeke's neck, as he kisses Zeke soundly. The other hand is rubbing himself.

I suck extra hard, and Zeke pulls back, looking down at me, his lips wet and plump from kissing Doug. He looks wrecked.

"Max," Zeke whispers, as he strokes my hair with one hand and holds tightly to Doug's bicep with the other. "I'm not going to last, and I—"

I take that as my cue to suck harder, deeper, as I wrap my hands around Zeke's tight, muscular ass.

Come inside me, I think, trying to communicate without words.

Zeke rubs his hand down my head, over the top of my ear, and lets go.

He comes hard into my mouth, his entire body relaxing with the release, as Doug holds him tight and sucks on his neck.

When Zeke's dick starts to soften, I swirl my tongue around him one more time and then pull off his body. I'm about to suggest that Doug should be next, when someone jerks on the handle of the doors. Which are locked, thankfully.

"Everything okay in there?" calls Samara's muffled voice.

"Shit," Zeke swears, quickly putting himself together while I hop off the floor, surreptitiously wiping the corners of my mouth and brushing off my knees. Doug rights his own pants, then checks to see that we're both decent before he unlocks the door, and Samara bursts in.

"Did you see this?" she asks, thrusting her phone toward Doug. His eyes narrow as he scrolls.

"What is it?" Zeke asks. "What's wrong?"

Doug shakes his head, his cheeks turning brighter shades of rose pink until they're nearly the color of the strawberries he always keeps in the fridge for Zeke. "Barton Asterstop," he says darkly. "He's what's wrong."

Max changed the group chat name to "Max's Gay School for Hot Vikings"

DOUG

I'm a viking too??

MAX

Of course!

ZEKE

lol having a hard time picturing Doug as a pillager, tho

MAX

I have no trouble picturing that at all [panting emoji]

Admittedly though I see Doug as the stay-at-home kind of viking. You know, chopping wood and keeping the home fires hot and burning

DOUG

I am rly good at keeping a fire hot!

MAX

Stop flirting with me. Actually NEVER stop

Zeke is a viking pirate as I've already explained

ZEKE

You've given this a lot of thought

MAX

You have NO idea

Max changed the group chat name to "2 Vikings and their willing hostage"

CHAPTER 17
DOUG

A week ago, the thought of Barton Asterstop writing another article about me was giving me nightmares. But a lot has changed since then. It's like so much is already packed into my head that Barton's words don't have much space to fill up.

It's hard to worry about grumpy newspaper editors and their stinging words when Zeke and Max are on my mind. Right now, though, even a passing thought about them is dangerous. I'm sitting at my desk in the mayor's office and I really need to finish signing the documents Marty set out for me. I can't do that if I'm salivating over the memory of staring into Zeke's eyes while I palmed myself over my briefs, and then—holy smokes—Max getting on his knees for Zeke. Seeing Zeke's naked body, his hard dick sliding into Max's mouth, and then the look on his face and the sounds he made when he came…

Focus, Doug, I order myself, and pick up my pen. It's already well after nine. I came here straight from the old firehouse, and I was put to work by Glenn, the Holiday-Off volunteer coordinator, writing thank you notes to citizens who donated holiday decor for the Holiday-Off. Glenn assured me that thank you notes were a much better response than an email blast, and I hope he's right, because I think my hand went numb after holding a pen for so many hours.

I can't wait to get home, even though I don't expect to see either of the two people I can't stop thinking about. Zeke is midway through a shift. Max is *still* editing photos from the shoot today, and he's happy with how they look, according to his sporadic, excited messages in our group chat. I can't believe how hard he's working to help our fundraising efforts. Whatever the Icebreakers make at the Holiday-Off should be named after him.

"Hey, Marty, could you come in here for a minute?" I call.

Marty, who just walked by carrying a box heaped with child-sized elf hats, doubles back and pauses in the doorway of my office. "Yeah. What's up? Have you seen these yet?" He puts one of the elf hats from the box on his head. With his curly hair and slightly pointed nose and chin, Marty makes a pretty good elf.

"Are they the ones we're passing out for free at the Holiday-Off?"

Marty nods. "Yup! Every kid gets one."

I frown. "Those *are* for kids, right? That one looks like it fits you."

"Oh, well, I have a tiny head. Huge brain, though!" He drops the hat back in the box. "So, what did you need?"

I know that we're completely alone in the town hall. The last of the volunteers and the other staff members all left hours ago. Still, I have to resist the urge to pull Marty the rest of the way into my office and close the door behind him.

"Well," I say, "there's some town business that's come up. I don't want to drag you into it in case it gets hairy. I'm hoping you could do me a favor related to this… business… without asking any follow-up questions."

Marty's eyebrows shoot up. "But I always want to know everything."

I chuckle, nodding. "I know. I promise I have a really good reason to withhold certain details, though. I'm worried the whole thing could get—"

"Hairy. Right. So you said." Marty looks pained, but nods decisively. "Okay, yes. I will refrain from follow-up questions."

I stand and give his shoulder a soft slap. "Awesome! Thanks, Marty. So, your little brother Marcus works in Montpelier, right?"

"He's an intern for the Department of Agriculture," Marty confirms, nodding.

"And he knows Vermonica's people."

"He knows one of her handlers pretty well. They met playing softball I think. Their team was called Udder Greatness. Not that original, if you ask me, but you didn't. And neither did Marcus, or I would have helped him come up with something *way* better."

"Right. Well, do you think you could text Marcus and ask if his friend knows about anything being, I don't know, *irregular* when it comes to Vermonica?"

Marty's eyes narrow. I hold up a finger, and he sighs. "Right. No follow-up questions," he mutters. "Sure. I can text him right now." He takes his phone from his pocket and his thumbs fly. "He should be at home, so hopefully he'll reply right away. Wait, how did you word that exactly? Is there anything *irregular* going on with Vermonica?"

I nod. "Will he want to know why you're asking?"

"Nah. We text about Vermonica all the time. He sent me the cutest photo of her a few weeks ago. Look!" Marty holds up his phone, which shows a text string between him and someone referred to as "world's most egregious PITA" who I assume must be his brother. There's a blurry photo of a Holstein standing in a mound of straw behind a velvet rope, and a man in a suit appears to be feeding her something off of a fork.

"Oh, he's replying already. He says that she's on a scheduled hiatus." Marty looks up at me. "A little weird this time of year, but they do send her back to her original farm so she can have a break from the high life from time to time. That's probably where she is." His expression darkens. "That way she'll have plenty of rest for her visit to Atherton."

"Right," I say, my thoughts going a mile a minute. "Okay.

Well, thanks Marty. And you should definitely keep one of those hats. They look really good on you."

When I finally get home, the house is dark, and thoughts of Barton Asterstop catch up to me. After a half-hour of tossing and turning, I give up and go downstairs, open my satchel, and get out the newspaper I brought home from the town hall.

I should just forget about Barton's article. Why dwell on something negative when there are so many positive things in my life?

What is it about this man's words that I can't help letting them get under my skin?

I make my way to the kitchen and turn on the little lamp on the counter that Grandma used to switch on to read recipes.

"Mayor Goes from Merely Incompetent to Complete Clown," the headline announces. I read every word of the article I only skimmed on Samara's phone, and each syllable leaves me a little lower than the last. Literally. I start out reading on my feet, then I lean against the counter, then I slide to my butt on the floor.

Could Barton be right? Am I too caught up in the contest with Atherton, and for the wrong reasons?

On the floor by the back door there's a salt lick I picked up earlier for Vermonica but haven't taken out to the garage yet. It's like it's there to remind me that whatever my reasons, I've pretty much for sure taken the contest too far.

There's an unlawful Holstein in Grandma's garage for Pete's sake.

Groaning. I drop my forehead to my knee. Then the thought of Grandma reminds me of her text earlier in the day: *Don't let a petty old man get you down, Douglas. This is an occasion for ice cream.*

Someone must have sent the article to her. I wish she hadn't read it, but I appreciate her advice. A bowl of ice cream does sound pretty good. Good enough that I manage to get up off the floor and go to the freezer.

"Thank God!" Max shout-whispers, scaring me so badly I jerk the freezer door open reflexively and bang the corner of it into my nose.

"Oh, shit," Zeke exclaims as I stagger backward, clutching my face. "Sorry, babe. We didn't mean to scare you. Max heard a noise down here and woke me up."

"It's okay," I say, voice muffled by my hand. My eyes are watering and I can't see them in the dark, but suddenly Zeke is there beside me, rubbing my back and tugging my hand away from my face. He touches the bridge of my nose, which is sore and throbbing, but his touch still feels nice.

"I'm soooo sorry," Max chimes in, putting his arm around my waist from my other side. "It's just that I thought you might be a murderer. So I got Zeke."

"And I pointed out that it was probably you downstairs, considering that you weren't in your room," Zeke says reasonably, smiling fondly at Max.

"And I pointed out that it was possible you were the first victim," Max returns, standing on his tiptoes to give Zeke a quick kiss. He looks up at me and bites his lip. "Do you need some ice?"

"No. But I'd take some ice cream."

Max grins and kisses me, his lips soft. I'm starting to get used to his casual affection, and I really like it. "Oh, that's a great idea. I'll join you. Zeke?"

"Sure," Zeke says, guiding me toward the kitchen table and pulling out a chair. As I sit down, he squeezes my shoulder. "You sure about that ice?"

"Yes," I tell him. "It's nothing."

"Yeah, but the nose always hurts a shit-fuck-ton."

I point to the spot on the kitchen wall beside the grandfather clock. Zeke rolls his eyes and plucks the swear jar off the shelf.

"What is happening? Why is Zeke writing on a jar?" Max asks, returning to the table with the quart of vanilla ice cream from the freezer and three spoons.

"It's the swear jar," I explain. "Haven't you seen it yet?"

Zeke finishes making a hash mark on the paper label I taped to the jar at the beginning of the month and then holds the jar up, the stubby pencil dangling from its glued-on string.

"Zeke never has cash, so the swear jar is mostly on a credit system at this point," I tell Max. He shakes his head and sticks a giant spoonful of ice cream in his mouth as he hops up onto the edge of the heavy wooden table, his legs swinging.

"We settle up on the last day of the month," Zeke adds.

Max swallows his bite of ice cream. "What are you doing with all this wealth, Doug?" He nudges me with his toe. He's wearing fuzzy green socks, and I catch him by the ankle and squeeze, making him giggle.

"I mostly just pay all the streaming video subscriptions," I confess. "Which is the opposite of a penalty for Zeke, because he loves TV and movies more than he will ever admit."

Zeke reaches for the ice cream and grunts, but at least he doesn't try to deny it. "So," he asks me as he carves out a bite. "Am I finally allowed to tell Bart Asterstop what I think of him?" He extends his leg so that his calf slides between mine, and Max scoots down the table until his feet are basically in my lap. Having them close makes it hard to think about Barton Asterstop, but I see the paper lying on the kitchen counter where I left it and the words pile up in my brain all over again.

"No," I tell Zeke, dragging my hands through my hair. "But maybe the third time's the charm. I don't get what his problem is, you know?"

"He's like Scrooge," Max says, shrugging. "Maybe you should sic Zeke on him, like a very grumpy ghost." I frown, confused, and Max's eyes widen. "Come on. Haven't you seen *A Christmas Carol*?" I shake my head and he digs out another spoonful of ice cream, and instead of eating it, holds it out toward me. I laugh softly and open my mouth, letting him feed it to me. We make eye contact as my mouth closes around the spoon, and the playful moment melts into a hot one, the same way the bite of cold, sweet vanilla ice cream melts on my tongue.

"I've been wondering," Max says. He drops the spoon on the table and scoots off the table and into my lap, straddling me. His hands make their way up my torso. "How did you feel yesterday, touching yourself while Zeke watched you? And then watching me go down on him?"

My hands slide slowly along his thighs, and I'm dizzy with how he woke my body up, like the weight and warmth of his body flipped a switch. "Um, I felt good," I admit. "Really good." I bite my lip as he grinds on my rapidly swelling dick. I can feel the soft weight of his balls against my leg. That's a sensation I never really thought about before, much less realized how hot it would feel.

Max has plenty of feminine qualities that I find sexy, but his masculine ones intrigue me just as much. Which is confusing, because I don't think there's a single feminine detail on Zeke's body, and I'm drawn to him too. But the attraction feels different, and I'm not sure whether that comes down to the physical, emotional, or historical.

Ugh, my thoughts don't even make sense to myself in this moment, but I don't know how I'm supposed to think when Max is dragging his thumbs up my chest and making circles around my pecs.

My head falls back. "If you want me to talk, you're going to have to stop doing that."

I hear a deep chuckle and then feel Zeke's fingers slide over my temple, combing back my hair and sending tiny little bursts of electricity into my scalp.

These two guys are blowing my mind.

And that's not the only thing I want them to blow.

I'm not a virgin or anything, okay? I've actually done a lot of sex stuff. I used to consider myself experienced.

But of all the ways I've touched and been touched, nothing felt as intense as watching Max give Zeke a blow job, or feeling Zeke's hand in my hair while Max drops open-mouthed kisses on my neck.

The past several days have been amazing, really confusing, and if I'm honest, exhausting. I've barely slept. I've been stressed out and pacing my room. But my head is so full of spinning thoughts, and all I have to show for it is the feeling that I know pretty much nothing about sex and attraction after all.

"Okay, I won't make you talk. You can just nod, or shake your head," Max says, speaking quietly with his mouth right next to my ear. The sound of his voice and the feel of his breath are the best kind of torture. "Zeke told us one of his fantasies, and I told you one of mine. Now I'm wondering if you've ever fantasized about what it would feel like to have a dick in your mouth?"

I groan and nod my head. Maybe I haven't had the fantasy for long, but it's *definitely* been on my mind for the past few hours. The idea makes my mouth actually water. Which is vaguely surprising, because I felt pretty conflicted and unsure about the idea, as hot as it was watching Max and Zeke. But now, with Max's sexy voice in my ear and my throat still damp where he left a trail of wet kisses? Heck yeah. I want to suck his dick.

And I want to do it right now.

I pick Max up and put him back on the table and kick back my chair in one movement, as single-minded as when I hear the alert to gear up for a call at work, but Max makes a squeak that breaks the spell just as I drop to my knees between his spread thighs.

I blink up at him. "Did I hurt you?" I ask worriedly. "Was I too rough?"

Max stares down at me. His shirt is rucked up, and I can see a strip of his soft stomach. I want to bury my face in the skin there.

"N-no," he manages. "I just meant—I didn't mean *me*."

Zeke rises from his own chair and runs his hand up Max's arm. "You don't want Doug to blow you, baby?"

Max actually whimpers. "Um, no. I mean *yes*. I do want him to."

"Mmm. I'd like to see him do it, too." Zeke is doing the sex voice again, and I can't resist the urge to lean in and breathe against Max's inner thigh. He groans, and Zeke puts his arm around his shoulders. "Lay back, sweetheart," he murmurs to Max. "We'll take care of you."

Max mutters something that sounds like *holy-fucking-shit*, but the swear jar is the very last thing on my mind. Once he's lying sprawled on the table, Zeke rubs his chest, then slips his hand down Max's body and unties the drawstring on his typewriter pajamas so I can pull them off his legs. He's not wearing any underwear, and his cock is hard. It's almost as thick as mine, but narrower at the tip, and his neatly trimmed pubes are soft. Before I can think about it too hard, I lean in and take the tip into my mouth, sucking gently to taste the salty wetness already collecting at his slit.

"Oh, fuck," Max moans.

"You're not fucking kidding," Zeke agrees. He puts his hand on the back of my neck, and I think my eyes roll back in my head. I take Max deeper, eager to feel him, and palm myself because I'm rock-hard just from this.

In fact, I think I'm going to come before Max does. Zeke's thumb strokes my clavicle, and my dick jerks against my hand. I suck harder, not sure what's making me more wild, Zeke's encouraging touch on my neck or the smell and feel and taste of Max.

"Does it feel good, baby?" Zeke asks. "You look so fucking hot."

"Feels so good," Max whines. "Are you sure you've never done this before, Doug?" He breathes out a laugh that turns into a cry as I deliberately graze his shaft with my teeth. I move my head back and forth, stroking him with my mouth.

I've definitely never done this before. But I know what *I* like, and Max is so open and expressive with his whole body that it's easy to notice what he likes and do more of the same.

I open my eyes and look up at Zeke, standing above us, one hand on Max's thigh and the other still rubbing the nape of my neck. I hadn't expected him to be looking down at me. Our eyes lock.

And I can't help it anymore. I gasp around Max, take another deep swallow of him, and come on the spot.

Max is right behind me. He tastes so good I moan, rocking against my hand and swallowing everything he gives me until we're both spent, and Max is laugh-sobbing and tugging at my hair so I'll let him go.

I obediently pull off, wrap my arms around Max's hips, and rest my forehead on his sweaty thigh.

I might be having an out-of-body experience. I've never felt so good or so high in my life. Not even that time that Chev Lacosta tricked me into trying mushrooms.

But I snap right back into my body when I feel Zeke's breath on my neck where his hand was, and then the soft press of his kiss against my shoulder.

"That was," Max says breathlessly, "amazing." He sits up and hooks his arms around me and kisses me, his tongue tangling with mine. Apparently he doesn't care that I taste like him. "You're a great pupil."

Zeke snorts.

Max and I both turn to him, and I notice Zeke's huge erection at the same time Max falls to his knees. He and Zeke work together to take out Zeke's hard cock.

I've seen Zeke naked tons of times in the locker room over the years, but it's not exactly considered good manners to stare at your naked teammate. When Max was blowing him in the firehouse, I was mostly focused on Zeke's face... and our kiss.

Now, though, I can look my fill.

Zeke's erect cock is a reflection of him—gorgeous, wild, hot, and, I have a feeling, extremely sensitive. While I'm thinking about how to give him what he needs, Max is already on it.

"Come on me," Max whispers, and he opens his mouth, holding out his tongue. Zeke gets the message fast and starts stroking the head of his dick. At first, he's watching Max with these heated, adoring eyes. Then he turns those eyes on me, and it's one of the sexiest, most intense things I've ever experienced.

Grunting, Zeke closes his eyes, and I grab his hand as his entire body shakes with tension and excitement. Watching him come across Max's tongue and cheeks feels hot and dirty in the best of ways, but it also feels more intimate than maybe any other sexual experience I've had.

But it's quickly surpassed by watching Zeke slide his thumb through the spots of come on Max's face and Max glancing slyly at me as he sucks Zeke's finger clean.

I groan, and Zeke bends down to kiss Max, and then me. I feel his lazy tongue and groan again. How could I have ever thought of Zeke only as a best friend? Not that he isn't my best friend. But there's so much more building between us, and it feels so *right.* How did it take so long for us to connect?

I know the answer to that question. We hadn't met Max.

I wonder: what will our lives be like once he leaves? My chest feels heavy as I try to imagine this scene, this moment, without Max in it.

But he's not leaving yet, I remind myself. I vow to enjoy every second Zeke and I have with Max—illegal cows and holiday contests and angry newspaper editors be darned.

From the group chat "2 Vikings and their willing hostage"

DOUG

Okay, I fed and watered Vermonica

ZEKE

I don't think we should be using her real name in texts. Let's erase this chain and find a code name or something.

MAX

Bovine FBI over here, hahaha. But yeah, maybe you're right.

Honestly, I had no idea taking care of a cow was so much work! Thank goodness she's in her dry spell now.

ZEKE

I think farmers just call her a "dry cow" Max

MAX

OH, got it. Must have been thinking of my life before I arrived here… [string of flame emojis]

Now I just wait for you both to dress up as Vikings wearing firefighter gear

ZEKE

Turnout gear, babe

MAX

Or just keep calling me babe and we'll see what happens…

DOUG

Babe babe babe bab babe babe babe?

*Babe

CHAPTER 18

MAX

"How long can it take to frost those buns, Doug?" I complain. "I'm dying, here. They smell so good." My stomach growls as if on cue, and Zeke, sitting in the chair beside me, laughs and squeezes my thigh.

"Patience, Rivers," he instructs. "I promise Doug's buns are worth the wait."

I narrow my eyes at him, but his expression betrays nothing. Could that pun have possibly been accidental? Surely not, it was way too good. But Zeke just sips his coffee with a completely straight face, mystifying me.

"I know I, for one, can't wait to try Doug's buns," I say just as solemnly. "How about you? Are you looking forward to having a taste?"

Zeke's lips twitch and his cheeks get red. A slow grin of triumph spreads across my face, and I'm doubly rewarded when Doug crosses the kitchen to place a steaming, perfect cinnamon bun in front of me. He's wearing an apron and a sweet, proud smile that reminds me of the one he gave me after he sucked my brains out through my dick. And on his first try!

"This looks amazing," I tell him, grabbing my fork. "We should bring some over to the 3way."

"Good idea. I always bring them eggnog, and everyone knows eggnog goes great with cinnamon buns. The recipe is Grandma's, but I can never get them to come out as well as when she makes them," Doug says modestly.

"When do I get to meet your infamous grandmother?" I ask him. "Does she ever come back from Florida?"

Doug's whole expression brightens, like Vermont sunshine between the gray clouds of the December snowstorms. "She says she'll try to make it back here for the Holiday-Off this year, but she may not if she gets into the championship round in her golfing league."

Because of course Doug's grandmother is also a high-caliber athlete.

"I'm just bummed she won't be at the decorating party we're holding this weekend," Doug says. "Nobody trims a tree like Grandma."

Zeke and I exchange smiles.

Doug brightens. "But she told me she already preordered a copy of our calendar! I can't believe how quickly you got it up for sale, Max!"

I preen a little when he says that, because there's something about Doug's praise that makes me crave more and more of it. "I called in some favors. Preorders and online sales should be where the bulk of our profits come from, but stores up and down Vermont are going to be stocking them as well. It's too early to tell exactly how much the town will make, but we might be in good shape to book the Icebreakers."

"And maybe we won't need them." Doug bites at his lip. "I mean, we do have Ver—"

"Don't say her name," Zeke interrupts. He leans over to kiss Doug gently on the cheek, and I marvel at how much more comfortable they are being intimate with each other than they were just a few days ago.

"Okay, we've got the Secret Cow," Doug corrects himself.

"Nothing suspicious about that title whatsoever." Zeke rolls his eyes and smiles fondly at Doug.

"Secret guest?" Doug tries. "Oh, I know! The MVB! For Most Valuable Bovine!"

Zeke laughs, and I hide my smile and stuff a bite of cinnamon bun in my mouth. Then I moan, which makes both Vikings stare at me in startled fascination.

"Did I make a sex noise?" I ask when I swallow. "Sorry, but this is orgasmic, Doug."

His cheeks pinken, and he seems to be watching my mouth as I lick some icing from my bottom lip. "Thanks—I'll, uh, tell Grandma you said so."

Zeke snorts. "Maybe don't use those words exactly."

A loud pounding on the front door interrupts us. Zeke and Doug instantly get on their feet because they have the instincts and reflexes of Vikings, and I saw off another bite of cinnamon bun with the side of my fork because I'm sure they have it handled. A violent intruder won't keep me from licking my plate clean.

Zeke looks out the kitchen window while Doug heads for the front door. "What the fuck? That's Barton Asterstop's car in the driveway."

"Seriously?" Okay, maybe a violent intruder wouldn't separate me from breakfast, but Barton Asterstop is another story.

Zeke and I hurry after Doug, who's already opened the front door by the time we reach the foyer.

Sure enough, there's Barton on the doorstep, a legal pad under his arm. He's wearing his customary frown. His effort at looking imposing is somewhat impeded by the fact that his glasses are all fogged up in the chilly air.

"Douglas McEmbirk," he says in the same tone a TV cop would use before reading someone their rights. He's definitely looking at Doug like he thinks he's a criminal.

Zeke's face is basically one giant scowl. I push myself in front of him, a little worried that my beloved Viking pirate is about to take out an aging journalist. "Barton!" I say cheerfully. "Great to see you. Thanks for stopping by. Would you like a cinnamon bun? Doug made them from scratch."

Barton's nose twitches and his frown falters. *Aha!* I think. Investigative journalist, remember? I can read people. And Barton Asterstop very nearly weakened at the offer of cinnamon buns.

He's made of stronger stuff, though, and only falters for a half-second, then squares his narrow shoulders beneath his wool coat. The lapels fall back enough that I can see he's wearing purple suspenders with brass buckles. Honestly, with a few minor adjustments, Barton would have a real look going. But I remind myself he's the enemy, not the hero in need of a glow up in my personal episode of *Queer Eye.*

"I'm here to ask a few questions about a certain *fundraising initiative* I was made aware of." He whips his legal pad out from under his arm and clicks a pen. "Do you have any comment, *Mayor* McEmbirk, in response to allegations that it's inappropriate for an elected official to sexualize himself in exchange for money?"

"You goddamn—" Zeke begins, but I grab his arm and beam at Barton.

"You mean the calendar! Oh, good! I'm glad word is getting around. Did you have any questions about how you place a bulk order? Lots of businesses around town are planning to sell copies at retail."

"I will be placing no such order," Barton tells me tartly, then swings his glare back toward Doug. "Well? Any comment?"

Doug puts on a very mayoral face, all solemn listening. Except in his case I know it's genuine, not political. He really wants to please everyone. Even Barton Asterstop. My heart goes out to him, because I know that sooner or later, he'll figure out that it's impossible to please all people all the time. That realization is definitely going to hurt him.

Before Doug can say anything, though, a long, loud, and

distinctly bovine bellow reaches our little party from the direction of the MVB's quarters in the garage.

Barton peers over his shoulder. "What on the good hills of Vermont was that?" he asks.

Zeke stiffens beside me, and I think we're both too horrorstruck to react.

Amazingly, nothing in Doug's body or serene expression changes at all. "Sounded like a cow to me, sir."

Barton turns back to us, scowling harder than ever. Maybe I've been spending too much time around Zeke, but I find Barton's glares more cute than threatening. "Yes, and isn't that something of a surprise in the middle of town? Not to mention a zoning violation?"

Doug chuckles. "Come on, Barton. You know as well as I do that if someone wants to keep a sick cow or a bottle calf close by for a couple nights in the dead of winter, people look the other way. Not to mention there are several cow pastures within a stone's throw of town limits."

"And just a few days ago," Zeke adds, "someone's stray wandered up. We stalled him in the garage for the night with some straw bedding and a couple panels we had lying around. As soon as we got a hold of the owners they came and moved him out of there, of course. Still need to get that mess cleaned up."

Barton looks at Zeke like he has laser vision and can read his thoughts if he just glares for long enough. Then he asks Doug, icily, "So is that *your* habit, Mr. Mayor? Aiding and abetting illegal acts? Or just 'looking the other way'?"

Before Doug can say anything, another long, low *moo* comes from the garage.

Barton's eyebrows fly toward his wispy hairline. "That animal must be on this very property, as close as it sounds. Maybe our local politicians 'look the other way,' but I for one have some integrity." He starts down the porch steps. Thank goodness he's only able to get down them one leg at a time, because that gives

Zeke time to charge out from behind me and jump off the porch steps to block his path onto the sidewalk.

"Listen, Mister Asterstop," he says in a calm, respectful voice that I wouldn't have thought he could muster at all, much less toward a man who's probably caused him to add a year's worth of streaming subscriptions to the swear jar. "I understand that you don't approve of Doug's leadership. I've been persuaded not to challenge your opinion no matter what nasty things you print about him in your paper."

I'm so fascinated by Zeke's speech, I almost don't notice when Doug leaves the doorway and sprints toward the back of the house. Barton certainly doesn't.

"I understand," Zeke goes on, "that you're entitled to write whatever angry, bullshit untruths you care to in your paper. And honestly, I think freedom of the press is important, and that ninety-five percent of the contents of your publication are necessary and meaningful to the community, so that's another reason I've worked so hard not to come to your house and give you a piece of my mind."

All I can see is Barton's back and the rigid set of his shoulders, but I have to credit him for not taking a backward step with Zeke looming over him. "Does this little speech have a point, kid?" he bites out.

I catch a glimpse of movement out of the corner of my eye— it's Doug, hurrying Vermonica out of the back door of the garage. Her mouth is filled with the fancy, bright green hay she loves best and is only supposed to have in small quantities.

Of course Zeke was staging a distraction while Doug relocated the cow. *Damn.* Even in bovine-related capers these two are perfectly in sync.

In front of Barton, Zeke spreads his arms. "Of course it has a point! A point I'm making right now. You know, not all of us have the exact words ready in the moment. Some of us have to work our way there."

"Yes, son, and if you could hurry up and get there, I would appreciate not standing out here in the snow freezing my—"

Doug is out of sight. I meet Zeke's eyes over Barton's head and raise my hand in a thumbs up. Zeke catches my eye with the barest nod and puts his hands on his hips. "Right. The point I'm making is that you have no right to be on our property uninvited, and I'd like you to leave. Please."

"Of course. I'll just make a note right here that I was stymied in my investigation of the sounds of cattle coming from the property." He clicks his pen. "Anything to say about *that*, Mr. Mayor?" He whirls around toward—well, just me, standing in the doorway of the house. My heart plummets. Shit. Cattle caper failed.

And then I jump when Doug's hand lands on my shoulder. "I wouldn't want anyone to feel *stymied*, Mr. Asterstop. Did you want to have a look around? We don't mind, do we, Zeke?"

He's not even winded. And it's not like the garage is two feet from where we're standing. I've got to watch some of his and Zeke's firefighter training regimens sometime.

Their eyes lock for half a second, and then Zeke shakes his head and steps out of Barton's way. "Not at all."

Barton lifts an eyebrow as he studies Zeke for a long moment. I swear, neither of them blink. I'm starting to wonder if Barton might have been something of a Viking pirate himself back in his day. "That won't be necessary," he finally says, and sticks his pen behind his ear. "Just to confirm, before I go, you have no regrets about exposing yourself, *our mayor*, in a photograph designed to titillate?"

Hearing a white-haired man in suspenders say the word *titillate* tests my self-control, but I do *not* giggle.

"It's a calendar designed to raise money for a cause the town cares deeply about," Doug says smoothly. "And no, I have no regrets."

"I see." Barton sends him one more glare before he turns around and stalks off down the driveway. He climbs into a rusting Buick and quickly disappears down the snow-packed driveway.

Doug lets out a low whistle. "Max, I probably should have asked you this a long time ago. But is it safe to assume everything that happens on this property involving the MVB is staying off the record?"

I nod and give him a kiss. "I think we're keeping a lot of things off the record."

From the group chat "2 Vikings and their willing hostage"

DOUG

So, I was watching some porn last night and I
have a sex question.

MAX

[gif of someone doing a spit take]

DOUG

What? I thought some research would be a good
idea.

ZEKE

…

DOUG

Anyway, that whole thing where people have sex
with other people's thighs. What's that called?

MAX

Oh! You mean intercrural sex?

ZEKE

I don't think I can text about this

MAX

Oh, no problem! Believe me, I would MUCH
rather have this conversation in person.

DOUG

Sounds good to me!

CHAPTER 19
DOUG

"I just need to get a little higher," I say, bending my knee to step up one rung on the ladder.

"McEmbirk, don't you *dare*," Zeke growls.

I bite my lip. Ladder safety is practically a sacred oath among firefighters, but I'm missing the four crucial inches I need to put a star on top of this dang Christmas tree, and the A-frame ladder I'm using is barely four feet tall. What's the worst that could happen, a couple of bruises?

Mind made up, I put my foot on the top platform of the ladder. It creaks ominously under my weight, and Zeke swears. But I plop the star into place, and I'm back into the safe zone lickety-split.

"See?" I ask Zeke. "No big deal." I plug the star into the hidden wires in the tree, and it lights up, multicolored and twinkling. Max applauds, and even Vermonica *moos* appreciatively.

No, we didn't bring the Holstein into the living room. We're in the garage. She seemed lonely, so we brought Christmas to her. And three lawn chairs and a pile of blankets, where Zeke and Max have already settled in, passing back and forth a thermos of hot chocolate.

"Okay, everybody ready?" I ask them. Vermonica tosses her

head like she's nodding *yes,* but I'm pretty sure she's just excited about the extra alfalfa Max snuck her when he thought no one was looking. She's festive, too, in a red plaid blanket from the feed store. It's made for horses but seems to fit her just fine.

Zeke may have gone a little over-the-top when he went out to do some shopping for her. It reminded me of the time right after Shay was born when he bought out half the baby aisle at Target.

"What are the movie options, again?" Max asks.

I use my sleeve to dust off the screen of the TV/VCR that's been in the garage for quite a few years, but still turned on when I tested it a few minutes ago. "There used to be a bunch, but the attic window broke in a storm in '03, and got all the boxes wet," I tell him. "The only VHS tapes to survive were *Pretty Woman* and *Breakfast at Tiffany's.*"

"Oh, old school," Max says approvingly. "I'm thinking *Pretty Woman.*"

I glance at Zeke, who nods, so I slide *Pretty Woman* out of its case. "Grandma loves this movie," I tell them. "Well, she loves both of them, which is why they weren't in the attic with the rest."

"When I met Doug, he had never seen a movie released later than the mid-nineties," Zeke tells Max.

I shrug. "Grandma says why watch something you might not even like when you can *rewatch* something you know you'll love."

"I think your grandma is onto something," Max says, pulling up his feet and hugging his knees. "I love to rewatch movies. Especially this time of year."

"Doug still does, too," Zeke says, putting his arm around the back of Max's chair and cupping his shoulder. "But no matter how many times I see Doug's favorite movies, I still don't know what the fuck is going on."

"Oh, yeah? What's his favorite movie?" Max asks curiously.

"*Cloud Atlas,*" Zeke says, and I can *hear* him rolling his eyes.

"Actually, it's in a three-way tie for my favorite movie," I correct him. "With *Inception,* and—"

"*Memento*," Zeke finishes for me, and shudders. "No, thank you."

Max looks fascinated. "And what are *Zeke's* favorite rewatches?" he asks me.

"Zeke isn't as into rewatching, but he still has his comfort zone." I wink at Zeke, who grunts.

"Let me guess—based-on-real-life sports dramas?" Max says eagerly. "Or true crime? Okay, don't leave me in suspense."

"Anything in the Hallmark holiday movie catalog," I say.

"Aw, babe," Max says, kissing Zeke's cheek. "I adore your sweet and sensitive side."

"If I wanted to be confused or depressed, I'd watch the news," Zeke mutters, grumpy, but still tilting his head into Max's kiss. "Now, what about you?"

I grab the remote and squeeze into my seat. "Yeah, what do you like?"

Max's eyes sparkle a little, and not just from the lights from our haphazard Christmas tree. "I'm really into horror. The gorier the better."

I narrow my eyes, studying his face for signs that he's kidding.

Zeke snorts. "I believe it. So, what's your all-time favorite?"

Max snuggles against Zeke's side, and I reach up to cover Zeke's hand, still resting on Max's shoulder, with mine. He smiles at me over Max's head as we lace our fingers together.

"Probably the very first *Saw* movie," Max says thoughtfully. "It was truly groundbreaking."

"Never seen it," I admit.

"Well, you wouldn't have, since it came out in the last few decades," Zeke says with a little grin.

"In the beginning, a guy has to cut off his own arm. I mean, what could be better than that?"

Zeke stiffens and pales. "He does *what*?"

"Oops," Max says, wincing. "Sorry. Yeah, not the right movie for you."

But Zeke's expression shifts from alarmed to thoughtful. "No, I want to see it. If it's your favorite, I mean."

I glance at Max, whose eyes widen a little, then he nods. "Really?"

"Of course. It will help me get to know you better."

I nod. "You can cover Zeke's eyes before the scary parts."

Zeke rolls his eyes at me and Max laughs. "Blindfolded for the whole movie then. Is that another one of your fantasies?" he winks at Zeke.

"*No*," Zeke says, then hesitates. "Unless you'd be into it."

Max tilts his head thoughtfully. "I don't really want to blindfold *you*, but I definitely could get behind *you* blindfolding *me*."

It's still pretty cold in the garage, or I'd be more than a little hard already. When the three of us are together I feel like I'm going through puberty all over again. Constant boners.

Max gets the smug little smile that shows he knows exactly what he's doing to me and Zeke. I *love* to see that smile. He nestles back into the blankets. "Yeah, sounds fun. Maybe we can squeeze it in before I leave."

The lightness of the moment fades for me at the reminder that Max is just visiting La Fierte. He has a life he'll go back to in DC—very, very soon.

But right now I don't want to think about that. So I press the play button, and slightly staticky music comes from the TV along with the opening credits.

I relax into the familiarity of a movie I've seen a dozen times at least, but with the new element of camping out with Zeke and Max and a cow in a drafty garage in December.

I have to say, I can't think of a place I'd rather be.

But before the contentment can fully steal over me, the lights flicker slightly, and then the whole garage goes dark.

"Fuck," says Zeke. "Did we blow a fuse somehow with the tree lights? We were so careful about the outlets we used."

I wait until my eyes have adjusted enough to make out shapes, and then I make my way over to one of the high garage windows.

The street is pitch black, the window of every house around us still and dark. "Nope, looks like a full power outage in the neighborhood," I tell them. "Dang." My phone buzzes in my pocket, and I fish it out to find a text from the local power company. "Electric company says it's nothing serious," I report. "Just a down line. They estimate a few hours until it's up and running again."

"Probably Linus George again," Zeke says, shaking his head. "That guy should not be allowed near a chainsaw. Speaking of saws."

Vermonica lets out another low moo, as if she's agreeing with him.

"Well, there goes our holiday movie night with the Hungry Heifer." I click on my phone's flashlight, blinking in the sudden illumination as it casts new shadows in the dark garage. "We decide to give ourselves one night off from everything else that's going on right now, and it all gets ruined by a power outage."

Zeke grunts.

Max sits up. "But maybe... our night doesn't have to be ruined?" He grins, his eyes dancing. The more time I spend with him, the more I love the way he looks when he's excited.

"What do you have in mind?" Zeke asks. His voice is curious. A little cautious.

"Well," says Max. "If the power's out, we should all get safe and warm in one place, right? Maybe... one bed? And then we'd need to light some candles so we can see. Not too many candles, of course," he adds quickly. "Wouldn't want to create a fire hazard. And then we'd need to snuggle to get warm. With lots of blankets in that one bed."

Zeke jerks up out of the chair like someone just electrocuted him. "I'll get the candles and blankets," he says, fumbling for his phone. "Where the fuck is that fucking flashlight app?" he murmurs to himself. He's either anxious, or excited, or a whole lot of both. And I completely understand the feeling.

Max looks over at me and winks.

Thirty minutes later, the three of us are all standing around the king-sized bed in the room I inherited from Grandma. It's one of the only rooms in the house not decorated in a farm-animal theme—Grandma didn't like all those eyes staring at her while she tried to fall asleep. I got Vermonica settled in for the night while Zeke raided the house for candles and blankets and Max set up *the ambiance,* as he calls it. He's got soft, choral music playing on his phone. The bed is layered in possibly every blanket contained in this house that's *not* an heirloom quilt, and candles are scattered around the dressers and end tables—at safe intervals, of course. Zeke and Max's faces are both bathed in soft, flickering light, and I can't stop looking back and forth between the two of them.

I couldn't have imagined this moment a month ago, but now that I'm in it, I know I'm exactly where I'm supposed to be.

I take a breath and slowly lift my shirt over my head. Zeke lets out a low growl and Max gasps, which is pretty flattering, to be honest. "I will never look at your abs and not be amazed," Max teases. "Holy genetics, Batman."

Zeke laughs and pulls off his own shirt. Now Max moans. He puts the palm of one hand on Zeke's chest, and the other on mine.

"I swear, the fact that no one recruited you two for a spicy calendar years ago is a crime against humanity." He rips off his clothes at record speed, and then his entire naked body is bathed in flickering candle light, his dick half-hard in front of him. "Come and get me, Vikings." He dives under the covers and then stares up at us, smiling.

Zeke shakes his head, his mouth turned up in a half smile. The two of us are stepping out of our jeans, and for a moment I watch him, undressing next to me—something I've seen so many times in so many locker rooms over the years. The intersection of the familiar and unfamiliar squeezes my chest in an unexpected way. I lean across the bed slightly to fit my mouth against his, feeling the electric current as our tongues touch.

Max moans. "You two," he says, his voice low. "I am going to need you in this bed *now*." He moves his tongue slowly around his lips, from top to bottom, and Zeke and I waste no more time getting naked.

I climb in on one side and Zeke takes the other, until we're making a Max sandwich. He giggles as we wedge him between us, pulling the blankets up high.

And then… no one says a word. The best way I can think to describe what happens next is *exploring*.

I explore Max's neck with my tongue while Zeke explores my cock with his fingers. I think Max explores my nipples with his lips while Zeke explores Max's ass with his thigh. Hands are everywhere, mouths are everywhere—there's heat, slow movements and fast, small gasps and moans. I'm aware of everything that's happening, and at the same time I almost feel like I'm enveloped in some kind of dream, like the details of everything around me are encased in a blur. I manage to find my container of lube in my bedside table, and soon all three of us are slick and my ears are full of moans—theirs, mine, all tangled together and rising above the music that continues to fill the candlelit room.

At one point, my cock is even with Max's, and he's wrapping his hands around the two of us, holding them together while he nibbles sweetly at my neck. Over his head, I catch Zeke's eye just before he plunges his mouth against mine. I move my own hands down Zeke's thighs and realize that Zeke's cock is in a somewhat unexpected place—he's thrusting it between Max's thighs, fucking himself between them.

Ever since Max gave me the crucial key word of *intercrural*, I've been fantasizing about this, and seeing Zeke do it is somehow even better than doing it myself. Max moans and grips our cocks harder. I move my hand so that every time Zeke thrusts, the head of his cock bumps against my fingers.

Zeke cries out as Max mewls and pumps his hand faster. The friction, the force, the feeling of these two men and the way our three bodies are so perfectly in tune—I can't stop myself from falling over the edge, and my release comes just as Max cries out and Zeke shouts and pushes himself one final time between Max's slim thighs. Stickiness coats my fingers, my cock, as the three of us fall into each other.

Max snuggles into my neck as Zeke rests his head on top of mine. I let out a breath in the contented air of the room.

I know this isn't meant to last. Max will leave soon. Zeke and I will have to figure out whatever we are to each other without him.

But I'm not going to think about that right now. Right now, in this moment, nothing of the world outside us exists: not time or DC or stolen cows or angry newspaper editors or twin bullies or holiday contests. There's just the three of us, wrapped up together in a kind of peace and comfort I've never felt before.

From the group chat "2 Vikings and their willing hostage"

MAX

I know we're all criminal fugitives involved in underground operations these days, but I'd still really like to talk about that silicone dildo

ZEKE

Can we please fucking not?

MAX

Sex toys are nothing to be ashamed of, Zeke.

Really, they're just another expression of love

ZEKE

[Attachment]

MAX

HOLY FUCK YOU'RE KIDDING

THAT'S INHUMAN ZEKE

ZEKE

I was curious what size XXL looked like

MAX

[string of shocked face emojis three lines long]

CHAPTER 20

MAX

Doug, Zeke, and I are lounging in the inviting living room of Jeb, Embry, and Adam's newly remodeled farmhouse. It's quite festive here, inside and out. Besides the holiday lights lining the architectural features outside and the wreath on the door, a large Christmas tree covered with shiny decorations stands in the corner, and stockings for the three of them and their demon goat, Sherbert, are hung up on the mantel. Modern Christmas music is playing and the room smells like cinnamon. And to make everything even cozier, a light snow just started outside.

Zeke and Doug are sitting next to each other on the couch, close, but not quite touching. Jeb and Adam cuddle in a loveseat, with Adam between Jeb's legs and leaning against his chest. Adam had been sitting next to Doug and Zeke but moved when he came back with refills on cookies, leaving a space I'm wondering if I should go occupy. Embry's splayed across a recliner, his leg up on the arm, while I'm perched on a wooden chair that we've pulled up to make enough seating for all of us. Jeb tried to say that guests don't sit in wooden chairs, but I wouldn't hear of taking his place, and I didn't trust myself to get too close to Doug and Zeke. My hands might start walking, which might lead to our PG scene changing to a more adult rating after all the eggnog I've had.

We've been chatting for a while, getting caught up on the events at Stock Tree Farm and the status of the Holiday-Off. All of us except Zeke, our DD, are drinking Doug's famous—and, I'm learning, *very* alcoholic—eggnog, and eating another helping of Grandma's cinnamon buns as well as piles of Embry's X-rated Christmas cookies.

"I'm not going to be able to run from mall cops anymore if I keep eating like this," I say, feeling the alcohol in my brain. "I've never really liked eggnog, but this stuff is tasty. Even if it looks kind of like a fancy bucket of whipped come with nutmeg on top."

Five hot guys stare at me.

"Um, too much?" I ask in a smaller voice, pushing up my glasses.

Embry recovers first. "Mall cops? The closest mall is in Burlington."

"*That's* what stood out about Max's statement?" Adam says. He's looking dashing in a Fair Isle sweater. "Mall cops?"

"It happened in that very mall." I hiccup.

Zeke snorts. "Okay, what the fuck did you do?" he asks fondly.

Might as well tell the whole story, even though my cheeks are burning. "They were chasing me on Segways because they thought I'd taken a dildo from Spencer's. Since I was too embarrassed to take it to the register."

"*Had* you taken one?" Adam asks, amused, taking another bite of what looks like a frosted gingerbread penis cookie.

"I paid for it," I say indignantly. I cross my arms over my thin chest, then loosen them. "Okay, I left twice as much money as the toy cost on the counter and ran because I didn't want to actually have the sales clerk ring me up."

They laugh, although I can't help noticing that my Vikings are looking me up and down like they're imagining me with said dildo in hand and wondering what I'd get up to with it.

Damn, I really like it when they look at me like that.

"There's a thing called online shopping," Adam says, raising an eyebrow.

I shrug. "Not when you're sixteen and don't have a bank account."

"And you didn't want to ask your mom or whatever," Jeb supplies. "I totally get it." So he's the extra-nice one. Good to know.

"You paid for it," Doug points out. "So you didn't actually steal it."

"Right. Do you guys think I'm a serious criminal?" I ask in a small voice, nervous that I've blurted yet another cringeworthy truth to Doug and Zeke—and now their friends.

"I'm hardly one to judge," Embry says. His rugged good looks are set off by his burgundy corduroy shirt.

"Why? Have *you* stolen a dildo, Embry Matthews?" Adam asks, setting his elbows on his knees. "And if so, when can we use it?"

Embry rolls his eyes. "No, I haven't, and we don't need any other dildos than the sixteen we already have."

I giggle.

Jeb turns pink, which clashes with his red flannel shirt. My brain goes slightly haywire thinking about the three of them using sixteen dildos, stolen or not.

Embry continues, interrupting the prurient direction of my imagination, "But hasn't *everyone* done something a *little* illegal at some point? Driven over the speed limit or not stopped all the way at a stop sign?"

"Or harbored a cow?" I mutter. "Harbingered a cow? Napped a cow?"

"What?" Embry asks.

"Nothing," I cough. "I'm not talking about stolen cows. And I'm not drinky… er, um. Drunk. Not. I'm not that."

"Come here," Zeke commands gently, opening his arms from where he's sitting on the couch. I take the invitation to crawl into them. "Lightweight," he whispers in my ear, but it's done with a grin. I sit my ass in his lap and drape my sock-covered feet over Doug's thighs. Doug immediately starts rubbing the bottoms of my feet.

This. This is where I belonged. With these two men.

I'm too busy feeling good in Zeke's arms, with Doug's ministrations, to notice that the three remaining gentlemen in the room are blinking at us.

Adam clears his throat. "Um. So. We've heard a few things through the La Fierte grapevine."

"Yes, I'm bisexual," Zeke says immediately. There's a tremor in his voice as he says the words, and I squeeze his hand.

It's not easy to share important truths about yourself with people. Even your best friends.

"Me too!" Jeb says, his tone making me halfway expect him to hold up his hand for a high-five. I hide my smile.

"Is this a… thing?" Embry asks, gesturing at us.

"Yes," Doug says, then glances a little shyly at me and Zeke. "Well, we haven't talked about it. But I think so."

"So Doug, are you—" Embry begins, and then glances at Jeb, who's giving him a stern look, and grimaces. "Sorry. Your sexual orientation is none of my business."

"And he doesn't have to label himself at all if he doesn't want to," Jeb adds, so earnestly that I can't help but smile.

"That's what Lydia said," Doug says, nodding. "But I don't mind telling you guys that I'm bisexual. Or maybe pansexual."

"Wait, *Lydia,* as in Zeke's ex-girlfriend?" Adam's brow furrows. "But you *hate* Lydia."

Doug waves his hand around without his usual coordination, which makes sense considering he's refilled his eggnog cup twice. "That's in the past. We had a really good talk."

"Well, I can't say we're completely surprised," Adam says.

"When we first met you, Embry and I thought you belonged in a gay firefighter porno."

"Right?" I say, nodding, adjusting my glasses. "Exactly. And both of them at once, can you imagine? Well, I can. It's practically all I think about."

Wow. That eggnog is *really* strong.

Doug swallows hard and looks at Zeke over my head. Zeke squirms beneath me. If I'm not mistaken, his bulge is bigger than it was when I first sat down.

"Let's get some water into you before you get a hangover," Zeke says. Doug starts to rise off the couch, but Embry beats him to it. I think I hear him laugh as he shakes his head and heads for the kitchen.

"I'm not that drunk," I insist, flapping my hands. "I'm just saying, as fantastic as blowjobs are, there's *so* much more I want to do with you two."

Adam sits up straight, clasping his hands under his chin. "Oh? Do tell."

Jeb tugs him closer. "Shh. Don't make him say something he'll regret when he sobers up."

"Oh, I don't have a filter when I'm sober, either," I tell them. "Sorry."

"You don't need to apologize," Adam says. "Maybe it's unconventional, but if that bothered us, well, we'd have bigger problems." He smiles. "I think it's important to be candid with other people in the kind of relationship we have. Sometimes the logistics are tricky." He winks, and I laugh. "Friends don't force friends to resort to internet searches to figure out their relationship."

Jeb shakes his head adamantly and Adam leans his head on Jeb's knee and they grin at each other. Then, Jeb leans down to kiss him. Doug squeezes my feet and Zeke kisses the top of my head, and I don't think I've ever been closer to bliss.

When they break apart, another thought occurs to me. "Do you guys want to see the final proofs for the calendar? I just made a bunch of promo images." I grab my phone from my pocket.

"What calendar?" Embry says as he strides back into the room and hands me a glass of water. He brought one for Adam, too.

"You didn't hear about it?" Doug asks. "Max suggested making a calendar with photos of all the members of the fire department. You know, to raise money for the Holiday-Off. We're hoping we'll make enough to book the Icebreakers."

"How did we miss this news?" Adam looks appalled.

"Maybe because the only news we have time to pay attention to this time of year is the weather," Embry says, circling the loveseat to put his hands on Jeb's shoulders.

"Exactly how naked is this calendar?" Adam asks.

"Pretty naked!" I tell him cheerfully. I hand over my phone and watch his eyes widen as he scrolls through the photos.

"Oh wow," Jeb says, looking over Adam's shoulder. "I'm ordering ten copies. One for every room in the house.

Embry makes a noise that does *not* sound like agreement. But his eyes are definitely latched to the pictures too.

Zeke is squirming, avoiding looking directly at any of us while we talk about the calendar. Doug, on the other hand, is beaming with pride.

"Max says sales are off to a great start," he tells the 3way. "Hopefully it all works out and we get the Icebreakers. Otherwise…"

He trails off and his face falls.

Embry sighs. "Yeah. We heard about Vermonica."

I hope the other three men in the room don't notice how Zeke, Doug and I all stiffen at her name.

"Yeah, sorry, man. There's no way Atherton got her by playing fair."

An idea worms its way into my brain. "Hey," I say. "The three of you don't happen to have any connections to Vermonica's handlers, do you?"

Jeb laughs. "If only! Are you kidding? We'd have her up here for appearances all the time."

Hmmm. That makes sense. But then again, if they *were* the do-gooder cow-nappers, they wouldn't just confess. Not after leaving us that very secretive note in the garage.

But they do seem to care a lot about Zeke and Doug. And they are used to working with livestock. Or, at least, with demon goats.

Wait—what do demon goats have to do with bovine state mascots? Wow, this eggnog is *really* strong.

"Well," says Adam, "if you guys need someone to talk to, we're here."

"Definitely," Jeb says. "It takes a lot of thought and communication to understand all of the dynamics in a polycule, but it seems like the three of you have already worked out the most important thing—deciding to commit."

"We're not," I blurt out. "I mean, I'm not. I'm not staying here, I mean. Home is DC. I'm leaving when I finish writing my series about the Holiday-Off." Despite all the alcohol I've just had, I know those words are right. Accurate. The real ones I had to say.

"Oh, I'm sorry," Jeb says. "I just assumed—shit, I put my foot in my mouth, didn't I?" He stares down into his eggnog, and Embry rubs his shoulders.

"Well, it's cool that the three of you are hanging out for now," Embry says. "Maybe we all need some water, huh?"

I nod, torn between knowing that what I said was true, and feeling like *I'm* the one who put my foot in my mouth. Doug is frowning, and Zeke's back to staring at a spot on the opposite wall instead of looking at anyone else.

And me? There's a dull ache in my stomach that doesn't feel like it's from the eggnog.

One of the advantages of being freelance is that I determine my own schedule. But the lack of a nine-to-five job also means that I have to be a creative shark, constantly moving to survive. With or without a hangover.

Determined to have something to show for the past few weeks

—besides hot, unforgettable memories with two sexy firefighters —I rise early and spend most of the morning banging out an article defending Doug against *The Pigeon's* insinuations.

I mean, I write a *totally neutral and balanced* portrayal of a small town mayor doing his best to better his community.

Three thousand words later, I feel like the brainy one in *The Breakfast Club*, and give myself a pat on the back. My stealth advocacy for this sweet man also happens to be highly newsworthy.

I finally leave my room to find Doug and Zeke, following the sounds of the television into the living room. Then I skid to a stop on my stockinged feet because now that I'm allowing myself to really look at them… damn. They're *magnificent*. In sweatpants and thermal shirts, they're watching *Die Hard*, Doug leaning his head against Zeke's shoulder and Zeke resting his hand on Doug's knee.

Their comfy domesticity gets to me. These two are *supposed* to be together. They *have been* together for years, but now they're letting their relationship evolve.

While I can appreciate the beauty of them getting closer, it does make me feel like I'm intruding. I'm thinking about walking backward to my room when Doug sees me and smiles.

"Hey," he says warmly. "You done with work?"

Zeke pauses the movie. "Come over here."

"Okay." I circle the side of the couch, trying to get over the lingering feeling that I shouldn't be interrupting them. "I, um, finished my article. Do you want to read it?" In addition to trepidation over intruding on their movie night, I'm nervous to show them what I wrote. Any time I share something I created, I have the same worries. *What if they don't like it? What if they don't like me?* But with these two it's more intense than I can ever remember. In a short time, I've come to care deeply about how they see me and think of me.

No use dragging my feet. I want to send the article to an editor I work with regularly who I know will love the chance to get in on the discourse following Barton's initial viral article. And as the subject of my article, I promised Doug he could read it first.

"Sure!" Doug says, with his customary enthusiasm. There's a worried look in his eyes, though, which makes me want to hug him. Hopefully my words will be more effective in and of themselves.

"Just so you know," I say, sitting down on the edge of the coffee table facing them, "I would still have written all these good things about you even without the sexual favors."

They both laugh. Zeke rubs my thigh, which distracts me while I'm trying to send the article to them. But after a moment of fumbling thumbs, I hit send and wait while they each pick up their phones.

I move to the armchair, drawing my knees up to my chin and wrapping my arms around my shins, watching them.

Rather than use his own device, Zeke squints over Doug's shoulder so that they can read it at the same time. I think it's Zeke's way of being quietly supportive, like always.

As Doug reads, his shoulders gradually relax and the little furrow in his forehead smooths out.

"Hey, good point," he pauses to tell me. "I forgot that La Fierte means pride. Of course, our town has a lot of pride." He glances at Zeke. "Sorry, I keep moving. Can you still read?"

"It's okay." Zeke makes a go-ahead gesture with two fingers.

"I'll just read it out loud," Doug says, and he starts at the beginning.

"In La Fierte, Vermont, small children wait at a tree farm to be picked up for a hayride, the tractor driven by none other than the small town's mayor. It's a scene of wholesome Americana that's hard to find these days. In this small corner of the country, the community embraces nostalgia for its traditions while also embracing progress toward a more inclusive future. Residents take particular pride in simple pleasures done well. After all, la fierté means 'pride' in French. And that pride is no more evident than in the town's mayor, Doug McEmbirk."

Doug pauses for a moment to glance up at me, his lips pursed and his eyes soft.

"Technically, mayoral duties do not include part-time work at a farm, but for McEmbirk, it comes naturally: his friends own the farm. They need help. He shows up. Simple. He brings a humble spirit to everything he does because he cares about this place.

"McEmbirk is an unlikely mayor. Maybe it's his age (28), occupation (rural firefighter), or his hockey career (a high-school state champion and two-time Frozen Four qualifier), but people tend to underestimate him. That's a mistake."

Zeke glances over at me with a small smile before he squeezes one of Doug's shoulders and leans over to put his head against the other.

"Since his election, McEmbirk's administration has secured additional state financing for the fire department, purchased safe playground equipment for the elementary school, and is in the process of spearheading a Holiday-Off celebration, which pits two towns in a contest to see who has the most Christmas/Hanukkah/Kwanzaa/Solstice spirit.

"McEmbirk holds a bachelor's degree in fire science. He's a certified emergency medical technician. When he's not behind the mayor's desk—or the wheel of a tractor—he still works full-time for the town/county fire department as a firefighter and EMT. In short, he spends his days taking care of this New England town he calls home."

"Damn straight he does," Zeke murmurs. Doug stops to clear his throat before he goes on speaking.

"This attitude is not lost on the residents of La Fierte, including lifelong La Fiertan Jemima Ackerman, a retired choir teacher. Ackerman states that although she voted for McEmbirk's opponent in the last election, she won't make that mistake again. 'Doug's a young man with gumption and initiative. He's got my vote for as long as he wants to be mayor.'

"In addition to his other qualities, McEmbirk has a culinary reputation to rival that of his grandmother, Phyllis McEmbirk, who was a seventeen-time county fair champion prior to her retirement to Florida last year. Embry Matthews, a local farmer, says, 'Doug's berry pies are amazing. And you should try his eggnog.'"

Doug keeps reading to the end, and when he gets there, he keeps staring down at his phone for a second before he looks up and smiles.

I'm nervous. "So, um. Do you have any changes?"

He shakes his head.

"Is it okay for me to send in?"

Doug looks at Zeke. Zeke gives him a tight nod and smile. They both turn to me.

"Yes," Doug says, and he swallows thickly. Are his eyes a little red?

I'm still not sure what they really think, so I babble a little. "I was going to write more about the Holiday-Off, but I think that will be in the next article for this series I'm writing. I can stay a little longer here. If you'll have me."

Zeke nods, then looks at Doug and slides his hand over the back of Doug's neck, giving him another little squeeze.

Doug blinks. His eyes are *definitely* red. "Max, thank you," he says quietly. "I've never had anyone say such nice things. Well, except Zeke. And of course you can stay as long as you like."

"*This* is the article you should be keeping in your pocket," Zeke tells Doug. Then he turns to me. I figured I was out of reach on my perch in the armchair, but my Vikings are so tall that when Zeke leans toward me he can easily reach out and touch my knee. "You really captured who he is, and the spirit of the town. It's an amazing story."

"Would you come over here, please?" Doug asks, opening his arms. I hop out of my chair and into his lap, and he gives me a fierce hug, burying his face in my neck. "Thanks for making me sound like a real mayor, not a goofball."

I hold onto him until he leans back, and then I give him a quick kiss. "Just telling the truth. You're a treasure."

Zeke rubs a hand up and down my back. "Good job, Max. This is the way the world should see Doug. Not whatever the fuck that fucking article said about a child mayor bankrupting Christmas. Or whatever."

"Don't remind me," Doug groans.

"Sorry."

I smile and lean over, pecking Zeke on the lips, too. Then I glance at our phones. "Um, boys, don't we have somewhere to be? Aren't the volunteers gathering for Holiday-Off decorating? We can't miss it. I need more material for my next article."

"That's right," Doug says. "I got into the movie and completely forgot. Let's get changed and go. Wait, let me check on the MVB, and *then* we can go."

"Deal."

After he ensures that Vermonica is content, we put on hats, gloves, and heavy coats, and pile into Doug's truck.

My eyes are glued to the windshield during the short drive. Throughout the tiny town, Holiday-Off spirits are high. The white clapboard homes are snow-capped and almost every door is hung with evergreen green wreaths tied with red velvet bows.

The town square is bustling as we pull up. Volunteers on precarious ladders are wrapping every street pole and tree with lights that will look magical after dark. When we step out of the vehicle, I can hear holiday tunes drifting from the speakers rigged up outside the feed store. The tall elves that plagued Doug's budget are assembled like sentries by the bandshell, where a Christmas tree large enough to rival Rockefeller Center is getting festooned with the help of the local utility company—two cherry picker trucks and a team of workers in hard hats and reflective vests.

Walking between Doug and Zeke, I have the urge to take both of their hands. I stop myself, though. I'm not entirely sure what the protocol is here. Zeke is obviously out. Doug doesn't seem to be shy about anything, and hasn't expressed any worries about pursuing a relationship with Zeke. And I have been conducting interviews all over town and am known to be staying with the guys, so I have heard more than my fair share of gossip and conjecture about whether they're more than best friends.

I know La Fierte is a sex-positive and inclusive place, and that most people are excited by the speculation around everyone's favorite hockey-playing, fire-fighting duo. But what would they think about an interloping twink who has a crush on both of their hometown heroes? Adam, Jeb, and Embry's support may not reflect popular opinion, because of course they'd approve.

From the moment I found myself in the middle of Doug and Zeke, first as friends, and now as—well, whatever we are—it's felt perfectly right. But now, for the first time, I'm not sure. Am I getting between them in all the wrong ways?

PART THREE
OMFG

From the group chat "2 Vikings and their willing hostage"

MAX

TMI time. I think it's Doug's turn to share a fantasy.

ZEKE

What is TMI time? Is it on a recurring date and time? Should I set a calendar reminder?

MAX

Nope, it happens at random intervals according to my royal decree. You know, as TMI King.

ZEKE

I thought I was the king

MAX

You were king for a day, but I've reclaimed my throne. Remember the incident yesterday?

ZEKE

As though I could forget you telling the mailman you had hoped the box of holiday chocolates from Doug's grandma was actually the dildo you think I ordered?

MAX

Fortunately the chocolates are EXCELLENT so I've recovered from my disappointment. Partially.

MAX

Doug, don't think I haven't noticed that you're suspiciously silent. Not even a doctor's note can get you off the hook for TMI time.

CHAPTER 21
ZEKE

"Can you believe we're just standing around," I murmur, "raising up twelve-foot high dreidels and discussing placement of hot chocolate stands? When all the while we've got a secret cow stashed in our garage?"

Doug smacks my shoulder. "Zeke!" he whispers in a hiss. "I thought we agreed not to mention the MVB in public! You're the one who almost started a cow-mentions jar!"

"I know." I shove my hands into my pockets as I scan the citizens of La Fierte spread out across the town square, hanging fairy lights and erecting absurdly sized inflatable decorations. Max has already made at least six jokes about the size and shape of the twelve-foot candles currently standing at each corner of the square. "But with all of these people around, I can't help wondering which one of them put Vermonica in our garage."

"Maybe the cow-napper—I mean, totally legitimate cow borrower"—Doug hastily amends—"isn't here at all. Maybe they're from Atherton."

"Why would someone from Atherton sabotage the Holiday-Off in our favor?" I ask.

Doug shrugs, then bends to hit a switch at his feet. A large snowman inflates up into some sort of plastic existence. "Have you thought that maybe we shouldn't look a gift-cow in the mouth?"

I whirl on him. "Did you seriously just say that?"

He grins. "I did. But Max said it first. While you were in the shower this morning."

I snort with laughter, and then he does. As always when we get each other going, we're chortling every time our eyes meet for the next solid minute or two.

I wrap Doug up in a quasi-headlock and he pushes his knuckles into my ribs because once I've got him like this, the only way he can escape is by tickling, the cheater. Things between us are so easy and familiar.

Well, not everything is familiar. We also kiss now. *So much* has changed between us in such a short amount of time. Ever since we met Max.

Doug shrugs me off and puts his arms around me. Mine close around him automatically in return. Being with him, like this, so much closer on so many levels—it feels better than I ever even imagined it would. But even as I've watched so many of my dreams come true in a matter of weeks, it's been hard not to wonder if anything ever would have changed between me and Doug if Max hadn't arrived on our doorstep. I'd probably still be lying to my best friend, keeping my most important secrets from him and spending every night wishing for something I was certain I could never have.

"Oh, aren't you two just the most adorable!" Someone claps their hands behind me, and I immediately let go of Doug and turn to find Melinda and Norman Perkins standing right behind us. "I always knew the two of you would get together someday."

"She did!" Norman agrees. He pushes his wool hat up his forehead as he sighs with happiness. "So good to see you boys together at last. Any word on a wedding date?"

I'm fairly certain my heart actually stops beating at that word. *Wedding?* What the actual fuck? Doug and I *just* figured out how to kiss each other.

Then again, do I want to marry Doug? I mean, all I've wanted my whole life is to be with him. I should want to marry him, shouldn't I? But—

"Thanks, Mr. and Mrs. Perkins," Doug says. Always the consummate mayor, he leans across me to shake their hands. "So I'll take this endorsement as a sign that the entire town knows Zeke and I are dating now?"

"Of course!" Melinda says cheerfully. "I heard it from Sarah Elsby who heard it from Juan Ocon, who heard it from—"

"Wonderful, thank you," Doug interrupts smoothly.

"Marty from town hall's been telling everyone to give you both your privacy," Norman adds. "But we just saw the two of you over here together looking so happy, and we couldn't help coming over to say something!"

"That's right," Melinda says. "Well, we're off to help put lights up on the gazebo. You two take care now! Hope you find some mistletoe!" She winks, her face bright above the scarf that's covering her chin, and then the two of them start trudging through the snow piles in the square toward the gazebo in the middle of it.

Max jogs up to us, huffing. "I saw them accost you. I *told* Marty you both needed some space, but he warned me he might not be able to keep people away once they saw you together—I guess there was a bet going about whether you two have secretly dated since college?"

"Max, it's okay." Doug squeezes Max's shoulder with a large, gloved hand while he glances around at the crowds that are unsuccessfully pretending not to stare at us. "I appreciate you looking after us, but folks were going to find out eventually. You know what my Grandma says about La Fierte. Well, I guess you don't. She says, 'In this town, news travels faster than a January wind.' Right, Zeke?"

I hear Doug speaking but can't summon an answer. Why am I panicking about people knowing about me and Doug? I've always wanted to be with Doug. That's all I've ever wanted since before my voice changed.

So why the fuck do I suddenly feel like a goldfish in a teeny, tiny bowl of water it can never escape?

I never felt this way when people saw me with Lydia.

"Doug!" A voice calls from across the square, and I look up to see Marty waving at us from where he's standing next to a large blow-up pig wearing a Santa hat. Doug heads over, seemingly oblivious to my inner crisis, leaving me and Max standing between a box of ornaments and a large, tangled pile of fairy lights.

Max nudges my elbow with his. "You doing okay there, big guy?"

I'm not sure how to answer him. I open up my mouth and try to put the emotions swirling through me into words, but nothing comes out.

"Zeke!"

Oh no. *That voice,* at exactly the time I do not need to hear it. I barely have time to catch Max's grimace and wide-eyed, terrified glance over at me before my fucking twin, Jonah James, is charging into our space, nearly stepping on the pile of lights I was about to start untangling.

"You almost broke those," I inform him as evenly as I can.

Jonah huffs. "I knew exactly where I was going. I need to fucking talk to you!"

I close my eyes against the roar of something like panic that's suddenly pulsating through my body. There's no way he's appeared in the town square today to help me put together La Fierte's stage or our eight freestanding plywood reindeer. Frankly, I'm surprised it took Jonah this long to confront me. I'm still surprised he didn't accost me at hockey practice the morning after I made my big announcement at town hall that I'm—

Say the word bisexual, *Zeke. You have to be able to say the word* bisexual *to him.*

But what if I fucking can't? What if I can *never* say that word to him? I couldn't even look Melinda and Norman Perkins in the eye. How am I supposed to look at my own brother and tell him I'm not who he thought I was our entire lives?

And what the hell is wrong with me? Now that I've finally given myself permission to be myself, my real self, in front of everyone—why can't I do exactly that? Why am I hesitating to tell Jonah exactly what I've known since we were kids?

"I hope you're not here to steal our tree configuration plans for the Holiday-Off," I finally say to him.

Jonah snorts. "Hell, no. Don't pretend like you don't know exactly why I'm here. Did you really think I fucking wouldn't find out?"

Max is completely motionless next to me, frozen by Jonah's presence. "Jonah," I say, taking a deep breath and willing my heart rate to fall. "I. I, uh—"

Jonah throws his arms out wide. "What the hell is going on at those damn hockey practices of yours? Shay told me all about it today—did you really think he wouldn't? I've been dropping my kid off for *hockey practice*, and you've been sending him off to dance lessons instead!"

"Wait—what?" I'm so floored by Jonah's announcement that I can barely form words. He's here to talk to me about *Shay dancing*? Not about me being non-straight? I glance at Max, whose facial expression is equal parts horror and curiosity. All I want is to take Max's hand, to comfort him in the face of Jonah and all the memories he brings up. I reach over to take his hand—

But I can't. For some reason, Melinda Perkins's beaming face is in my head as I let my hand fall back by my side.

I manage to say, "It's not 'dance lessons.' It's strength and flexibility training. With music." I always knew Jonah would find out about all this eventually. I wouldn't tell Shay to lie to his dad, and he's a chatty kid, especially when it comes to how proud he is for mastering his chassé.

I straighten myself up to my full height, which puts me exactly point-three inches above Jonah. I know because we used to have very involved measuring competitions.

"So, yeah," I go on. "That training is run by a local dance instructor. And yes, Shay really fucking loves to dance. And yes, I let him dance more than I make him skate at practice. Because dancing makes him happy, and hockey doesn't."

Jonah throws his hands into the air. "You got my son thinking he's the next Billy fucking Elliot!"

I squint at him. "How do you know about *Billy Elliot*?"

"There was a movie—that's not the point!" Jonah shouts. "The fucking point is you need to keep him on the ice and away from that poofy dance shit!"

I'm still trying to process that Jonah's not here to discuss my recent coming out announcement when I hear Max's quiet voice next to me. "Why?" he asks.

Jonah whirls to face Max squarely, but Max doesn't even flinch. "What do you mean, why?" he asks.

"I mean," says Max calmly, "if your son likes to dance, why won't you let him dance?"

Jonah purses his lips. "He hasn't given hockey enough of a chance," he says. "As he gains some skill, he'll learn to like hockey. And when he does, he'll thank me for helping him toughen up. Otherwise he's gonna get the shit beat out of him in high school for being a pansy ass, and—"

"Oh. So that's what you're worried about." Max's eyes are wet, but his voice is steady. Once again, I feel the urge to grab his hand and hold it. And once again, something stops me. "You're worried somebody is going to treat your son the way that you treated me."

Jonah's mouth curls into that sneer I'm all too familiar with. The one that's identical to my father's. "Oh, for fuck's sake, Maxi Pad. You're not still pissed at me about high school, are you?"

"You broke my toe!" Max cries out.

"He did what?" I growl. Every muscle in my body instantly

tenses. Jonah fucking *broke one of Max's bones*? I take a step toward my brother.

"It was just a prank!" Jonah cries out as he backs away from me. "Yeah, okay, we went a little too far. But all we were trying to do was get a little Kool-Aid on your white shirt because you said you liked pink so much!" He shakes his head and crosses his arms over his chest. "I dropped that cooler by accident. I told you that. I said I was sorry!"

"You apologized for breaking my toe," Max says tersely. "You never apologized for making a fool of me every day, or making me feel like I was less than human just because I wanted to be myself and be out in public and wear what I liked to wear. You definitely never apologized for all the awful names you called me."

Jonah closes his eyes, his face pinching together. "Come on, Maxi—I mean, Max. I never—"

"You *broke his toe*?" My voice isn't loud, exactly, but even in my ears the words hold a dangerous note of warning. All my nastiest memories of Jonah are roaring through my brain right now: taunting me, siding with Dad when he called me names, choosing Dad over Mom and me in the custody battle. Growing up to be *exactly* like our father, in so many ways.

Something shatters inside of me. Before my brain can get my body to slow down, I'm pulling back a fist. And then I fire it directly at Jonah's nose.

Everything around us seems to move in slow motion as my fist hits his face with a *crack* and Jonah's head snaps back. Tiny drops of blood swirl through the air as I watch myself be someone I've always known I could be. Someone like Jonah. No, worse. Someone like my dad.

The town square has gone silent. Everyone's standing like they're frozen, and they're all staring at me. Jonah chokes out a gasp and holds his hands to his face as I look around at the shocked faces surrounding me. They all see me now. All the parts of me I've kept hidden for so long.

They see all of me now. Every one of them. Every single cell of me is on display for the world.

One face stands out, though. Max. His eyes are wide and unblinking, and his expression is one I recognize.

It's the same look that takes over his face when he sees Jonah. Except now, it's directed at me.

DOUG

Can I declare TMI time? I think it's time we heard
about another of Max's fantasies. :)

ZEKE

Yeah, what's your #1?

MAX

I mean, I have A LOT of fantasies. Some of them
are not to be discussed in polite company

ZEKE

Who the fuck said I was polite?

MAX

I do have one big one I have never, ever told
anyone about. And never will.

DOUG

Aw, Max! You can tell us anything!

MAX

[gif of person zipping their lips]

It's too TMI even for me.

CHAPTER 22
DOUG

"This has to be far enough," I call to Marty, who I'm following down the uneven brick sidewalk of Second Street. We're almost a block from the square now, and frankly, I'm surprised by how much ground Marty can cover when he puts his mind to it. My legs have to be five or six inches longer than his, and I'm hustling to keep pace.

Marty pauses and turns toward me, scanning the surrounding houses like he thinks someone might be peering out their windows at us. Finally he meets my eyes and sucks in a deep breath. "Doug. I mean, Mr. Mayor. I think I messed up."

"Oh." I shove my hands into my pockets. "Well, that's okay, Marty. Everyone makes mistakes. Just tell me what happened, and we can figure it out."

Marty manages a half-smile, but it quickly fades and his lower lip wobbles. Oh, shoot. Marty is made of tough stuff. He's the only one on the town hall staff who isn't afraid of the church ladies, which is why he's our go-to liaison with the United Congregational Choir. This has got to be serious. I squeeze his arm. "Take a deep breath." He does, but the exhale is pretty darn shaky. I give him another squeeze. "Now, just let it out."

His cheeks go hollow for a second, and then he says in a rush:

"I misappropriated town funds to put together a down payment for the Icebreakers." Then he claps his hand over his mouth and stares at me with huge, anxious eyes.

I was *not* expecting this conversation when Marty gestured to me from where he was standing next to a group of blow-up farm animals in holiday regalia. I'd just assumed there was an issue with the giant duck wearing reindeer ears. "What do you mean, 'misappropriated'?" I ask, trying to keep my voice calm while my heart beats at double speed.

Marty nods, dropping his hand from his face. "I transferred money from the street maintenance account. That is *not* permitted by the budget approved by the council, so, I'm basically a criminal." Now he puts both of his hands to his face and loses his cool completely, sobbing into his hands.

"You… what?" I ask, the words coming out very slowly. Not because I don't understand the conversation we're having, but because I'm distracted by the thoughts racing through my mind. *What should I do? What should I say?*

Marty nods miserably, and I rub his shoulder while he continues to cry quietly into his hands. Then I find my gaze straying to my right.

The place where, in moments like this, I expect to see Zeke.

Zeke is always at my side in the hardest moments. I need him there. He's the smart one, the quick thinker. He's the one who always knows what to do.

"They needed the deposit yesterday to hold the reservation," Marty says, sniffing and rubbing his eyes on his sleeve. "There wasn't enough money in the Holiday-Off account, though. Not even with everything we have from the calendar preorders. I figured, the money will come in, right? When we sell more calendars? And then I'll pay back the street fund. We don't fill potholes until spring, right?"

He looks at me hopefully. I know he wants me to tell him he did the right thing. Or, tell him what we *should* do to make it right. But all I can do is frown, searching my head for an answer.

Only I can't find one.

"No, you're right," Marty says, shaking his head, apparently hearing some kind of answer in my silence. "I need to call the Icebreakers' manager and tell him there was a mistake, and I'm stopping payment on the check."

"But then will we lose the booking?" The words roll off my tongue before I have time to think about why I'm asking.

Marty winces, then he nods. "If we don't pay their deposit now, they're not coming."

The course of action is obvious, right? We do what Marty said. Get the money back, explain to the town that we tried but couldn't get the Icebreakers after all, and that's that. Sure, I promised them we would have an event they'd never forget, *and* win the Holiday-Off in the process. But it's just a contest. Nobody should be compromising their integrity to win.

I bite my cheek. It's impossible to have that thought and not immediately picture the Holstein currently residing in my garage.

Marty's phone buzzes, and he peers down at the screen, his eyes widening at whatever he sees. "Oh, shit," he whispers, then looks up at me.

"What?" I reach for my phone, but I don't have any notifications. "What happened?"

"Zeke James is beating up Jonah James in the middle of the square."

"*What?*" The La Fierte gossip grapevine isn't particularly reliable, but generally it's not *absolutely ridiculous*. "That can't be true." But I'm turning to hurry back the way we came anyway to see what the heck is actually going on.

"Wait!" Marty insists, reaching for me. "We have to talk about this."

I hesitate. "I know," I agree. "Just give me a few minutes, okay? I'll follow up with you ASAP. I promise."

"Doug!" Marty shouts, but I can't stay here talking to him when something might be happening with Zeke and Jonah. They've gotten into it before, but I can't imagine Zeke would get violent with him. Or, can I? It's been a long time since I've seen Zeke really lose his temper, but I know that he has to work hard to keep a lid on it when his brother is around. Is it possible that he snapped? Yeah, it is, depending on what Jonah decided to let spill out of his mouth.

When I get to the edge of the square, I see none other than Jonah James, a wadded scarf held to his nose, jerking open the door of a truck parallel-parked on the street and climbing in. He doesn't see me, and I barely look at him. Instead I search the crowds of people, all stopped mid-decorating, to find Zeke.

There he is. Right next to the half-built stage, with Max. I break into a run in their direction. Just a few minutes ago the scene in this spot was entirely different. My heart had never felt lighter or happier. And now it's like there's a dark cloud over everything, including Zeke's face as he turns to me, his expression oddly blank, and his right hand half-curled into a fist.

Just like that, I'm sure he hit Jonah. The shock of it is still written on his face, and he looks down at his own hand like he's never seen it before. Max is staring at Zeke like he doesn't recognize him.

"Are you okay?" I say when I reach them, looking between the two of them. "What the heck happened?"

Zeke looks down. Max looks at me, blinking slowly. Neither one of them answers.

"Should we go home?" I try, but it's like neither one of them can hear me. Then I remember what just happened with Marty, and I wince. "I can't leave, actually. Not yet. Actually, Zeke, I need to ask you—uh," I cut myself off, not wanting to spill Marty's secrets in the middle of a crowd. "It's something about the Holiday-Off. Something really important."

Zeke's head jerks up and his eyes latch onto mine. The expression on his face startles me. It's not blank, not anymore. It's angry.

"Dammit, Doug!" he says. He's not shouting, exactly, but his words have enough force to strike me in the chest, like a punch. "Did it occur to you that this might not be the time for me to help you through any of your mayor-job bullshit? I have my own fucking problems, you know? I can't hold your hand all the time." I open my mouth to say something—I have no idea what—and he shakes his head. "I know what you're thinking. I'm being a fucking asshole, right? Well, that's nothing new. Everybody knows who I really am. You're the only one who convinced himself I'm any better than my dad. Or my brother. I'm gonna walk home." And just like that, he turns and leaves.

"Doug," a voice calls urgently from behind me, and when I tear my eyes away from Zeke's departing back to look over my shoulder, I see Marty, face pale between his fluffy earmuffs, his expression pointed.

"I…" I begin, and then a hand closes firmly on my forearm. I blink down at Max, who steps close to me and gives me a tight smile.

"You deal with whatever's going on," he tells me.

"But, Zeke—" I start, and Max shakes his head.

"You do what you need to do, Mr. Mayor. I've got Zeke."

There's something about Max that I haven't been able to put my finger on—something that's harder to see than his bright smiles and sparkling wit. Something quiet. Something strong as iron. I see it clearly right now, and I can't look away. I nod.

"And, Doug?" he adds softly. "You've got this. Okay?"

"Okay," I say. "Yeah."

Max smiles, and calm washes over me. Then he turns to jog after Zeke, and I take a deep breath.

I've got this, I think. When Max said it, it felt true. I'm still not entirely sure, but what I do know is that there's nobody to pass the puck to. I'm the mayor, just me. And I'm going to have to act like it.

From the group chat "Max and Zeke"

CHAPTER 23
ZEKE

"I'm not bending to your will."

I stare down my opponent, eyes fixed and unblinking. If I blink, he'll know he won.

"I'm serious," I tell him, my jaw firmly set. "You're not getting what you want here. I know everyone else just takes one look at you and gives in, but I'm not like the rest of them. Intimidation won't work."

He's still propped up against the fence in front of me, eyes steady as he stares me down. We've been standing like this for three minutes straight, neither of us moving. But he's not getting it. Never. I'm not giving him what's in my hand.

I need a win this week, and I'm fucking taking this one.

"I'm going," I tell him, "to walk right past you now. I'm not going to give you this apple. It's for Darla, the Clydesdale who fucking earned it because she actually did some damn *work* around here today. All you did was scare the small children picking out Christmas trees by standing up on your hind legs like the menace to society that you are."

He gives me a slight nod, as if to say *yes, yes I did*. And he's claiming it with pride, not shame.

I sigh. "But you *did* let that toddler put those neon sunglasses on you for a picture… oh, fucking fine. Here, you can have it."

I toss the apple into the goat's pen. Sherbert studies it for a moment before finally hopping down onto his forelegs to grab it with his teeth. I swear he nods at me again. Like he's acknowledging our standoff and being generous in his victory.

"You're spoiled rotten, Sherbert," I tell him.

"Looks like he knows it too," says a cheerful voice behind me.

Max is standing behind me, his hands shoved in the pockets of Doug's ski jacket. It's so long on him that it falls almost to his knees, and we had to roll up the sleeves four inches. I'm glad we talked him into borrowing it, though. His face is red with cold right now, and that's inside of a barn that's relatively warm with the heat of so many animals. I fight the urge to rush over to him and wrap my arms around him so he can be warm all the way through.

I doubt he'd want me touching him right now.

"How'd you find me? Or get here?" I ask.

Max shrugs. "You weren't coming home or answering my messages, so I called Jeb. Embry picked me up."

"Traitors. I'm never babysitting their demon goat again." I glance over at Sherbert, who's calmly eating his apple as though he wasn't staring at me murderously less than a minute ago.

"They care about you," Max says. "And I do too," he adds softly.

I sink down onto a bale of hay as he takes a few steps closer to me. It's impossible to look directly at him right now. "Hard to imagine why," I say. The image of Max's face after I punched Jonah is fresh in my mind, like a wound, and I can't imagine it will ever heal.

Max takes another step closer and holds up something I hadn't noticed in his hand. "Can I show you this?"

I scoot to one end of the hay bale. Max sits next to me, but I'm careful to give him as much space as I can.

Max draws in a deep breath as he holds out the item. It's a shoebox I remember rescuing from the impound lot. Bright orange, with the Adidas logo in white across it. "My mom gave this to me right before I got into that accident," he says.

"Fucking Dante. Thank goodness you were okay." Max blushes. "I'll never forget what it felt like to see you in that wrecked car," I tell him. I wonder why today, of all days, he wants to show me a pair of shoes.

"Mom said it's a box of my high school memorabilia." Max rests the box on his thigh, studying it. "I haven't been able to bring myself to open it up and see what's inside."

I grunt, then wince. *Dammit.* I should be more careful and use my words with him right now. Speaking in grunts is what cavemen do, right after they punch their brothers. But Max keeps staring at the box, apparently unbothered.

"Zeke," Max says slowly, "where's your mom? You don't talk about her much. I know Doug's parents both died when he was a baby and he's always lived with his grandma. But your mom's still alive, right?"

I'm not sure why he's asking, but I'm so grateful he's even speaking to me that I answer right away. "She moved to Arizona after Jonah and I graduated high school. Probably would have moved a lot sooner, but she wanted to stay as close to Jonah as she could after he chose to live with Dad." I shrug. "It was hard for her, being around Dad after the divorce. She knew that marrying my dad was a mistake. She said she never regretted it, though, because she had me and Jonah," I add. "But sometimes I wonder if she would do it all over if she could."

Max nods, and I find more words that I've never really shared with anyone—not even Doug—spilling out of my mouth.

"It was awful for her when Jonah picked Dad over her," I say. "Especially since Dad was even more of a piss-poor parent after she left. We both knew that Jonah was doing a lot of the work around that house. Cooking, cleaning. Taking care of Dad when he went on benders. But he always refused to come live with us. He said Dad needed someone around too, just like Mom did."

Max's eyebrows go up. "Wow."

"My mom's a great person," I tell him. "When I finally tell her that I'm—uh, well—"

"Whatever you want to tell her about you and Doug," Max interjects kindly.

"Sure. That. When I tell her that, I know she'll be happy for me. Because she always is." I sigh. "She's the one," I whisper to my lap. "She's the parent I always wanted to be like. But no matter how hard I try, I'm like *him* instead."

Max sets the box down and takes my hands in his. I still can't look directly at him, so I stare down at our hands, braided together.

"I don't know your parents. But I know *you*. You're Zeke James. You're kind and protective and loyal. Even though I've never met your mom, I can tell you have all her best qualities." He squeezes my hands.

"When I hit Jonah," I manage, my voice tight, "I saw the look on your face. And I don't blame you. I've tried so hard to make you believe I'm different, but…" I trail off, wishing I could vanish into thin air. But Max's hands hold mine tightly, keeping me in the moment, as hard as it is to stay.

"That moment definitely messed with my head," Max concedes. "Violence is never going to make me swoon, even when it's directed at one of my least favorite people. Some memories are hard to let go of, you know? But I want you to know that when I look at you, I don't see Jonah James anymore. I don't see someone who tortured and teased me. I see the person who wraps me up in down jackets and tells off newspaper editors."

I snort.

"I see the person who arranged clandestine dance lessons for his nephew. The person who always makes sure we watch the movie Doug would like best even when it's your turn to pick." He clears his throat. "I see someone who will always be more than *where* or *who* you came from."

Max leans across my lap and kisses me softly on the forehead, then on the lips. I swear Sherbert snorts at us in derision, but I don't fucking care. My body's being wrapped up in the sensation of warm, soft blankets.

When we lean away from the kiss, I pull him against me, holding him tight.

"Thank you," I whisper into his neck. I'm not sure exactly how to explain everything that I'm thanking him for, but I have a feeling Max understands.

"Thank you," he whispers back. "For helping me let go. And for so much more."

He's better with words than I'll ever be. I squeeze his shoulder gently as he shifts away from me to pick up the box again. "Hey," he says. "There's a fire pit behind this barn, right? Is it all covered in snow?"

I raise an eyebrow. "Yeah, there's a fire pit. Embry keeps the area clear so they can have fires when they do evening events here.

"Great." Max beams. "C'mon. Take me to it. Oh, and we need some matches."

"Why?" I ask as I stand up and dust off my jeans.

"Because!" Max beams. "We're going to have a memory bonfire!"

Sherbert hops up on his hind legs and lets out a *baaahhhh.*

Twenty minutes later we're standing in front of a low fire.

"I bet you know the exact regulations for how big this thing can be, don't you?" Max says wryly.

"Sure do," I tell him easily. "And we're well within them. Now, what the fuck is a memory bonfire?"

Max holds up the bright orange shoebox. "The definition is

right there in the phrase," he says. My eyes widen as he lifts the box up above the flames.

"You're not going to open it?" I ask. "See what's in there?"

Max takes a deep breath. "I think the point is," he finally says, "that it doesn't matter anymore."

"I respect that," I tell him. "Maybe just let me peek inside first to make sure nothing in there is toxic or explosive?"

"Oh! Good idea." Max passes the box over.

I turn it away from him as I pop up one side of the lid. Old newspaper articles. Pictures. Notebook paper. A blue ribbon of some kind. Nothing that should be too dangerous to burn.

Thank goodness. This moment is obviously important to Max. I didn't want to have to disrupt it like the time I had to interrupt Mary Brighton's lost love séance after she threw a tire into her fire and someone reported her.

She never did explain why she wanted to burn that tire so badly.

I wrap one arm around Max and hold onto him as he tosses the box into the fire. We watch together as the cardboard slowly starts to change shape and melt into itself in the heat of the flames. Max lets out a small noise when the contents inside become visible for a moment between the holes in the cardboard. Then they, too, begin to fold in on themselves and take new shape. Eventually they'll be nothing but ash.

I watch the flames of the fire burn before me, and I think about all disasters I've ever seen, all the calls I've ever answered, and all the ways I've watched people rebuild after tragedy.

Rebuilding from ashes. I always thought that was an act of hope. "How do you feel?" I ask Max.

"Good," he says breathily. "I feel really good." He stands up on his tiptoes to peck me on the lips with his. Then he nuzzles into my shoulder. "You know," he says into my coat, "for a lot of years I've barely been able to bring myself to visit Vermont. Lately, I kind of wish I could stay forever. With you and Doug." He shakes his head as he pulls back away from me. "That's super weird, right? I mean, you two are basically relationship goals. You're endgame."

I frown. "What do you mean?" I ask him.

He pulls his arms fully away from me to wrap them around his own body. "The two of you. You were always meant to be. *Just the two of you.*"

My brain feels like it's running back through every moment Doug and I have spent with Max since he's arrived; the images rewind in front of me until I feel almost dizzy. Max has been with us for such a short time, yet he's slotted into our lives so seamlessly. It's hard for me to imagine going back to life without him here.

But Max was always supposed to leave. Right? I'm supposed to end up with Doug. That's what I always wanted. *Endgame,* Max called us. It *almost* feels right. Except... I shake my head.

"I don't know about that." There's more I want to say. That as close as we were, there was a gap between me and Doug, but no bridge. I think Max is that bridge. I don't know if we could make it work without him, and even if we could, I don't *want* to.

But this feels like a conversation between three people, not two, and I don't want to get ahead of myself. I need to talk to Doug.

Too bad Doug might not be very interested in talking to *me* given the way I spoke to him before. I rub my forehead. Max sighs and slides his hand through my elbow, tugging me along.

"Come on. The fire's out. It's cold out here. Let's go home."

I snap out of my thoughts in an instant and start to unbutton my coat. "Do you need another layer?"

Max rolls his eyes and tugs again. "No, thank you. I'll be fine when we get moving. It's my feet that are cold—and don't you dare offer me your socks." I snort, and he looks smug. "I got a smile."

"I'm not smiling," I say automatically.

"I saw it. You can't gaslight me," Max insists, pressing his side to mine as we walk. "I love the lights," he says, gazing at the lights the 3way has strung up around the outbuildings that dot their property. "I even love the snow."

I look around me, trying to see everything through his eyes. But then I'd rather look at him, with the holiday lights faintly reflected by his glasses and the tip of his nose adorably pink from the chilly air.

From the group chat "2 Vikings and their willing hostage"

MAX

I was just working on my next article and wondering: has Barton always been so angry?

ZEKE

For as long as I can fucking remember

DOUG

Actually, he used to be a really sweet guy back when I was little. I remember his house giving out the best candy on Halloween. Homemade banana taffy… it was amazing

ZEKE

What the fuck happened?

DOUG

Well, the Halloween candy stopped the year his wife passed away. I haven't thought about that in a long time.

ZEKE

It probably didn't help that the paper has had to reduce staff at least a few times that I can remember.

MAX

Oh, wow. Poor guy.

Do you ever think about how we're all the heroes in our own story and probably the villain in someone else's?

ZEKE

Huh.

CHAPTER 24

MAX

By the time we reach the house, Doug is already sitting on the porch. Zeke has been quiet for most of our trip home, but I could feel some of the tension ebbing out of him. Now, it's back, and his arm is taut where it's looped through mine.

I can understand why he's not eager for this moment. He said some pretty tough words to Doug. But I hold to my philosophy about telling the truth, even if it leads to arguments. I know they'll come out of their conversation stronger than they went into it.

Doug stands up from his perch on the porch steps, his eyes moving from Zeke's face to mine. He smiles at me, and I give him a little wave with a gloved hand. "I think you two need to talk," I tell them. "I'll go check on the MVB."

I circle the house, stealing a last glance over my shoulder before they're out of sight. Zeke has stepped up to the bottom of the steps, and Doug stands over him from the step above. Zeke tips back his head, and I see his lips move around words spoken too softly for me to overhear. But I'm pretty sure they're *I'm sorry*. Doug just shakes his head and pulls Zeke in, Zeke's head to his chest. Zeke's arms close tightly around Doug's waist.

I smile to myself and continue to the garage. Vermonica startles easily for such a generally sleepy animal, so I crack open the door and peer inside, not wanting to shock her with a sudden entrance. She's napping, but her ear twitches like she can sense me. With her eyes closed, her eyelashes are so long and curly that she looks like a cartoon character. For a few seconds, I admire her, bathed in the soft glow of her personal Christmas tree, then show myself out.

As I re-emerge into the snow, I stifle a scream as a human-shaped shadow yawns across the side of the garage, cast by the ring of light from the yard lamp.

Before I can scream for help from the Vikings, I notice that the shadow is familiar. "Barton, is that you?" I ask the figure standing next to the trash cans.

"Yes, Mr. Rivers, it's me," Barton Asterstop mutters, shuffling into the light.

"What are you doing out here?" I ask.

His scowl deepens. "Technically I'm on a public street," he informs me, gesturing to the area around him. "I am perfectly entitled to be here. And I only live a few doors down."

I deliberately step away from the garage door, which I remembered to lock behind me, fortunately. Not that I expect Barton to race past me and force the door or anything. He looks more likely to flee. I see the way he glances down the street and shuffles his feet, like it pains him to stand here and talk to me instead of going about his business.

"I know," I hasten to tell him. "But it's cold, and getting dark. Not the typical time for a casual stroll."

"The cold helps me think."

I can't relate. The cold makes me feel like my thoughts have frozen along with my brain cells. I try not to look yearningly at the house and the warm, welcoming glow of the lights in the downstairs windows. Something is tugging at me, making me want to engage with Barton instead of hurrying inside.

He's hurt Doug, which is definitely *not* okay with me. But I have a feeling Barton isn't all bad.

"A lot on your mind?" I guess, based on the way he's gazing pensively at the snow-covered ground.

His eyes snap to mine, then narrow. "I'm sure you'd like to know."

I hold up my hands in the universal gesture of *I mean you no harm.* "I'm just asking."

Barton studies me with those narrowed eyes for a second, like he's gauging my sincerity. Then he sighs heavily. "Yes. You could say my thoughts have never weighed on me so greatly."

As a fellow wordsmith, I have to admire the way Barton speaks, like a man from another time. Which he is, I guess. "How long have you been with *The Pigeon*?" I ask him.

He seems surprised by the question, but after a moment's pause, he answers me. "I started the day after I graduated high school. Come May of next year, it will have been sixty years since the first time my name was printed under a headline."

"That's amazing," I say, meaning it. "I would never have guessed you were so—um, experienced," I add, narrowly avoiding using a word that would *surely* piss Barton off.

He gives a rusty chuckle, though, surprising me all over again. "The word you're looking for is *old*, young man, and you can say it. It's true, after all. I turn seventy-nine on January fourth. It all passes in a blink. I know you young folks hear people my age say that so often it's lost all meaning to you, but it's true."

I imagine Barton as an eager young newspaper man decades before. It's not hard. He probably banged out his articles on an old-timey typewriter and never left the house without a wool hat.

"Hard to believe it will all be over soon," Barton goes on, his voice faraway, like he's forgotten I'm standing there.

I frown. "What do you mean? Is it—oh, I'm sorry. Is it your health?"

"Of course not," he says, rolling his eyes again. "I'm not talking about my *life* ending. Well, not literally. It's the paper, I mean. It will have to close down at the end of the year. I got notice of another rent hike, and it's the last straw for this camel. My back's broke."

"I'm so sorry," I murmur. "I had no idea."

"Nobody does, except the staff. All three of them. I think they're holding out hope for a miracle, because they haven't even told their families yet." He looks so sad and alone, I want to bundle him up and take him inside the house with me. But before I can say anything, much less force him to let me warm him up, he stands up a little taller and nods curtly. "I'll leave you to your evening, Mr. Rivers. Good night." And he slowly makes his way along the alley until he disappears behind the neighboring house, leaving me staring after him, slightly dazed.

I hope the guys have had the time they need, because I'm seriously cold at this point. But just in case they're still talking, I sneak in the back door so I won't interrupt them. They notice, though, because they're waiting for me in the unlit kitchen.

"Oh, hey," I say, shedding my hat, coat, and gloves.

"Hey," says Zeke. "Were you talking to someone outside? I thought I heard two voices."

They're standing in front of me in their bare feet, jeans, and long-sleeved T-shirts. I want to squeeze in between them, and I'm in luck, because they both reach for me to pull me in, Zeke rubbing my upper arms, Doug unwinding my scarf and hanging it on the peg.

"Actually, I was," I say. "Barton Asterstop. He was just out for a walk."

They both stiffen, exchanging sharp looks.

"He wasn't being nosy or asking questions," I assure them. "Actually, he told me *The Pigeon* has to close soon. Did you two know?"

"*What*?" Doug asks, at the same time Zeke shakes his head, brow furrowed.

"We didn't know," Zeke says. "What did he say, exactly?"

"He said the rent's going up, and he can't afford it anymore, so everything will have to shut down."

"I can't believe it," Doug murmurs. "*The Pigeon* is a big part of life in La Fierte."

"In the whole county," Zeke adds, and Doug nods.

"My grandma probably has a few thousand clippings from the paper over the years. County fair results. High school sports columns. A ton of marriage and birth announcements. And obituaries."

"Yeah." I shake my head. "It's really a shame. But the print news industry has gotten really difficult. I can't say I'm shocked. *The Pigeon* was already something special for surviving as long as it did."

Zeke grunts. "I may not *like* Barton Asterstop, but before all this nonsense about the Holiday-Off, I always respected him. It's too bad about the paper."

I nod in agreement, then tilt my head. "What about the two of you? How are you doing?"

"We're fine," Zeke tells me. "We had a good talk."

"Oh, excellent." Zeke and Doug not talking to each other left me feeling uneasy. It's wild how attached I've become to the two of them as a pair in the short time I've been here.

They're Bert and Ernie. Peanut butter and jelly.

Two halves of a sandwich that I'm really enjoying being in the middle of from time to time. My stomach twists as I imagine what it will be like to leave these two. I'm really going to miss so many things about living with them, and *not* just the outstanding sex. There's also Doug's smile that warms me like sunshine, and Zeke's grunt-based language which, miraculously, I'm starting to understand.

I feel a sudden urge to enjoy every moment I do have with them. "Guys," I say hesitantly. "You know how we've been talking a lot about fantasies?"

Zeke's eyebrows go up. "Yes," Doug says slowly.

"And do you remember when I drank all that eggnog and said I wanted you two at the same time?"

Doug's grip on my knee tightens briefly, and Zeke says, "*Fuck.*"

"Well," I say. "How would you two feel about making some of this twink's fantasies come true?"

Doug lets out a squeak.

"Is that a yes?" I murmur, pressing myself back against Zeke's body while I slip my hands under the hem of Doug's shirt and glide my palms up his sides.

"It's a yes," Zeke says, breathing a little harder as I feel his bulge against my back. "It's a resounding yes."

The three of us bolt toward the stairway.

MAX

So you know how I have fantasies about your turnout gear, right?

ZEKE

I may recall that

MAX

Now you have to tell me about a fantasy you have about me and my job

DOUG

Easy. You, naked. Nothing but the glasses. Hunched over a typewriter.

ZEKE

Cosign.

MAX

Doesn't this house have a typewriter somewhere?

DOUG

BRB

CHAPTER 25

ZEKE

Since the night of the power outage, we've fallen into the pattern of sleeping together in Doug's bedroom. All three of us are a tight fit even in a king bed, but Max usually seems to end up sleeping on top of one of us.

"Clothes off, please," Max orders sweetly. We get naked in record time. Doug sets his hand on top of Max's cock, gliding slowly up and down. Max hisses. Is there anything harder than granite? Oh wait, there definitely is. My fucking cock.

"Let's talk for a minute. You're important to us, babe," Doug whispers to Max. "You know we're both new to this game. We want to make sure we can make you happy. Give you what you need," he adds in a low tone, and Max shivers slightly before he gulps.

"Okay, yep," he agrees quickly. He sits down on Doug's bed, and Doug and I sit down on either side of him. "Exactly what do you want me to tell you?"

I know my answer to that question. I drift a finger up and down his thigh. "I want to know more about your secret fantasies," I tell him. "I want to know about your number-one fantasy." I want whatever Max, Doug, and I do next to live so large in Max's brain that he thinks about it every damn day. Preferably for the rest of his life.

Max gulps. "Honestly? There is one that I never trusted anyone enough to share." He gulps again. "It's really weird, okay? I'm not sure I can tell you."

"Sweetheart." Doug leans over to kiss Max's cheek. "You can tell us anything. Truly."

I nod.

Max takes a deep breath. "Okay," he finally says.

Doug and I each hold one of his hands. If there's anything I've realized over the past few days, it's how fucking hard it is to be really, truly vulnerable with other people—even people who mean the most to you. And also, how the payoff is totally worth it. Whatever Max is about to say, I want him to know this was the safest fucking place he could have said it—and then I want to make him *so* happy that he did.

"So," he finally says. "You all know that high school was terrible, and Jonah bullied me a lot. I hated it."

Doug and I both nod.

"But, um. There were times—not very often, but once in a while—when it sort of… turned me on?"

I'll admit, his words set off a stun gun in my brain for a second, but I manage to keep my poker face on. Thank fucking goodness. Doug is Doug, of course. Always unflappable. He just nods. "Tell us more."

Max sighs. "He was awful to me. But sometimes when he was being all domineering and looming over me or whatever, it was like… there was something about the control, I guess. The idea that he was big and strong enough that if he really wanted to, he could make me do anything he wanted." Max shrugs. "I don't know. I guess I've always liked the idea of someone taking charge of me. Giving me the freedom not to have to make any choices. Sometimes, Jonah made me crave that."

"That makes sense," I tell him slowly. And actually? It fucking does. While I'll admit that my gut clenched initially as I imagined

Max being turned on by my brother, I get what he's saying right now. I *really* get it. "You know what?" I tell him. "It fucking turns me on, too. The idea of controlling you. Making you do whatever Doug and I want." I let go of his hand and start stroking up and down his thigh again. Max squirms underneath me.

"You'd corner me in the locker room," he says breathily. "Tell me there's no one else left around after practice, and you're going to do whatever you want. I can't stop you."

I move my fingers just a little bit closer to his groin, edging toward his hard cock, and he gasps again. "What else would we do?" I whisper in his ear.

He takes a deep breath. "You'd refuse to call my dick my dick. You'd call it my clit. You'd call my ass my pussy."

"Oh my," says Doug. His pupils are blown, and he's stroking Max's other thigh. "That's pretty hot, sweetheart."

Max closes his eyes and nods. "You'd take turns with me, using me. I'd tell you to stop, over and over, but you wouldn't listen—you'd know I didn't mean it. You'd know I liked it."

This conversation is driving every nerve ending on my body onto high alert. I know I can't wait much longer before we get this party started. "Safeword," I growl. "You need a safeword. Just to be sure we don't do anything you don't like."

Max nods, and I edge my hand a little closer toward his cock. "Sherbert!" he gasps out.

Doug lets out a chuckle. "I guess that'll do. But maybe let's not tell Jeb, huh?"

I snort.

"Okay, honey," says Doug. "Here's what's going to happen. Zeke and I are going to go out in the hallway. We'll come right back in. You should be in the corner. This is a locker room now, and you've just gotten undressed after working out. How's that sound?"

Max leaps off the bed. "Fuck yes!" he squeals. "And seriously, you can give it to me really, really hard, okay? I *love* having a cock in me. And it's been a really long time since I did."

Well, if I wasn't right on the precipice before, I sure am now. Luckily Doug hustles me out into the hallway and closes the door right before I jump Max and ruin the scene completely.

Outside we stand next to each other for a minute, both of us breathing pretty fucking hard for two guys who've been sitting on a bed for the last ten minutes.

"Zeke?" says Doug. "I just want you to know something. What we're about to do? I wouldn't want my first time doing it to be with anyone else. Not in the whole damn world."

I grab hold of his neck and pull him to me in a crushing kiss, letting our tongues and lips fight and dance and pound back and forth while we both cling to each other. My erect cock brushes against his, and I shudder. I love finally being able to touch Doug's beautiful body. We finally break away, and now we're definitely breathing even heavier. "Me fucking neither," I say.

And then Doug pushes the door open, and we step back inside his room.

Max is standing in the corner, slithering his tight, black boxer briefs—which he must have just put back on—down over his lithe legs. Doug nods at me and sends me a quick look, and just like that we might as well be back in the hockey rink, signaling plays to each other with our eyes.

I know what he's going to do. I know what he wants me to do. And fucking hell, I'm going to have a great time doing it.

I charge up to Max from behind and grab hold of his hips. "Hey, Maxi Pad," I whisper into his ear. "Saw you looking at my cock in science class today. Not surprised to find you here, waiting for it."

Max chokes out a gasp as Doug sidles up next to him. "Everyone in the rink and gym are gone," Doug tells him. "Just the three of us here now. We thought maybe it was time you made up for staring at Zeke's junk like that." He tilts Max's chin up. "I saw you looking at mine too, sweetheart."

"I wasn't—I didn't—"

"Sure you did, honey," Doug says smoothly. "But we're not mad, right, Zeke? Not too mad, anyway."

"Nope." I drift a finger up and down the cleft of Max's butt, pushing in gently to explore his hole. I stroke the sensitive nerve endings. "We'll forgive you, Maxi Pad. All you've got to do is let us both have your pussy."

Max grinds back against my finger as Doug begins to stroke his cock, up and down in a slow, steady motion. "You can't—you can't touch me there," he whispers.

"Can't touch what, honey?" Doug asks. "Oh, you mean your clit?"

Max nods jerkily.

"Baby, I assure you," Doug says. "I can touch you anywhere I want. After what you decided to do with your eyes in science class today, Zeke and I own you. You're not going to have any say over what happens to your pussy or your clit for the next hour. You understand that, sweetheart?"

"No," Max whimpers. "You can't. I won't let you! I—"

"You'll do whatever we tell you to, Maxi Pad," I growl in his ear. "You understand me?" And then I push my finger inside of him, with just enough pressure that I can be sure he'll feel it heavily in his entire body. Max lets out a loud groan as Doug presses his mouth against Max's.

The next few moments are a blur as I watch my best friend take total control of Max's mouth. I find a bottle of lube Max conveniently left out for us and begin prepping him. This is the first time I've done this for anyone other than myself, but every movement feels natural. Easy. I follow the guidebook of Max's whimpers and mewls, making sure he enjoys every motion. "You like that?" I whisper, as I slam one wet finger into him, back and forth, over and over again. "You like my finger in your pussy, Princess?"

Max nearly howls, and I decide to keep "Princess" in the repertoire. "You ready for another one, sweet thing?"

Doug's still stroking Max's cock, and he begins moving his

mouth down and across Max's pecs, teasing at his nipples. "No, don't," Max says.

Doug lifts his head. "What'd I tell you about that word, honey? You don't get to say no to us. I own this pretty little tit." He goes back to licking and sucking at one nipple and then the other, while Max whines and begs us to stop.

"Bet I could get my whole hand inside him, Doug," I say. "Imagine us spreading him out on the bed, taking turns dipping our hands in and out of his pussy."

"Please stop," Max begs, and all I hear is demands for *more* in his voice. I add another finger and thrust hard.

"Oh, I'm not stopping, Princess," I tell him. "I'm not stopping until my cock is buried so deep in you that all you can feel is me." I gesture for Doug to hand me one of the condoms on the small table next to him. While we don't have to wear them, for what I'm thinking, it's a good idea. "You're going to feel me for days, Maxi Pad," I whisper in his ear. "And then you're going to feel Doug. Doug, take care of Maxi Pad here while I fucking get myself ready to own his pussy."

Doug takes control of Max's mouth again while I roll on the condom and lube it up. And then, because I honestly can't wait one more fucking second, I do what I've been dying to since I first met Max.

I push him into Doug, bracing his tiny body against Doug's massive one. I take hold of his hips, and I thrust inside of him.

Holy fucking God. He's so tight and so warm around me. My cock's never imagined life could be this good, and I choke back a groan as Doug leans over, across Max's shoulder, to capture my mouth with his. I revel in the feeling of his tongue playing with mine as I thrust hard into Max, over and over, hitting a spot that I've only ever known from theory and porn before today. Max calls out, louder and louder, but the words are pretty incoherent now. I think I make out "stop" and maybe "you can't," and each one pushes me to slam into him a little bit harder.

"Fucking hell, Princess," I tell him. "You've got the tightest pussy I've ever been in. I wonder how often you play with this pussy. You ever play with it in class, under the desk? While you're watching me and Doug?"

Max mutters something else I can't understand, and Doug laughs. "I bet you do, don't you, sweetheart? Zeke, hon, I know you're teaching the princess a lesson back there, but I've got to tell you that I won't last much longer. If you could—"

"No problem," I tell him. "Wait for it, Princess. I'm about to come in your mouth while Doug takes your pussy." I'm so close that all it takes is a few strategic moves in Max's tight body before I'm ready for a change of scenery. I pull out fast, making Max gasp again, while Doug's holding up a condom. Max shakes his head, and Doug positions himself behind Max where I just was. Then I shove Max down on all fours on the rug, lose my condom, and jam my cock hard into his mouth.

Doug pistons into Max's hole, and soon the two of us are fucking him at the same time. We hit a rhythm right away, Doug driving Max into me and then me driving him back into Doug. "Oh, Princess," I tell Max. "Your mouth's almost as good as your pussy. Now be a good little Maxi Pad for us and come when we tell you to, okay?"

"Nnnh!" Max says around my cock, and that vibration is almost enough to send me over the edge.

"Oh, yes you will," Doug tells him. "Or we'll have you right back here in this locker room tomorrow. Same time, same place. And you'll like it just as much." He thrusts his cock hard into Max, and Max's perfect mouth envelops me. "Now come for us, sweetheart."

Max screams around my cock as his body shakes, and that's it —I can't wait one more moment. I come hard in his mouth, grabbing hold of his head and making him take everything I pour into him while I stare greedily at Doug, who's losing himself in Max at the same time. His eyes are open, his gaze locked on mine, and he separates his lips quickly in a pout as he lifts his head and purses his lips together.

He's sending me a fucking kiss from across Max's body. I swear, I nearly come all over again.

We end up on the bed in a collapsed heap, with Doug and I cradling Max between us while Doug cleans him off and I stroke every part of him I can touch. "You did so good, baby," I tell him. "You were amazing. Absolutely perfect. Was it everything you wanted it to be?"

Max blinks hard, eyes so big they seem to be taking over his entire face. "Oh my *god*, yes. That *totally* worked for me. It felt like my fantasy, but better. Safer. I knew you'd take care of me, and you weren't actually going to hurt me."

"Right, babe. Never," I assure him.

He nods. "It's amazing to feel so safe with you."

"That's the best thing I've ever heard," Doug says. "Because I gotta admit, while it was hot, it also felt like… I don't know. Like I was playing a role. And what if I did it wrong?"

"You didn't," Max says.

"I had a different fear," I confess. "What if it made me more like my brother?"

"You're totally different from him, and I know that."

"Even though I hit him?"

"Even then," Max says.

We lapse into silence. My fingers trail up and down Max's chest, and he snuggles into both of us.

"I'm so excited for the Holiday-Off," Max says in a small voice. "But at the same time, I never want it to get here. Because then I have to…"

Leave. We let the unspoken word echo through the room. I can hear it banging against each one of the walls around us.

Max's breath catches slightly in his throat, and Doug gives me a small nod.

It's time for me to tell Max what we both agreed on downstairs earlier while Max was outside.

"Max," I say. "You matter to us. A lot. Both of us are really enjoying figuring out what we are to each other. But neither of us can imagine being together without *you*."

Now Max's eyes are filling with tears. Doug brushes them away from his cheek with a soft thumb.

"Zeke and I want to be together," he tells Max. "All three of us. We can try long-distance if you want to go back to DC. We know Vermont is a hard place for you to be, and I can't exactly leave La Fierte anytime soon. But we want to give this a shot. Whatever this is."

"You don't have to answer right now," I tell Max. "Take some time to think, okay? We just wanted you to know how we feel."

Max lets out something like a sob, but I think it's a happy sob. "You Vikings," he says, his voice strangled. "What kind of after-care is this? You're not supposed to ravage me and make me cry right afterwards!"

The three of us start laughing, and then we cuddle some more, and then we fucking go to sleep. Because it turns out being in a threesome is not only exciting, sexy as hell, and the most fulfilling thing that's ever happened to me—it's also *tiring*.

From the group chat "2 Vikings and their willing hostage"

DOUG

There's something I really want the three of us
to do.

MAX

Ohhh! Do tell! You know I'm always primed for
fantasy-fulfillment. ;)

DOUG

Oh no, it's not a fantasy

Well, maybe it is, but not a sexual one.

ZEKE

Tell us, babe.

DOUG

I want to hike up to Rocky Point.

ZEKE

That old trail north of town?

DOUG

Yeah. I've never gone up there. But it's where my
parents got married. Grandma showed me a
picture a long time ago. They carved their names
in a tree.

MAX

Oh, honey.

ZEKE

You never told me about that.

DOUG

I never wanted to see it. It felt too hard. But when
I think about going there with you two, I don't
know. It still feels hard, but in a good way. Does
that make sense?

ZEKE

Absolutely, babe.

MAX

[heart emoji] You just tell us when, and we'll go.

MAX

[heart emoji] You just tell us when, and we'll go.

CHAPTER 26

MAX

The morning after Zeke and Doug made my deepest, most secret fantasy come true—and then proposed a Serious Relationship with me—I wake up slightly worried that things might be awkward or feel strange between us. But Doug and Zeke are their usual selves, and we go through our usual morning routine. Doug makes coffee and eggs, Zeke tidies the bedroom and makes the bed, I drink caffeine and try not to be too grumpy while I wait for it to kick in.

In other words, everything is perfect. I collect the breakfast dishes while Zeke stretches his arms up over his head. "I'm going to go take a quick shower. Be right back." He jogs up the stairs while I finish placing mugs and forks into the dishwasher.

"How are you feeling?" I ask Doug. "Just three days until the Holiday-Off. And you seemed pretty upset about something back at the square yesterday."

Doug frowns and shakes his head. I know that look: he needs cuddles. "C'mon." I reach out my hand for his, and he takes it, following me into the living room. I push him down onto the couch and lie down so I can settle my head into his lap. He plays with my hair, curling it up gently in between his fingers.

"Spill," I tell him. "Are you okay?"

He sighs. "*Okay* might be a bit of an overstatement. Marty got creative to pay the Icebreakers' deposit, and now I've got to decide if we're going to stop payment on the check or not."

"Why would you need to do that?" I ask. "We've made enough money from the calendar to pay the Icebreakers."

Doug's body goes still, and he grips at my hair. "I'm sorry, what?"

I sit up and snuggle into his neck as I pull out my phone to show him the calendar's order updates. "We had a massive bulk order yesterday from a chain of Vermont tourist shops. You've got more than enough money to pay the deposit, and you're on track to pay the Icebreakers' entire bill with the calendar earnings."

Doug blinks. "Holy Guernseys," he murmurs.

I burst out laughing. "I don't know exactly what that means, but okay. You did it, Doug! I know you still haven't decided what to do about Vermonica, but you've got the money you need for the ice sculptors. There's every chance in the world we'll beat Atherton in the Holiday-Off."

Doug shakes his head in amazement as I set down my phone. "I guess there is," he whispers.

I sigh. "Have I told you how much I love the way La Fierte has come together for this Holiday-Off? It kind of reminds me of my favorite Pride festivals."

"I've never been to one of those," he says. "I don't think Zeke has either."

"Oh, I can't wait to pop your Pride fest cherries!" I snuggle up under his arm. "I know it might sound like an odd comparison—but the way the entire town has united to put on the Holiday-Off? Even after Atherton pulled their stunt with Vermonica and no one was sure you could win?" I grin. "It all really reminds me how Pride always feels. Pride's about everyone gathering together to say they love who they are and they love their community. It's all about people having pride in one another, I guess."

"I like that," Doug says softly. "I like that a lot."

I sigh. "It really is sad that Barton Asterstop's paper won't be a part of this community anymore. I know he's acted like an ass to you lately, but it sounds like he's always been a big part of the town pride here in La Fierte. I guess not everyone gets their holiday miracle, huh?"

Doug frowns and nods. He's not looking at me, though. Instead, he seems to be staring at some unknown spot on the wall across from us. Then he gently eases me away from his body as he kisses my cheek.

"Babe," he says. "I have to go do something." He stands like a man on a mission.

"Huh? What?" I ask him.

"You'll see."

"So, any idea why this mayor of yours is holding a surprise press conference?"

"Mom!" I throw my arms around her as she arrives next to me. "What are you doing here? I thought you had to work this afternoon."

She kisses my cheek. "I did, but the whole county's talking about this impromptu press conference Doug McEmbirk called. Especially since he said it was about the Holiday-Off and didn't include any other details. Seeing as how my son is one of the intrepid reporters covering said press conference, I had to come. How are you doing, sweetheart? Do you have any idea what this is about?"

I shake my head. "Nope. Doug won't tell me or Zeke anything." All I know is that in the few hours since Doug announced a "press conference critical to the La Fierte Holiday-Off," he's spent all his time holed up over at the town hall.

"I hope he's not planning any confessions that are going to get him arrested," Zeke muttered to me as the two of us drove over to the town square. Neither of us could rule that out, though. Every time we've texted or asked Doug we get the same response.

You'll see. Trust me.

Now, with the La Fierte square buzzing with people and a lectern set up on the gazebo in the center of the action, we're about to find out what Doug has planned along with the rest of the town.

"Well, then I guess we'll both learn things together today." Mom hugs me around the shoulders. "Now, tell me how you're doing. How's the writing going?"

"Really well. The same publication I'm writing for wants to give my entire Holiday-Off series top billing in the new year."

Mom beams. "Honey! I'm so proud of you. I can't wait for all the articles to be published." She kisses my cheek. "Of course, that means you'll leave again, and I'll be so sad to see you go. I wish I could keep you here forever!"

I blush. "You know," I tell her, "for the first time ever, I sort of want to stay."

Mom's eyebrows go up. "Tell me everything!"

So I do. How I became a love tutor for two giant Vikings and got more involved with them than any one of us probably intended. I tell her how much they've come to mean to me, and I tell her that they've invited me to be with them. And maybe stay here, if I want to.

Mom nods the entire time, never interrupting or judging. She's great that way. "Wow, sweetie," she says when I'm finished. "And you're thinking about it? You're considering moving back to Vermont?"

"I'm not sure." I shake my head. "You know what this place is like for me."

"I know," she says quietly. "Wish I could have done more for you back in school. A mother always wants to protect their child."

I take her gloved hand in mine and squeeze it. "I might be moving past all that now," I tell her. "I'm not sure. But I'm also worried: what if I am getting in the way of what the two of them could have together? And we never realize it, because I never leave?"

"Oh, Max-love." Mom's childhood nickname for me sends a wash of warmth through my limbs. "What if you leave and the three of you never realize what you could have been together?"

That question is like a jolt of icy water rushing over my head. I'm temporarily frozen in place, words stuck in my throat. Then I hear a grunt behind me. Zeke's back from his bathroom trip.

"Zeke! Meet my mom."

"Ah, the famous Zeke." Mom accepts his handshake. "I have to be honest and say I've never been the biggest fan of your brother. I hear you're a better version of the genes?"

I snort-laugh, and Zeke looks like he's trying not to smile. "I certainly do try to be, ma'am."

"Good." She pulls him into a hug that he definitely didn't ask for. "Then I look forward to watching you take excellent care of my son. I saw that black eye Jonah has, so I'm already convinced you'll be a good protector. Now, let's discuss important things. I hear Doug's set up an eggnog stand somewhere? Can someone tell me where that is?"

We send her in the right direction, and Zeke smiles at me. "Your mom is great."

"She is," I agree, smiling fondly after her. Then I narrow my eyes at Zeke. "Have you gotten anything out of Doug? Any idea what he's going to say?"

"Nope," he says. "And believe me, Doug is *not* good at keeping secrets. I'm sure that's why he's avoiding us. If he spends ten seconds with us, I bet he'd spill everything he has planned. Which makes me worry that he thinks we'll try to talk him out of whatever it is."

That statement is disconcerting. "Think we need to go find him? Convince him to tell us?"

Zeke frowns as he considers the questions. "No," he finally says. "Doug says he can handle this on his own. I believe in him."

I smile. "So do I."

Just then, Doug steps into the gazebo. The crowd gradually falls silent as they take notice of him too.

Zeke reaches out like he's thinking of taking my hand. Then he glances at the crowd around us and pulls back again.

Vulnerability really is hard. But he'll get there, my Viking pirate. I'm sure of it.

"Thank you all for being here this afternoon! I appreciate everyone making the time to come out to hear what I have to say." Doug's face is pink from the cold, but he looks calm as he speaks into the microphone. He's really good at this. I can see him getting somewhere in politics at a higher level—if he had any interest, that is.

I have a brief but vivid daydream of being a senator's husband. I think Zeke and I would bring a lot to the role, in our own special ways. The world could use some polyamory in its politics, I think.

"This afternoon," Doug continues, "I want to start by saying how thankful I am that Atherton and La Fierte are able to hold the Holiday-Off this year." His voice echoes through the square, clear and bright and earnest—quintessentially Doug. "I know this started off as a competition, a way to earn bragging rights. But for what it's worth, I think this competition has become a whole lot more than that."

The crowd murmurs its agreement.

"Someone recently reminded me what our town's name means: pride," Doug tells the audience. "And I know I'm *so* proud of the work we've done as a community to prepare for this event."

I can't help but preen a bit. Doug referenced my article!

"I'm proud of each and every one of us—each and every one of *you*—for coming together, helping each other out, donating decor and supplies, and volunteering your time, so that the Holiday-Off can be something La Fierte can be proud of. We might win, and we might lose, and that's okay. Because either way? We built this together, La Fierte. And what matters most isn't what anyone else thinks of what we built—what matters is what *we* think of what we built."

The crowd cheers loudly, vigorously. Doug waits for the applause to wane and then starts speaking again.

"But before the Holiday-Off kicks off a few days from now," he says, "I do have some important announcements to make. The first is that I've decided to cancel our final event of the Holiday-Off—the appearance of the renowned ice artists, the Icebreakers."

A rumbling of discontent rolls through the crowd, and Zeke stiffens next to me.

"As you know," Doug goes on, "the fire department volunteered to be featured in a calendar we've used to raise funds for the Icebreakers. We were proud to support La Fierte by doing what we could to benefit our community. But that money would be better spent in service of a much more important cause. A pillar of our community: *The Pigeon*."

"The newspaper?" a voice calls out incredulously.

"The newspaper," Doug answers. "Rent increases have given Mr. Asterstop no choice but to close his doors. But *The Pigeon* has been a part of this town for generations. And ever since they lost their own papers, other towns in the county have made it a part of their communities as well. *The Pigeon* has chronicled every good and bad and indifferent thing we've ever done here. It has kept us together through hard times." He glances around the crowd for a long moment. "And on occasion," he adds, "it has held mayors accountable for their choices."

His quip earns a few laughs, but it's clear the crowd isn't entirely on his side.

Doug goes on. "I can't in good conscience spend money on an event that will be over in a day when I could instead preserve a key part of La Fierte's past, present, and future. And so, we've paid the annual rent for *The Pigeon* for the next two years, and we will continue to look for a long-term funding solution. Which may or may not include another edition of a calendar." He smiles.

The crowd remains silent, as though everyone is collectively trying to figure out how to respond. Then someone behind me claps. Slowly, at first. Someone joins them, then someone else, and soon the entire crowd is clapping and cheering. Shouts of "Good choice, Mr. Mayor!" and "Way to save the paper!" echo through the audience.

"An actual slow clap," I murmur to Zeke, as I clap as loudly as I can with mittens on. "I thought they only happened in movies."

"Now," says Doug, after the applause has diminished enough for him to be heard. "I have one more announcement to make. Not long ago, someone left something in my garage. Something that they said would help us even the Holiday-Off playing field with Atherton."

"Oh, shit," Zeke whispers.

"I've gone back and forth on what to do with this item in my garage," Doug tells the crowd. "Frankly, it's become quite the monkey on my back," he adds. "Except, it's, uh, not a monkey. Well, yesterday I realized that there's no way I can ever let La Fierte win the Holiday-Off because I didn't play fair. This town has too much pride for that—and *I* have too much pride in our community. So I'm coming clean right now. I'll show you what I found in my garage, and then I'm taking it straight to Atherton." He steps down the stairs of the gazebo.

"Wait, did he say he'd *show us*?" I hiss at Zeke. "Is she actually *here*?"

Zeke gulps. "Doug never does anything halfway. Including confessional press conferences, apparently. I really hope Deputy fucking Johnson isn't here right now," he murmurs.

Me too. I hold my breath as Doug returns to the stage, a long length of rope in his hand. He gently urges Vermonica—who I am not surprised to see doesn't love stairs; she's a bit of a diva—up onto the stage next to him.

I swear, the crowd gasps in *complete unison*, then breaks out into borderline hysterics as they recognize Vermonica.

I'm a Vermonter *and* a personal friend of Vermonica, but even I can't understand how there's *this* much hype about a Holstein with questionable eating habits.

"It's her—Vermonica!"

"How is she here? In La Fierte?"

"Look, it's her maple leaf!"

My heart's pounding so hard in my chest I'm honestly amazed it hasn't popped out in front of my body. Zeke looks like he's fighting every urge to rush the gazebo and hold the crowd back from Doug if he needs to.

Doug rubs Vermonica's neck and leans into the lectern to speak into the mic again, his face solemn. "I was told that whoever left her with me had authority to deliver her, and I confirmed that no one at the Capitol was looking for her. But regardless, I don't want to be the reason that she doesn't appear in Atherton for the Holiday-Off. They booked her, for better or worse, and that's where she should be."

"Wait!" Jemima Ackerman calls out. "That can't be Vermonica!" She holds up her phone. "Vermonica's already in Atherton. My cousin just posted pics on Instagram! Her handlers brought her to town early."

Phones pop out of pockets across the crowd as everyone investigates. I'm no exception. Sure enough, when I pull up Atherton's Instagram page, I see dozens of photos of a cow sporting a very distinct maple leaf patch right on her stomach.

"If *that's* Vermonica," Zeke murmurs next to me, "who's the MVB?"

And that's when it happens. *It.* A moment that will certainly live in La Fierte infamy. Doug whirls around to face Vermonica, his eyes widening in surprise. "What the fuck?" he says.

Right into the mic.

From the group chat "2 Vikings and their willing hostage"

MAX

OMG Zeke and Doug are the sweetest sexiest guys ever

ZEKE

M, I'm guessing you meant to send that to Reyna

MAX

Nope! Just reminding you both that you're awesome

DOUG

AWWWW NO YOU'RE AWESOME

ZEKE

You two are about to start blowing up the chat with emojis, aren't you?

MAX

[long string of multi-colored heart emojis]

DOUG

[long string of heart-eye emojis]

ZEKE

I mean, FINE.

[long string of kissy-face emojis]

MAX

I knew we'd break him eventually, Doug.

CHAPTER 27
DOUG

"Well." Deputy Eric Johnson crosses his arms. "The sheriff may be willing to give you the benefit of the doubt, but if it were up to *me*, I'd arrest all three of you right now."

"What for?" Jemima Ackerman stops scrubbing at the dyed hair on not-Vermonica's belly and puts her hands on her hips. "We don't even know who this cow belongs to, for goodness' sake." She shakes her head and stares wistfully at the fading maple leaf on Vermonica's side, which looks more and more like it's been ripped in half as Jemima continues to scrub with a solution she concocted from warm water and vinegar. "Imagine," she mutters. "Giving a dye job to a cow to make us all think it's our state mascot!"

Eric snorts. "Sure seems like theft of some kind happened here. You're the mayor, Doug. Can't believe you let yourself get mixed up in all this."

I drop my head down between my knees. Someone pats my back comfortingly. "Put yourself in our shoes," Max says. "You read the letter! We didn't know what to do. And Doug *did* check with the capitol. They confirmed she wasn't missing."

"He *says* he checked, but he won't name his source," Eric says wryly.

"Listen." Zeke's voice is far less patient than Max's. I've still got my head in my lap, so I can't see his face, but I'm guessing it's his I Am Two Seconds Away From Running Over You face. "Eric, I get that you want to break a big case here, but the most heinous crime committed today was Doug McEmbirk swearing for the first time in his life over a hot mic. Other than that? Nothing's happened. Someone needs to reclaim a cow. That's it."

"They should own up to a pretty darn good paint job, too," Jemima says cheerfully. I glance up and watch as she finishes wiping down not-Vermonica's belly with a soft cloth. The white expanse is almost painfully blank now. "Think I got it all off. I'll head out now. Whoever did this has got some good artistic skills."

Not-Vermonica moos, as if in agreement. Ever since we got her back into our garage she's been content to chew on her favorite hay and look on while Deputy Johnson interrogates me, Zeke, and Max.

I'm tired of hearing the men in my life defending me, especially when I don't deserve defending. I stand from the haybale where I've been sitting and wave to Jemima as she leaves. Now it's only the four of us here in the garage. "Eric, consider this me turning myself in—for whatever you need to arrest me for. Unlawful bovine possession. Using a swear word in public in front of small children. Failure to report a possible cow-napping. Or, my personal favorite, being a complete disaster of a mayor."

"You're not a disaster of a mayor!" Max throws his arms around my neck.

"Definitely not," Zeke agrees. "But Eric, you're a fucking disaster of a deputy right now."

Eric squares his shoulders and opens his mouth. I'm preparing to spend the night in jail with Zeke when the garage door swings open and Barton Asterstop rushes through.

"I confess!" Barton manages, panting with exertion. "I confess to it all. I'm the culprit. The cow belongs to my niece. She uses the dye on her show animals, and I asked her to dye this one with Vermonica's markings as a joke for a friend. Then I borrowed a rig and trailered her over here when I knew the mayor and his friends would be away and placed her in the garage with a note." He leans down, wheezing. "I hope the county jail has an oxygen supply. I swear the hill outside of this house gets steeper each year."

I grab a small bottle of water from the garage's minifridge and thrust it at Barton. "Here, drink this. And what on earth are you talking about?"

"He tried to frame you, is what he's saying," Eric tells Doug, scratching his head as he turns back to Barton. "Didn't Doug just save your paper? Why were you trying to frame him?"

Now Barton scowls. "First of all, Deputy, I wasn't framing him for anything! But if the question is why did I resort to such, erm, extreme measures, then the answer is that I wanted to prove once and for all that he doesn't care about the town, only the superficial *glory* of winning a silly contest." Barton pushes himself upright, still wheezing, and I hold onto his elbow just in case he needs the support. "I left the cow here to see how the mayor would react. If he would knowingly sabotage Atherton in the contest, then I had plans for an exposé. I thought I'd show the town that he's not a mayor we can trust."

Barton turns to look at me. "My ridiculous plot failed, of course. You told the truth."

I wince. "It took me a while."

"Still. You did not yield to temptation. And even setting aside all… cow-related matters… I realize I was wrong about your motivations. Don't get me wrong, I still think you were foolish to spend exorbitant amounts of the town's money on inflatable penguins," he says, pointing a gloved finger at me.

"But they're *caroling* inflatable penguins," Max protests. "They have inflatable sheet music! And inflatable stocking caps!"

"They are the most ridiculous thing I have ever seen in my very long life," Barton tells Max evenly, and then meets my eye again. "Still. You didn't want to win for the sake of winning, like one of your hockey matches. You wanted to bring this town joy.

Togetherness." He frowns. "My niece may have seen one of the videos of you bringing that cow on stage. She gave me quite a piece of her mind."

Max coughs. "So, your change of heart doesn't have anything to do with Doug saving your paper tonight?"

Barton leans on me as he pulls himself upright. "Well, it didn't hurt. Without the rent to squeeze into our budget, we'll not only stay open, we'll be able to expand our coverage. Keep giving folks a place to get their news other than that TikkerTokker."

"TikkerTokker?" Max says in a strangled voice.

Barton nods solemnly. "Yes. But putting aside the mayor's newspaper heroics, I can also admit when I've done wrong." He sighs. "I was just so determined to prove you were a fraud, Mayor McEmbirk. That day I stopped by your house and acted as though I wasn't sure where a cow on your property might be—that was all a ruse, of course, to see if my plot was working. I'm ashamed now when I look back on my behavior. Clearly, I've taken my own struggles out on you in an unfair and borderline ridiculous manner."

We all turn to look at not-Vermonica, who's chewing serenely in the corner.

"Okay, let me get this straight." Eric peers down at the notepad in his hand with a wrinkled brow. "The cow was *not* cow-napped?"

"She was borrowed," Barton clarifies. "With permission."

"And you were trying to make people think Doug cow-napped her?"

"No, I was trying to make *the mayor* think that someone else cow-napped—no, I'm not using that silly word—that someone else *stole* her."

"But she wasn't stolen," Eric mutters, glancing up and looking more confused than ever.

"No! She was *borrowed* with *permission*," Zeke repeats, and Barton nods. "What he *didn't* have permission to do was to leave a large, destructive animal on Doug's property and let her destroy shit until we found her."

I watch Eric's eyes slowly narrow and imagine the galaxy brain meme. After a second he shakes his head. "I don't know what the hell it is, but there's definitely at least one crime being committed in that scenario. Mister Astertop, I'll need to take you into custody while we sort this all out. Please come with me, and we'll—"

"No," I interrupt.

"Huh?" Eric wrinkles his nose. "Come on. The only part of this that's clear is that this guy tried to set you up for *something.*"

"He did." I purse my lips as I study Barton. Just a few days ago, I couldn't think of the guy, much less look at him, without hearing some of the most biting lines in his articles about me.

Now, though? All I see is a member of my community who needed help and wasn't getting it. Someone who thought he was going to lose everything and then lashed out. Someone my community needs, flaws and all.

"I don't want to press charges of any kind," I go on. "Let's put this all behind us, okay? It's the holiday season. The Holiday-Off is in a few days, and the town is going to celebrate. Win or lose." I glance over at not-Vermonica again, and then to Zeke and Max, who are both smiling faintly at me. "We can't celebrate togetherness if one of our most well-known citizens is sitting in the tank. He's got local reporting to do, after all."

Barton looks at me solemnly. "Thank you, Mayor."

"Okay, whatever." Eric shakes his head. "If that's what you really want. What are we doing about this cow, though?"

"I can get her sorted out," Barton says. "And I can pay for any damage done to your garage," he tells me, then hesitates. "Though I may have to make payments over time."

"You don't need to pay for anything," I'm quick to say. "She just made a little mess, that's all. Zeke was exaggerating." I ignore Zeke's grumbles. "I can help you take her home. Your niece is probably missing her."

"Not at all, actually. She's an odd cow. Doesn't fit in at all with the others. My niece had put her up for sale, which is why I chose her for my little… project."

My eyes widen as I look over at not-Vermonica, her eyes half-closed and a string of green drool trailing from her lower lip as she enjoys another bite of alfalfa. "She's going to be *sold*? To who?"

"To *whom*, you mean," Barton corrects me. "And heck if I know who will buy her. I only know that she's for sale."

"How much?" Max asks, rushing over to not-Vermonica's pen to rub between her ears. "I'll take her."

"That is not how you negotiate a sale," Zeke tells Max, but I can see he's trying not to smile.

Barton blinks. "You want to keep her?"

"*Yes*, we do," I say emphatically. "Not here, though," I rush to add. "I'm aware of the zoning issues, don't you worry, Mr. Asterstop."

"If that's the case, then she's yours. It's the least I can do to make amends. I'll settle up with my niece."

Max claps, then slings an arm around not-Vermonica's neck and leans against her side. "You hear that, Ver—actually, what's her real name?"

Barton says, "It's Sorbet."

Zeke turns to stare at him. "Sorbet… as in, sorbet the food?"

"Like Sherbert," I murmur, floored.

Barton shrugs. "I guess it is."

"Oh my," Max murmurs. "Maybe some things really are meant to be."

From the group chat "2 Vikings and their willing hostage"

ZEKE

Being on shift when everyone else is conked out
and I can't sleep is the worst

DOUG

Too bad we're on opposite shifts this week. I'd
entertain you!

MAX

[gif of someone drooling]

We'll keep you company, babe

[Photo attachment]

ZEKE

Sheesh, now you're just making me wish I
was home

DOUG

We're already drawing up plans for how to make
it up to you the second you walk in this door

ZEKE

[gif of countdown timer]

CHAPTER 28
DOUG

"No, Sorbet," Max groans, tugging at her lead. "You can't eat that! *Or* that!"

He manages to drag the Holstein away from the Wise Men in the nativity on the Tesfayes's lawn, and then the giant candy cane decoration strapped to their mailbox.

I rock back and forth on my heels, containing the urge to go and help. "You got her?"

"For the twentieth time, *yes*," Max says, huffing and puffing a little as Sorbet relents and follows him along the street. "But I am glad we're almost back home."

After the big reveal, we don't have to keep Sorbet hidden. So we've been trying to give her more exercise to make up for all those days she was cooped up in the garage. I'm not sure she really cares about the change of scenery, but it does feel good to know she's at least stretching her legs.

I know we've made the right choice deciding to board her at the Stock Farm as soon as they can free up some space. She's going to love Jeb's open fields and wide pastures.

I hurry ahead to open the garage door. Sorbet lifts her head, her sleepy eyes getting wider, as she spots her hay pile. She practically drags Max after her inside, but he's laughing, not complaining, as I close the door behind us.

"Are we ready?" Zeke asks a couple minutes later, appearing with a giant bowl of popcorn and a handful of candy canes. We found out that Sorbet *really* likes them, and I hope cows can't get cavities, because we've been feeding them to her almost constantly ever since.

"Yes!" Max says brightly. "Cow-inclusive movie night, take two." He plops down in the middle of the three lawn chairs, naturally, and unfolds a blanket. Zeke puts the popcorn in Max's lap, then takes his chin in one hand and kisses him. I love the look Max gives him when they break apart—surprised, warm, and happy. I want him to feel that way all the time.

Zeke brushes his hand across my back as he passes, then studies me while he holds out the candy cane bouquet for Sorbet. "Tomorrow's the big day. How are you feeling?"

It's not that I *forgot* that tomorrow was the Holiday-Off. It would be impossible, considering that today I spent ten hours straight working through the last-minute details with Marty. But hearing Zeke mention it out loud does make my heart race for a second.

"I'm nervous," I admit. "I want everything to go well. But I know I did everything I could." I shrug. "It'll be what it'll be."

Zeke smiles and puts his arms around me. I'm surprised, and he must feel the tension in my body, because he pulls back to look at my face, his smile fading. "What is it?"

I shake my head, pulling us together again. "I don't think you've ever hugged me before—you know. Lately," I say, my chin hooked over his shoulder.

"That is false," he says flatly. "We've hugged a thousand times."

"I hugged *you* a thousand times."

He snorts, but he wraps his arms around me again, more tightly. "Then it sounds like I have some making up to do."

I relax into the feeling of Zeke's arms, strong and safe, and the *thud* of his heart that I can feel against my chest, and the hard columns of his thighs pressed to mine. And then I'm not exactly relaxed, because *jeez*, his body is so close and warm and…

We simultaneously lean our heads back so we can stare at each other. Zeke's face looks the way I feel: very surprised.

Because where we're tightly pressed together, hip to hip, I'm getting hard, and so is he.

Zeke's surprised expression turns into one that I've only seen before when Max is in the middle. It's one that *smolders*. My breath hitches, and we both lean in, perfectly in sync. As we kiss, Zeke grasps my butt, pulling me even harder against him.

When we separate, we're panting.

"I'm sorry, girl," Max informs Sorbet as he hops up from his chair. "But movie night is canceled. Again. Vikings, in the house. I need you upstairs. Naked. Now."

We don't waste any time.

A while later, I'm on my back, Max is sprawled on top of me, and Zeke just climbed off the bed where he'd been kneeling between my knees. He heads to the bathroom for a washcloth to clean us up.

I rub a hand up and down Max's sweaty back. "How do you feel, sweetheart?" I ask softly.

His face is buried in my shoulder, but he raises his head to answer my question. "I feel like I have no bones."

"How did reality compare to the fantasy?" Zeke asks, returning from the bathroom. He climbs back onto the bed, and Max rolls off of me so Zeke can wipe the come off my stomach and from between Max's legs.

"Reality slayed my fantasy yet again," Max says happily. "You two are amazing. When can we play 'good top, bad top' again?"

"Whenever you want," I say.

Zeke chuckles, and I lean over to kiss Max softly on the lips while Zeke leaves the bed once more, probably to toss the washcloth in the laundry hamper.

"Hey, Doug," he calls from the other side of the room. His voice is low, almost upset. "What the fuck is this?"

I push myself up on my elbow. It takes a second to focus on whatever Zeke is asking me, because the moon is shining through the bedroom window, and it makes Zeke's naked body look like a work of art.

"Uh," I manage, blinking, and notice that Zeke is holding the jeans I just stripped off in one hand, and a folded piece of newspaper in the other.

"I thought we agreed you weren't going to carry this around," Zeke says.

Max sits up. "Oh, babe." He puts his hand on my chest. "I thought you'd gotten over that article."

"I'm never going to get over that article," I say, sitting up the rest of the way. "How could I? Zeke, maybe you should take another look."

Max puts his arm around me and cuddles into my side. Zeke looks back down at the article, and after a moment, his scowl relaxes.

"I see what you mean," he says. "Anybody who reads this would have to believe that every word of it is true."

"Zeke!" Max exclaims.

"What?" Zeke asks. "He's an extremely talented writer."

Max is adamant. "He's not *that* talented."

"I have to agree with Zeke on this one," I say as Zeke walks back to the bed and holds out the article. I take it and hand it to Max. "He's the most talented person I know."

Max gives me a last astonished glance before turning his eyes on the article. Then he laughs as he reads his own words on the page. "You two are terrible." He bites his lip as he looks up. "You've really been carrying this around in your pocket?"

I nod, taking the article back from him and carefully refolding it. "I told you it meant a lot to me, didn't I?"

Max nods. Zeke gets into bed on his other side, and once I have the article safely on the nightstand, we settle into our usual positions—Max on his side, facing me, his knee between my thighs. Zeke tucked behind him, a hand splayed on his hip, and the other one curved over Max's pillow. I link my fingers with Zeke's and push a lock of hair out of Max's face with my other hand.

"I can't thank you enough. Both of you. Zeke for standing behind me for all these years when I couldn't really trust myself. Max for coming here and proving to me that I could. I love you both so much."

Zeke squeezes my fingers. Max smiles and wriggles closer, then lays a row of three quick little kisses on my cheek and two more on my chin.

My eyes widen. "Oh, was I not supposed to say that yet?"

Zeke snorts, and Max smiles.

"You're supposed to say it whenever you want to say it," Max tells me warmly.

"Of course Doug said it first," Zeke says gruffly. "He's fearless."

I frown. "What do you mean? What is there to be afraid of?"

"Technically, you told Doug you loved him first," Max reminds Zeke, twisting to look over his shoulder. "Don't sell yourself short. You are very fucking brave."

Zeke's scowl softens as he gazes at Max. "You're the brave one."

Max rolls his eyes, but he's blushing a little, and he looks pleased.

"I have to agree with Zeke," I say. "You're amazing. I should thank Barton for writing that article, because if he hadn't, we might never have met."

"That's probably true," Max murmurs. "I hadn't thought about it like that."

I touch my thumb to his cheek, then the tip of his nose. "I

know you haven't decided if you'll stay here," I tell Max. "But either way, I'm glad you know how I feel."

Zeke strokes from Max's hip to his thigh and kisses his shoulder. "I love you too. Both of you." His eyes meet mine as he presses another kiss against Max's skin, this time his neck.

"You don't have to say anything if you don't want to," Zeke murmurs into Max's ear. Max closes his eyes for a moment, and suddenly I realize what they meant—why telling someone you love them can make you afraid.

Because what if they don't say it back?

Before I can panic, Max opens his eyes. He smiles at me, then Zeke. "I love you. And you. I love *us*. You know?"

Zeke and I nod silently. I squeeze Zeke's hand again and swallow the lump in my throat, kiss Max's temple and breathe him in. I've said it before and I'll say it again: nobody is better with words than Max Rivers.

"Okay, team." Marty claps his hands together, frowning at the crowd of tiny humans before him. "Maybe you've been told that tonight is all about having fun. Holiday cheer. Community. And don't get me wrong—it is." He takes a deep breath and puts his hands on his hips. "But tonight is also about something else that's very important: *winning*."

Nina Burton, who's standing in the front row of the La Fierte Elementary School Choir, raises her hand. "Mr. Marty?"

Marty closes his eyes. That's his I'm Trying to Be Patient but I Don't Feel Patient face. I know it well—he uses that one on me all the time. "Yes, Nina?"

"What if I have to pee-pee while the judges are watching the show?"

"You have to hold it," Jamira Aldez informs her. "Mom says we have to beat Atherton! They beat us at basketball one year while she was in high school, and she's still really mad about it."

"My dad said they stole our town's Easter Bunny costume once!"

"Wait, is the Easter Bunny just a costume?"

"My sister says we have to beat them because it means we'll get more tourism money. What's tourism money?"

"Mr. Marty, what do we get if we win? Do we get a pony? I want a pony. Or a drone."

Marty's getting a wild look in his eyes now. I decide it might be best if I step in before we end up with a sobbing bunch of children and no act to open the La Fierte Holiday-Off Extravaganza.

"Okay, kiddos." I give the fifteen kids in front of me my best smile as I kneel down in front of them. "Here's the thing. We want to win the Holiday-Off. But we don't really want to win the Holiday-Off for money or because of basketball or ponies. You know why we *really* want to win the Holiday-Off?"

"Why?" Jamira asks.

"Because we love La Fierte!" I say, throwing my arms out wide. "And when you love something, you want to give it your best effort. Right?"

"Oh, okay." Nina nods. "Like when my dad takes his blue pill before bed because he says Papa deserves the best he's got."

Next to me, Marty quietly chokes on his next breath. "Yes, Nina," I say calmly, "Just like that. We all want to be the best singers we can be for La Fierte tonight, right?"

"Yeah!" The munchkins cheer in unison, and I give them high-fives. Maybe they will make it through their rendition of "Frosty the Snowman" without any potty accidents after all.

"Great!" I give them another smile. "Then follow Mr. Marty over to the gazebo and he'll get you all set up." The kids line up like ducklings behind Marty, giggling and poking each other. They're all decked out in bright red snow jackets and green pants, and I do have to admit they look cute as heck.

I take a moment to appreciate the scene we've managed to create. We, meaning the whole town. I've seen La Fierte come together as a community before—I mean, no one holds a barn raising like La Fierte—but what we've pulled off for the Holiday-Off judging day is pretty darn spectacular.

Main Street is glittering with string lights of every shape, size, and color. They're wrapped around and strung between every lamppost, guiding visitors into the blocked-off area of the street where there are booths for everything from gourmet hot chocolate to maple Christmas trees to tiny knit stocking ornaments that read "HOLIDAY-OFF: LA FIERTE" in miniscule letters. Tables wrapped in Christmas paper are heaped with supplies and instructions for holiday arts and crafts projects—that's something the Stock Tree Farm did at their carnival a few years ago that everyone seemed to enjoy, so we borrowed the idea.

Volunteers in elf costumes are passing out maps of downtown that point out all the activities and photo ops. Massive dreidels and cows in Santa hats and reindeer have taken over basically every inch of real estate we could find. The stage and the gazebo in the center of the square are both wired for sound, and Grandma's friend Stewart Pash set up fancy-schmancy stage lights that look all kinds of professional when they're lit up over the performers. Thank goodness we haven't had a big snowstorm yet this season. We didn't have a contingency plan if we ended up with three feet of snow the week before Christmas. Folks have been working overtime to shovel away the snow we have gotten, and the hardware store donated a few big heaters to place around the rows of folding chairs to make sure people don't get too chilly during the performances.

And boy, do we have some excellent performances lined up. The United Congregational Church choir, of course, followed by the elementary school choir. The local dance studio is also doing a big number.

The judges will be watching it all—and hopefully deciding that our celebration is better than Atherton's.

"You did great, babe."

Zeke's low voice is in my ear now. I turn around to find him standing there, in his puffy black ski jacket and an old knit hat with our college's logo on it. His eyes are shining under the street-lights, his cheeks red with the chill of the air, and I just want to grab hold of him and kiss him. Hard.

It's strange. There was a time when I wouldn't have ever imagined wanting Zeke's lips against mine. Now that's all my brain can focus on as I lean forward.

Zeke's still not really comfortable with PDA, but we're standing behind the gazebo right now, and no one's in our general vicinity. He pulls me close against him, our coats bumping into each other like we're two giant stuffed animals. Kissing outside in Vermont in winter comes with all kinds of practical challenges, that's for sure. But none of that really matters much as our lips dance in time with one another and quick spikes of joy flash through my body.

I don't want to let go of him, but I know it's getting close to the time when the judges arrive and the Extravaganza performances start. "Is Atherton's judging over?" I ask when we finally manage to pull away from each other.

Zeke nods. "Max is on the phone with his mom right now. She said it went pretty well, which fucking sucks." Zeke scowls. "Ver-monica was a huge hit. Sounds like the judges kept saying they couldn't believe Atherton pulled out all the stops to get her."

I nod and take a deep breath. We knew that winning tonight would be an uphill battle, but we're going to fight. Everyone in La Fierte is ready for the challenge, and we're not going to lose to Atherton lying down.

Max comes jogging over to us, and Zeke and I take turns leaning down so he can peck us on the cheeks before he pulls his bright green scarf up tighter around his neck and face. "Well," he says, "right now everyone's betting on Atherton to win. But Doug, you did an amazing job! La Fierte looks fantastic." He wraps his arms around me in a quick hug and then releases me. "If you don't win, I'm totally writing that La Fierte was robbed."

Zeke snorts and pulls Max against him while he kisses the top of his head. "Always good to have a journalist on your side."

Max shrugs and looks around, sniffling against the cold as he studies the lights and sounds around us. "Winter Wonderland" is playing over the speakers. "You ready to speak to this crowd? Again?" he teases.

"Can't go worse than last time," I joke. I turn to look at the microphone positioned dead in the center of the stage. "I'll try not to say any four-letter words in front of everyone this time."

"Cows?" Max asks innocently.

"Fork?" Zeke adds.

"Funny." I lean over to kiss them each gently as Marty appears on the side of the stage, gesturing at me. "Looks like it's time," I tell them as I squeeze their shoulders and head up the short flight of stairs to the stage.

"You've got this!" Zeke calls after me.

The spotlights on the stage are warm as heck, and I actually had to take off my down jacket to kick off this extravaganza. But even standing in front of the giant crowd that's gathered here right now, I'm not nervous. I know what I need to tell all these folks, and I'm ready to say the words.

"Thank you all for being here tonight."

"Hi, Mister Mayor!" Jemima Ackerman waves at me from the back of the crowd. Max and Zeke are off to the side of the gazebo, staying as close as they can without physically being on the stage. Toward the back of the crowd I think I might see Jonah and Shay, but I can't be sure. Marty's on the other side of the gazebo whispering to Samara.

I can't help but chuckle to myself. I wonder if he'll ever work up the nerve to ask her out.

"I said a lot of important things about this celebration at my press conference the other day," I tell everyone. "So I won't get too repetitive this time. I just quickly wanted to touch on something I started to talk about that afternoon: pride."

I see some surprise, now, on the faces of folks in the crowd, particularly the judges in the front row. Supposedly they're an impartial group of people from around the county, but I saw the

Atherton mayor's cousin come in with them. Once upon a time that might have bothered me. Right now I don't much care.

"Sometimes," I tell the crowd, "I think we can get real hung up on what other people think. We start to believe that our pride has to come from those other people." I glance at Max and Zeke. "But lately I've figured out that true pride comes from places a whole lot closer to home. Pride can come from loving ourselves. Loving the journey we're on. It can come from feeling the love we share with the people we know and care about the most."

Max wipes a tear out of the corner of his eye, and I'll be darned if Zeke doesn't reach up to swipe at his face too.

Dang. I don't think I've seen Zeke cry since we were teens.

"So whatever happens tonight, La Fierte," I say, "I just want you to know that I'm proud to represent you. But more than that, I hope you're proud of yourselves. I hope you're proud of all the wonderful memories we've built here tonight. Because win or lose, those memories are what will matter most in the years to come."

I step off the stage to what I guess might be a standing ovation. Zeke hugs me from one side, and Max hops up and down excitedly on the other, pulling himself up to kiss my cheek. "We're proud of you, too, Mr. Mayor!" a loud voice calls.

"Was that Barton?" Max asks, incredulously.

Maybe it was, and maybe it wasn't. All I know is that not a single La Fierte Elementary School singer needs to go potty during "Frosty the Snowman." All I know is that later, when the judges announce that Atherton won the Holiday-Off, nobody in La Fierte really seems to care.

We're all too busy dancing and eating and singing and being together.

Then the local dance troupe takes the stage, and Zeke's eyes nearly bug out.

"No way," he whispers. "Is that Shay?"

MAX

So, just putting it out there: you two ever wear short shorts?

ZEKE

You'd think by now I'd be used to you asking questions like this out of nowhere.

MAX

I am who I am, babe [gif of person throwing confetti and dancing]

DOUG

I'd wear short shorts for you, Max!

ZEKE

I would consider it. Only if you chose the cut, of course.

MAX

[gif of person jumping up and down excitedly]

DOUG

[picture attachment]

MAX

WAIT YOU ALREADY OWN SOME?!

CHAPTER 29

MAX

"What. The. Actual. Fuck."

Zeke's staring at the stage, his eyes wider than I've ever seen them. I swear, his mouth is actually *hanging open.*

"Oh wow! That really is Shay!" I'm shocked to see that Zeke's right: the kid on the left side of the stage, wearing a purple tutu, a bright red ski jacket, and reindeer antlers, the one twirling in perfect time to Mariah's "All I Want for Christmas is You," is undeniably Zeke's nephew.

"He's got great moves," Doug says. "Excellent balance must run in the family." He nudges Zeke gently in the side.

"Am I hallucinating?" I ask, squinting toward the stage. "The last time you and Jonah talked about Shay dancing, you ended up punching him, Zeke!"

"Yup. He sure did," says a low voice.

I nearly choke on the sip of eggnog I've just taken. Jonah James is standing behind us.

At least seeing him next to Zeke is far less of a mindfuck than it used to be because now it's easy to tell them apart. Zeke's hard, grouchy shell protects the most sensitive heart I've ever known. Jonah is the opposite, a veneer of charm hiding what I always thought of as darkness, but have lately come to suspect is mostly insecurity and self-loathing. I don't have any idea if he can be redeemed, but I would like to hope so. Him letting Shay dance in a purple tutu is a pretty good start.

The song comes to an end and the kids take dramatic bows. Shay's is more of a curtsy, and a very solid one at that. He's been practicing, for sure. The instant the instructor dismisses the kids, Shay runs straight over to us. "Dad, Uncle Zeke, did you see me?" He tugs excitedly at Jonah's jacket and then Zeke's glove. "Did you see me dancing on the stage?"

"I did, kiddo." Jonah lifts Shay up into a hug and then sets him down. "You did good. Real good."

"Okay, I'm definitely hallucinating," I mutter.

"Can I talk to you, Max?" Jonah asks, and I give him a point for not reflexively calling me Maxi.

I don't hesitate. I know Doug and Zeke have my back, but I don't need them to fight my battles for me. Not only do I think Jonah *won't* hurt me, I also think he *can't* hurt me anymore. I've returned to Vermont and let go of some old memories while creating new ones. I can be the person who once had to worry the world would never accept me, and I can also cherish being lucky enough to find so many people who love me just as I am.

I give Jonah my most magnanimous, and likely supercilious, gaze. "Sure."

Zeke and Doug send me simultaneous nods. "Hey, Shay," says Zeke. "How about Uncle Doug and I take you to find some hot chocolate?"

"Yes please!" he chirps. They each take one of his hands, and the three of them wander toward the food stalls, my giant Vikings flanking the boy in the purple tutu.

I'd pull my camera out and snap a picture if I wasn't busy trying to figure out how to handle the externalization of my childhood trauma.

Jonah jerks his head to the side, indicating that he wants to talk in private, so I follow him to a quiet area behind the gazebo.

Fairy lights cast quick, jumping shadows around us while three life-size nutcracker dolls look on.

Jonah runs a hand through his thick, dark hair. "Look," he says. "What you said, the day Zeke punched me? You were right."

I take another swig of eggnog, because more alcohol sure isn't going to hurt this conversation. "I'm sorry?" I say.

He shrugs. "You were right. I've been worrying about Shay, about him growing up and getting treated like shit because of who he is and who he wants to be. I'm worried somebody will treat him like I treated you. What I did is not okay. It wasn't then, and it isn't now." He shakes his head. "I know it's been a lot of years, and it's probably too late to be saying all this. But you coming back here, and then saying what you said to me, has really got me thinking about a lot of things. So I wanted to say that you were right. And I'm sorry."

"I can honestly say that I have no idea how the fuck to respond to that," I tell him evenly.

He shrugs. "I can't blame you for that. But I needed to say it." He turns to walk away.

"Jonah," I call. He turns around again, and I go on. "Zeke's told me a little bit about his—your—childhood. I know things weren't easy for you back then. But you really did fuck me up. Recently it hasn't been getting to me as much, but for years, I couldn't even visit my mother without feeling jumpy out in public and having awful nightmares about all the bad shit. But nowadays, I have some much better memories to replace you." I glance over toward the food stands, where I can see Doug paying a hot cocoa vendor and Zeke managing to hold several cups in his enormous hands.

Jonah nods. "That's fair. I don't expect you to forgive me—"

"I have. Forgiving you is a present for me, not you."

Jonah looks completely startled. He stares at me for a long few seconds, frowning. "Can I ask you a question?" he finally says.

"You can try," I tell him. "I'm not making any promises that I'll answer."

He glances over in the direction of Doug and Zeke. "Are those two together now? And are you… with them? Like, um, that way?"

"Like *dating*?" I say, and I take a moment to enjoy the way he squirms at the word. "We're still figuring that out," I finally tell him.

Jonah frowns. "So Zeke's gay?"

"That's not really my information to share, Jonah."

"Yeah, I guess not." He swallows hard, looking at the ground and then back up at me. "If you're here to stay for good, I hope maybe you won't mind being around for Shay the way Zeke is. I think you'd be good for him, Max." He shrugs. "I'm not always the best dad, but I do try. Shay's the most important thing in the entire world to me." Jonah looks over toward the hot chocolate stand again, and this time his eyes glisten with wetness.

Holy fucking shitballs. Is Jonah James *crying* in front of me?

Holiday miracles never cease.

"If I stick around," I say, "then yes, I'd love to be part of Shay's life. He seems like a great kid. And for what it's worth, letting him perform, and express himself, makes me believe that you want to do right by him."

Jonah wipes at his eyes. "I do. I really do. I know it doesn't mean much, but thank you. For helping me to see how I might be able to do that a little better." He smiles, a small, wistful smile. "He looked so happy on that stage tonight. Way happier than he ever looks playing hockey."

"He did look very happy," I agree.

Jonah clears his throat. "Yeah. Well. So. I'm going to talk to Zeke next. Tell him that I plan to cut Dad out of my life. I don't want his shit around my son, you know? That punch really was a wake-up call for me. It's time for a lot of changes."

I shake my head. "Wow, Jonah. You and Zeke are going to have a lot to talk about."

"I know. Anyway," Jonah goes on. "Maybe you and I can be—I dunno. Friends? Or something?"

I don't want to be a dick and say no, so I give him a noncommittal shrug. If cows can appear in garages, pigs might be able to fly.

"Maybe with the spirit of the holidays, we can agree to move on," I finally tell him. "It's a new year soon enough, and it's time for a fresh start."

Jonah nods. "Thank you. And I really mean that. Thank you, Max. For letting me say all that. Without punching me or anything."

I snort-laugh. "Don't think I didn't consider it."

Shay waves to us wildly from across the square, splashing hot chocolate across the snow, and we head back toward where the three of them are standing next to a large bow-tied snowman.

"Dad, I got extra marshmallows!" Shay says excitedly. "Hey, Max, can I call you Uncle Max the way I call Doug Uncle Doug? And are you still going to be here next week? Because I'm dancing in the New Year's recital, and I want you all to come see me!"

I squeeze myself in between Doug and Zeke. They're both watching me, waiting to see how I'll answer.

I think carefully about what that answer will be.

I think about how right I feel anytime I'm with them. Next to them. Between them.

I think about all the exploring and discovery we still have to do together. *Could* do together.

I think about how different Vermont looks to me now than it ever has before: here, in the December cold, surrounded by light created in the name of community and hope and unity. And *pride*.

I remember Mom's words from the day of the press conference: *What if you leave and the three of you never realize what you could have been together?*

"You know what, Shay?" I tell him. "I'll definitely still be here next week. And I'd love to watch you dance."

From the group chat "2 Vikings and their willing hostage"

MAX

Soooo you two ever wear pajamas?

ZEKE

Probably not since I was eight years old. Why?

MAX

Never mind! No reason! This has definitely absolutely NOTHING at all to do with Christmas!

DOUG

Uh oh, Zekers! I think I see matching Christmas jammies in our future.

ZEKE

What are the odds I can get out of this in exchange for shirtless pictures in front of the tree?

MAX

[gif of person looking intrigued]

I'd consider negotiation

CHAPTER 30
MAX

When I was a little kid, I'd wake up before dawn on Christmas morning and race out to the tree to see what Santa brought me. Even in high school, my mom still kept up the tradition of Santa bringing gifts, even if they were delivered with *a wink-wink, nod-nod.* "Oh, what did Santa bring?" she'd ask, with a faux-innocent tone but a genuine smile.

Well, this year, Santa totally outdid himself: he brought me two tops.

Best present ever.

I have one of my guys to each side of me, giving me enough room to move around a little, but not so much that I'm out of reach. Even in their sleep, they're all over me in the best way. Doug's arm is draped over my waist and his hand is splayed over my butt. Zeke's legs are tangled up with mine.

We're burrowed under an extra patchwork quilt. This one displays a variety of embroidered tractors. The room is warm and quiet, lit only by the glow of the night light in the hall and the digital clock on the nightstand.

Outside, wind whistles past the wood-framed window. Christmas morning is coming in cold and dark, and the contrast with the outdoors makes my spot in the warm bed feel even cozier.

Before Zeke and Doug wake up, I take a moment to reflect on the past few weeks. I came to Vermont to write a story and hopefully catch the wave of La Fierte being in the news. I've ended up shooting a highly successful firefighter calendar campaign, tending to a misappropriated cow, saving a tiny newspaper from bankruptcy, using my license to twink to help two best friends admit that they're more, and learning that I shouldn't drink eggnog without strict supervision. I've also come to terms with the bullying in my past.

Most importantly, though: I've fallen in love. Love that is returned two-fold.

Sneaking out to use the bathroom to freshen up—and do a little prep—I return and slide back in between them, scooting into Doug's arms. He moves to cradle me, my back to his front, his nose buried in the nape of my neck. He still breathes evenly, clearly asleep. Facing me, Zeke is also asleep even as he throws a protective arm around both of us. While I should stay still and enjoy the way this feels, I'm squirmy. In part because Doug's amazing hardness is nestled against my satin-covered ass, and in part because my own morning wood is now pressing against Zeke's muscular thigh.

I *adore* being the Max filling in a Viking sandwich.

Doug and Zeke gave me a pair of red satin boxers last night, telling me to wear them to bed. I obeyed, and the smooth fabric is lighting up my senses as I move. I can't help a little wiggle—both to make Doug's dick align better with my ass, and also to get some friction against Zeke's leg.

Of course, my movement stirs them to really wake up. First Zeke, then Doug.

Zeke's dark hair is mussed, making him look even more pirate-like than usual. He needs to shave, but the stubble is super sexy on him. He obligingly presses his leg closer to my hard cock, letting me rub against him, and he scoots to kiss me.

"Morning," he rumbles as we break apart, his voice low and gravelly.

"Merry Christmas," I whisper.

"Merry Christmas," Doug says from behind me, and stretches, then thrusts his pelvis against my butt, wrapping me deeper in his arms. He sucks along my neck, kissing where it joins my shoulder, and groans happily. A blissful moan slips out of me too.

Zeke raises himself on one elbow, leans over me, and kisses Doug, the heat of his body pressing into mine.

Yessss.

Seeing these two be intimate with each other is my new favorite thing. It's not just that they're hot, with biceps that strain as they grip the back of each other's neck to kiss. It's what it *means.* They've been in love with each other for a very long time, and now that they've finally figured out how to express it, it's a wonder to behold the vulnerability and freedom when they touch, much less make out over me.

What's even more wondrous? Their feelings for each other also extend to me. They say I'm integral to their relationship, and not only do I believe it, but I can *feel* that it's true.

They break apart, eyeing each other and doing that speaking-without-talking-out-loud thing that they do so often. Zeke gives me a devilish grin, and before I can think, he's diving under the covers, sliding down my new boxers while Doug's grabbing lube. They both peel off their underwear, so we're very quickly naked.

"How about a Christmas present for you, babe?" Zeke asks, turning me onto my side.

"Oh, yes, and good morningggg," I moan, as he catches my hard length in his mouth and sucks. Meanwhile Doug's cool, slick fingers find my hole. I spread my legs as best as I can, placing my heel on the side of my knee to give them both access.

Zeke's tongue swirls around my cock. Between the warm wetness of his mouth and the pressure he's putting in just the right spots, it's bliss. Add to that Doug's ministrations in opening me up, and I'm starting to chant swear words that probably aren't appropriate for baby Jesus's birthday. Not that that's going to stop me.

When Doug gets two fingers well into me, I start begging. "Please, please, please fuck me."

"Of course, gorgeous," Doug murmurs, as he withdraws his fingers and then lines up his cock. He enters me achingly slowly, my body first naturally rejecting him until he gets past the initial resistance. I reach down to do my best to haul Zeke up from my morning blowie. I can't get him to budge without his assistance, of course, but he scoots so that his cock is rubbing against mine and he's kissing me deep.

This overwhelmed feeling—of having them take care of me—is so damn decadent.

Zeke reaches over, and without missing a beat, Doug hands him the bottle of lube.

Doug's thrusts inside me are slow, but short. He's not moving that much, but it's as if every micro-movement matters. Like he's concentrating on giving me as much pleasure as possible. But as he whispers compliments behind me, I know he's *taking* his pleasure too. Like, "Max, babe, you feel so, so, so good." And, "You're incredible, sweetheart. This is amazing."

While Doug makes love to me, Zeke lubricates both his cock and mine and begins to stroke us together. I'm just trying to hold on, so I clutch Zeke's shoulders as we kiss. Zeke's paw is so big that he easily grasps both of us.

"This. This is what I wanted," I whisper. "Both of you."

"I'm going to come inside you, and then Zeke's going to have a turn. Does that sound good?" Doug asks, his voice becoming strained.

"It sounds absolutely wonderful," I pant out. I'm trying to hold on so I don't come too early. Which is very hard—pun intended—with Zeke lavishing attention on my dick.

Doug's movements grow erratic, which is one of my favorite things—having him come apart. His hand grips my hip as he starts to thrust deeper inside me, and now I'm just hanging on for the ride. Doug's cock is a monster, but... size queen over here, I love it. Having that rod be all up in my business is the absolute best.

Before long, he bites the meat of my shoulder and shoves hard into me, his body pulsing.

"Oh, fuck yes," I whimper as he rides out his orgasm.

Letting Doug come down, I stay put until his movements slow and he pulls out. Then, giving a wicked grin to Zeke, I flop over on my other side and line up against him. He easily presses his lubed cock into my slick hole, and we both groan loudly.

Now I can see Doug's face, and he's sated, with an expression so full of contentment. Like he loves that Zeke is getting what he needs and that I'm getting what I need and he got his, too. Doug scoots closer to me to kiss me, so his spent cock slides against my thigh. We're so messy, and we're definitely going to have to change the sheets, but I don't even care. Doug's tongue belongs in my mouth, and I grip his face as we kiss.

Zeke's rougher than Doug, but not in a way that hurts me; it's in a way that I fucking *adore*. I love that he can drill me—hell, pillage me—and I can take it.

"Fuck me," Zeke mutters. "This is so fucking *fuck fuck-shitdamn*."

Doug breaks apart long enough to mouth, "Swear jar," which makes me giggle. That giggle turns into a moan as Zeke shuttles in and out of me.

Doug reaches down to hold my cock, focusing his attention on rubbing the head against his palm. It makes me almost fold in half in delight, because that's the way it feels best.

Zeke keeps going, and Doug keeps rubbing, over and over and over again.

"I'm going to come," I warn.

"Babe, Max, honey, you feel so fucking... fuck," Zeke grunts, as his hips piston against my ass. The fullness inside is almost too much to take—but I adore that too-much feeling.

"Come in me, love," I whisper, and Zeke's thrusts get the same artlessness that Doug's had earlier, only now, Doug's helping me get to my own powerful orgasm. As he kisses and strokes me, and Zeke fucks me and sucks on the back of my neck, his hands clutching me to his powerful chest, I let go.

My body starts shuddering when the climax overtakes me, and I shoot into Doug's hand. His tongue is in my mouth. Zeke's licking my nape, and his dick's rubbing my prostate just right.

Intense waves of pleasure flash through my body, bounding and rebounding until it's all a blur.

Zeke lets out the most delicious groan as he empties into me a few thrusts later, then he holds me to him so tightly I melt.

He's panting. I'm panting. Even Doug is still breathing hard.

We're a sweaty, slick mess.

I've never been happier.

Zeke pulls out of me, and I flop on my back, then put one arm around each of them, dragging them into me. Laughing, they both curl into me, one on each side. We kiss each other and touch until the stickiness is a little too much.

"Shall we clean up?" I ask. "And we can open presents?"

"I think this was a pretty damn good present," Zeke says.

"I agree," Doug says.

An hour later, we're drinking coffee around the kitchen table, while Doug's cardamom coffee cake bakes. My mug says "WORLD'S BEST GRANDMA," and really, I wouldn't have it any other way.

We've opened presents. Zeke definitely loved the "naughty toy box" and the framed photo of his hockey team that Doug and I got for him, even though he pretended not to blush when he opened the toy box. I thought Doug was going to cry when he opened up the autographed picture of John LeClair Zeke and I gave him. (Zeke had to explain to me that John LeClair is a Vermont hockey legend; I had no idea.)

And me? I definitely *did* cry when I opened up the vintage typewriter the two of them had waiting under the tree for me. The card said only this: "To Max, who changes lives with his words."

Yup. I ugly-cried, and I have zero regrets. And now, more than ever, it feels like time to share my news with Doug and Zeke.

"So, I had a chat with Barton," I say.

"You did?" Doug asks.

I nod.

"When?"

"After the dance troupe last night. He said that he knew I was freelance, and he wanted to find out if I'd be interested in taking over the editorial job. Now that the paper's safe for the foreseeable future, I guess he wants to take some steps back. Make sure it's going to have a future after he's gone."

"Wait, so he wants you to be the editor?" Zeke asks.

I nod. "Apparently the other staff aren't interested."

"Are you?" Doug can't hide the excitement in his eyes.

"I am. I told him yes, I'd love to. So, you're looking at the new editor of *The Pigeon*."

Doug opens his arms. "C'mere."

I set down my mug and launch into his lap as he chuckles. "That's great!"

"I know! I'm going to keep freelancing, and there's this LGBTQ magazine that's asking me to do a regular column. So I've got a lot of work to do."

"Wow." Doug shakes his head. "This makes everything so real. You're staying in Vermont, babe!" He stands me up, twirling me around in his arms while Zeke smiles.

"You're ridiculous," I tease as he sets me back down. "Of course I'm staying. How could I not? I love you two Vikings."

"Me too," Doug says softly. "This… everything about it just feels right. In a way I could never explain—probably never will be able to explain—to anyone but the two of you."

"We're making this official, right?" Zeke asks. "The three of us?"

I nod, and so does Doug.

"Yes," I croak. No way I'm even going to try to pretend that I'm not about to burst into happy tears at any moment. Zeke pulls me onto his lap while Doug hugs us both.

When I first started college, I remember reading Thomas Wolfe's *You Can't Go Home Again* and thinking how true that title would always be for me. I kept a copy of that book under my bed for a long time, as a reminder, I guess.

I'm so glad Thomas Wolfe turned out to be wrong. I'm home again, and I'm sure I'm exactly where I'm supposed to be.

MAX

Zeke, did you go to the Stock farm to see Sorbet today?

ZEKE

Yup. She moos hello. She continues to enjoy her life with Jeb's menagerie.

MAX

You gave her the really expensive hay, didn't you?

DOUG

He spoils her rotten.

ZEKE

She's a good girl. She deserves some pampering.

MAX

I swear, I'm not as spoiled as that cow.

DOUG

Clearly we're not doing our boyfriend jobs very well, then.

ZEKE

Clearly not. Doug, let's talk later. I have ideas…

MAX

[gif of person clapping excitedly]

CHAPTER 31

ZEKE

"Are you sure you're okay being here?" Doug laces his fingers through Max's as we walk up the street toward Atherton Eats, the main hub of dining in Atherton. Their specialty is pancakes. Everything else sucks, but we're not going for the food.

"I am," Max says as he pulls himself up to his full height. "This is important for Zeke. I get why it's a bigger challenge for him than eating out in La Fierte would be. And I want to support him. I want to support you both." He shrugs. "Plus, being in Atherton doesn't make me want to curl up inside the janitor's closet at the high school anymore. Life is progress, right?"

He's right, I think. And that's why I asked him and Doug if we could come to Atherton Eats today for breakfast. Because I'm ready for progress. And I know what I want the next step of my own progress to be.

I want to eat out, very publicly, with the two men I'm dating. And I want to do it with more courage than fear.

My whole chest gets tight, I'm so full of appreciation and gratitude that they came here with me today. But all I manage to say is a gruff, "Thanks."

Max winks at me. "Of course, babe."

"We're so glad we can do this with you. And we've got your

back every step of the way," Doug says confidently. I grunt again, because words are hard right now. My palms are sweating more and more with every step we take toward the diner door.

My father eats here almost every morning since he's a fucking terrible cook. There's a very good chance he will be here today. There's a good chance I'll see plenty of other people I know from the county. And if I'm going to be myself with Doug and Max, then they're going to see a side of me hardly anyone has seen before.

I stop in front of Eats and take a deep breath. "Hold my hands?" I ask, my voice gruff and low. "If we're doing this, we're fucking doing it all the way."

Doug grabs one of my hands, and I'm suddenly reminded of the time in tenth grade when we cliff jumped together. I was terrified, but Doug wasn't remotely worried. He took me by the hand, and it was like some of his confidence passed into me through our skin. I felt so free, and knew I could launch myself off that cliff.

Max grabs my other hand. "Whatever you want or need," he whispers. "We're here for you, Zeke."

The words and touch are everything I need right now. I nod, and Doug pushes open the door.

We step into a space I know all too well. The shabby decor, the pictures of vintage tractors decorating the walls. The peeling laminate tabletops. I used to spend every other weekend with my dad, and we always came here. I know every faded poster and discolored ceiling tile by heart.

Yet walking into this restaurant, hand in hand with someone I've secretly loved for half my life, and someone else who's taken hold of my heart in a matter of weeks, I see the cafe with new eyes.

"Zeke! Doug!" Damon Lucas, a guy that Doug and I used to play hockey against in high school, calls our names from across the room. "Heard you two are finally dating. Right on, guys! Lemme buy you some pancakes!"

"Hey, Damon!" Doug waves at him, squeezes my hand, then

jogs over to say hello. Max nudges me, looks at the large sign that says "Please Seat Yourself," and starts leading me toward a booth. "Is it weird," he whispers as he chooses one and slides in, "that everyone around here seems to have just assumed you and Doug would get together eventually?"

"Probably weirder for me than you," I whisper back. Then I call, "Thanks, Damon," over the back of the booth, because *weird* doesn't necessarily mean *bad*. And I guess Doug and I have always been a couple on some level.

I mean, we've been living and working together since we were eighteen years old. I know married couples who don't spend as much time together as we do.

Doug slides into the booth across from me. "So," he says cheerfully, "Damon was serious about the pancakes. I ordered a stack of pecan. What else? A few orders of sausage? Maybe some bacon? Eggs?"

"You Vikings," Max mutters to himself, but he's smiling. "Sure, all of that sounds good. Zeke, are you doing okay?"

I fidget on the vinyl booth seat, which squeaks beneath me, a sound mostly drowned out by the drone of other diners' breakfast chatter. "Kiss me?" I blurt out.

"Come again?" says Doug.

"I want one of you to kiss me," I clarify.

"Oh! I can do that." And in typical Doug fashion, my best friend—boyfriend? All the things?—leans across the table and plasters his lips to mine.

I'm not sure I'll ever get used to having my dreams of kissing Doug come true. Right now, as his lips move gently and sweetly against mine, I can feel every nerve in my system humming in perfect harmony.

Doug pulls away. "How was that? Did I do okay?"

I reach across the table and take his hand. "You did great," I tell him.

He smiles. "You're doing great too. You really are, Zeke."

Those people who think Doug's head is in the clouds and that he doesn't notice things? They really don't see my friend at all.

"You're both totally crushing life goals," Max agrees. "Oh, and I was thinking that later, we can—"

"Uncle Zeke!" Shay appears next to the table and makes a beeline for my lap. "I didn't know you'd be here!" I grunt as his skinny knees dig into my thighs.

I grab Shay's arm to steady him, laughing in surprise. Jonah appears behind him, looking sheepish.

He and I haven't talked much since the Holiday-Off, when he shocked me to my boots by *thanking* me for punching him. He said I'd forced him to re-think a lot of things that day. Me and Max both.

"Hey there," he says. "Shay, let's go find another place to sit, okay? We don't want to bug your uncles while they're having time together."

He says it so easily, so simply. *Your uncles.* Max coughs and kicks me under the table, and I know what he's suggesting I do.

"Sit with us," I blurt out. "We've got plenty of room."

"Yay!" Shay claps and wedges himself between me and Max while Jonah slides into the booth seat with Doug.

Pancakes come. We eat them, because they're really fucking delicious. We make awkward small talk with Jonah about his job at the hardware store, Max tells us about the Holiday-Off article he's finishing up, and Shay gives us a move-by-move breakdown of his dance steps for his upcoming recital. I'm laughing at his attempt to show Max the different ballet positions from his booth seat when I hear *that voice* behind me.

"Guess it's all true, then," Dad says, his voice a rasp. He's standing at the edge of the table, and he looks even worse than the last time I saw him.

"Hi, Grandpa!" says Shay. "Look what I just colored!" He holds up his place mat, showing off holiday decorations perfectly shaded in blue and red and purple and yellow.

"Hey, kid." Dad turns to Jonah, his eyes narrowed. "I see

you're not changing your mind. About what you told me. Picked them over me, did you?"

I tense, but Max squeezes my knee as Jonah clears his throat.

"I made a choice," he says softly. "I'll see you around, Dad. Maybe. You know what you need to do if you want to be part of our lives."

Max, Doug, and I all look carefully at Shay when he says that, but the kid's basically oblivious to the conversation. He's engrossed in coloring a goat that looks oddly like Sherbert.

Dad draws himself up to his full height and snorts. "Okay, then. Guess that's all I needed to know."

And then he turns and walks away.

Our entire table is silent, save the sound of Shay's crayon scratching over paper. "I'm not sure what just happened," Max says finally, "but why do I feel like we just climbed Mount Everest or something?"

"I think we might have even made the summit," says Doug. He frowns and reaches over to rub my wrist with his thumb. "You two okay?" He asks me and Jonah.

Jonah's studying Shay, who's got his tongue pressed between his teeth in concentration as he colors. "Yeah," he says finally. "I really think I am."

I look around me, at the diner. At this room full of people who welcomed me, Max, and Doug with open arms. And if they hadn't? Well, that would've sucked. But we would have taken care of each other and gotten through it. I believe that.

"I'm good," I finally say. "Better than I've ever been."

I press one knee to Doug's and one to Max's under the table, and Max grabs Doug's hand and mine. We're our own circle of connection that can't be broken—the three of us, linked together.

We've got so much to figure out together. So much to learn—I know that. But right now, I'm holding hands with two men I can't imagine being apart from. I'm more at peace with myself than I ever thought I could be.

And that's not nothing.

MAX

I'm pretty sure that February is my favorite month

DOUG

Why? Is it your birthday?

MAX

No. It's the best calendar pic of Zeke, though.

ZEKE

Wedding rings for commitment ceremonies for polycules

DOUG

...

MAX

Um. Zeke? This isn't Google.

ZEKE

Shit.

[Unsent the message for everyone]

MAX

Doug, are we letting him get away with that?

DOUG

Nope.

ZEKE

SIGH. I was getting a little ahead of myself. But I fucking love both of you and want to show you how much.

MAX

You make me melt. I love both of you too.

DOUG

Me too!

EPILOGUE—MAX

Holding my hand up to my eyebrows, I squint at the busy rink, trying to make out the action on the ice. I'm watching Zeke's under-eights play their qualifier for the semi-finals in their league. The stands are full of parents cheering for their children, and the energy is electric. I'm also taking notes so I can write an article about La Fierte's hockey team for *The Pigeon*.

The problem is, I don't understand the game at all.

"Okay, so that tiny one with the helmet is doing something with a stick," I say to Doug, who's reclined in the orange plastic seat next to me, clapping every time any kid does anything. He's looking sexy AF in jeans and a hockey jersey in the same colors as our half of the kids out on the rink.

Doug grins at me. "Well, I'd say that's true."

I scribble down notes, which are basically a bunch of question marks. "And she's trying to get the puck into the net..."

"That's the goal, yep. Or, I mean, the goal is to get the puck into the goal to score a goal."

I think I understood that. "Then why does it look like absolute chaos? There are sticks and skates and bodies flying everywhere!"

"Oh, hey. Number eighty-one just deked number sixteen on the other side. Nice."

I throw up my hands. "I give up. I don't understand hockey."

"Don't give up! You can do this. I'll help."

Doug proceeds to narrate what's happening as the kids go zooming by. Periodically, Zeke whistles from the sidelines and claps, and trios of kids hop over the boards to skate while others come back in.

In my humble (and correct) opinion, Zeke's more interesting than the game, so eventually I start watching him instead. And he's an easy subject to study. While Zeke will always have a scowly, intense look, he seems almost relaxed these days. Especially when he's working with his team. Like he knows that these kids need to have fun first and learn how to play second and win third. He's got his priorities straight.

Inspiration pings. I can write a story about *that*. I don't have to report on the game, which I'm totally unqualified to do. I start scribbling down my impressions of Zeke, thinking that he deserves an article as much as Doug did. One that celebrates who he is and his contributions to the community.

"He's really in his element, isn't he?" I say to Doug, my eyes not leaving Zeke.

"He is. He's great with kids."

After I scribble down a few more impressions, I scoot closer to Doug. These seats aren't set up for cuddling, and we watch our PDA in family situations anyway, but it doesn't stop my mind from wandering.

I'm thinking about what it felt like to wake up this morning between my men. I made breakfast, and I'm mighty proud of my blueberry pancakes. I'll never be as good in the kitchen as Doug, but it's nice to let him be the one who gets taken care of from time to time.

As I study him in that hockey jersey, I'm wondering if he'd let me borrow it. I'm wondering if he and Zeke would do things to me while I was wearing it.

Maybe it's time to share another fantasy.

Thank you for reading! You may also enjoy *ILYBSM*, a holiday MMM romance by J.E. Birk, Rachel Ember, and Leslie McAdam.

ACKNOWLEDGMENTS

We would like to thank Birkie's handwriting translation software for autocorrecting "Doug" to "dong." Every. Time.

We would also like to thank our past selves for naming Zeke's girlfriend "Lydia," when we really wanted to call her "Desi."

We thank the "find and replace" feature on Google Docs for changing "desires" to "Lydiares," when we tried to automatically fix Desi/Lydia's name.

We thank all forms of autocorrect, our past selves, and technology for the sentence, "Dong has Lydiares, okay?"

We would like to thank Sherbert for volunteering his name as a safe word.

In all seriousness, writing *TMI* was quite a journey. We hope you love our trio (and if you do, please feel free to leave a review!)

We're so very grateful for Megan Dischinger's beta reading, Kari Shafenberg's edits, and Katy Cuthbertson's proofreading. Thank you also to Cate Ashwood for our lovely cover. Our hearty, holiday thanks to *you* for reading.

ABOUT J.E. BIRK

J.E. Birk was raised in Vermont and is now adulting in Colorado with intermittent success. She is a long-time lover of stories, and she writes and reads in worlds where imperfect characters find their happily ever after. Snag free bonus content and stay up-to-date on J.E. Birk's news and releases by signing up for her newsletter at www.jebirk.com.

ALSO BY J.E. BIRK:

Booklover
Counterpoint
Fauxmance in the Falls

facebook.com/jebirk
instagram.com/jebirkwrites
tiktok.com/@jebirkwrites

ABOUT RACHEL EMBER

Rachel lives in the Midwest United States with her two young sons and a menagerie of pets. She has always loved love stories, and having the chance to share her own tales still feels too good to be true. You can learn more about Rachel and read the first chapter of all of her books at www.rachelember.com.

ALSO BY RACHEL EMBER:

Wonderland
Long Winter
Night & Day

facebook.com/rachelemberauthor
instagram.com/rachelemberauthor

ABOUT LESLIE MCADAM

USA Today bestselling author Leslie McAdam is a California girl who loves romance and well-defined abs. She lives in a drafty old farmhouse on a small orange tree farm in Southern California with her husband and two children. Leslie's first published book, The Sun and the Moon, won a 2015 Watty, which is the world's largest online writing competition. She's gone on to receive additional literary awards and has been featured in multiple publications, including Cosmopolitan.com. Her books have been Top 100 Bestsellers on both Amazon and Apple Books. Leslie is employed by day but spends her nights writing about the men of your fantasies. Learn more at www.lesliemcadamauthor.com.

ALSO BY LESLIE MCADAM:

Ambiguous
Studious
Unmanageable

facebook.com/lesliemcadamauthor
instagram.com/mcadam_leslie
tiktok.com/@lesliemcadam